divine misguidance

November 2004

For Nick –
   The grandson of my best friend.

[signature]

divine misguidance

a detective novel

jerry maples

Ms. Tree Publishing
Scottsdale, Arizona

Copyright © 2004 by Jerry Maples

First U.S. Edition 2004

10 9 8 7 6 5 4 3 2 1

ISBN: 0-9759816-0-9
Library of Congress Catalog Card Number: 2004110890

Cover image from Getty Images

All rights reserved. No part of this publication may be reproduced, stored in, or introduced into a retrieval system, or transmitted in any form, or by any means (electronic, mechanical, photocopying, recording, or otherwise) without the prior written permission of both the copyright owner and the publisher of this book.

This book is a work of fiction. Names, characters, businesses, organizations, places, events, and incidents either are the product of the author's imagination or are used fictitiously. Any resemblance to actual persons, living or dead, events, or locales is entirely coincidental.

Ms. Tree Publishing
Scottsdale, AZ

Printed in the United States of America

*For Linda,
my best friend and my wife.*

Acknowledgments

This story was born on a walk.

During daily morning walks with my wife, Linda. I mentioned that I wanted to write a mystery novel and we explored topics where controversial topics could be combined with criminal activities. Due to its amazing controversy, euthanasia soon surfaced as an especially interesting subject. Views on this matter are varied and strong. In fact, there is not even a consistent legal approach to euthanasia throughout the country.

My ties to the Midwest and a good friend, Dr. Walter Peterson, made the city of Dubuque an easy choice for the setting. Walter not only encouraged me, but was my resource for everything about Dubuque.

To be credible, this story required expertise beyond my own. I am indebted to three individuals whose knowledge and willing assistance assured realism. Dennis Hawkins, a former police chief in Iowa, made sure the police procedures were accurate. Dr. Matthew Hummel, family practitioner, guided me through the medical aspects. And Stephen B. Jackson, attorney-at-law, took care of the legal end. Convincing accuracy would not have taken place without their help.

Numerous drafts of this manuscript did not have a natural flow until I shared it with Sallie Coonts. Her advice and constant, polite badgering transformed the work into an account that came together.

I am indebted to the multi-talented Bob Hoffarber for his input on the book cover design, as well as proofreading the manuscript.

My expectation of a hurried up check on grammar, etc. could not have been further from the truth in working with my editor, Jim Veihdeffer of *Words in Action*. Jim, a tough taskmaster, questioned every part of the work, again and again. His suggestions, diligence and constructive criticism have honed a less than perfect attempt into something better.

Thanks also goes to Lisa Liddy of *The Printed Page* for her transformation of the manuscript into a well-designed book and for taking Bob's cover design to completion.

Thanks to all of you for your encouragement and guidance.

"It is not, what a lawyer tells me I *may* do;
but what humanity, reason, and justice, tell me I *ought* to do."
—Edmund Burke (1729-1797)

ONE

Molly Starr was dead. Dubuque's maiden philanthropist had made her last donation in person. Her assets exceeded twenty million dollars.

The police department's lead detective, Zachary Gerrard, knew the community would be shocked by its loss. Half a million or more in annual gifts would be greatly missed.

Why would anyone who did so much for so many resort to taking her own life? At forty-eight, she was in the prime of her life.

The death scene, which he had been examining for the past three hours suggested this was a suicide caused by a drug overdose. But for the detective, the pieces didn't fit. His intuition told him it might have been staged. Supposedly, the victim had died from ingesting too many sleeping pills. If that was the case, why did she have that horrid pain-induced grimace on her face? Why were her prints on the water glass, used for taking the pills, placed in a seemingly improper position for drinking? What was the explanation for a minute speck of what appeared to be vomit behind the toilet? The bathroom floor was otherwise spotlessly clean. These were the questions Zack pondered while waiting for the coroner to arrive at the crime scene.

~~~

Dubuque's newest detective was unaware that events of a week earlier in another part of town would become so critical to solving the biggest murder spree in the city's history. Those happenings began in the home of a wealthy business leader who had astutely transformed his significant inheritance into a mega-million fortune. He was discussing the difficulties of his failing health with his son, a seminary graduate about to be ordained a priest.

"Dad, can you hear me?"

"Er…ah…yeah. Just resting. How're you doing, Riley?"

"I'm okay. I'm concerned about you"

"I'm gutting it out. Right now, I wish the end would come. I'm so damned tired…all the time. But I need to talk to you in private. Anyone else around?"

"Mom's in the kitchen. She's fixing you some soup."

"God, I'll bet it's chicken noodle again. Go tell her I need to rest for a while. When you come back close the door and sit by me on the bed."

Theodore Whitcomb knew his dutiful son always did what he was told—at least he had every time, except for that one disastrous incident. Right now, he wanted Riley to help him end his life. Unable to rest, his pain and fatigue were all-consuming. Latter stages of his terminal illness were taking their toll, mentally as well as physically.

A few moments later, the father, in his mid-fifties, heard the door shut, followed by a shift in his bed. His youngest child, who would soon take the vows of priesthood, lowered himself carefully onto the mattress.

"Mom said she'd wait until you're ready to eat. What'd you want to talk about, Dad?"

"I'll try to make this short, Son. I can't make it anymore. You have to help me meet my Maker."

"I know the cancer's terminal. Doctor Brown says he'll help you near the end."

"Hell. I can't wait that long. Listen to me, will you?"

"Sure, Dad, go ahead."

"I want to depart with dignity, Riley. I met another oncology patient who has a way. Evidently, there's a local group practicing euthanasia. And they can perform this service with the utmost confidentiality."

"Dad, that's against our religion!"

"I know. But please, just listen. No one has to know how my end comes about. It would kill your mother if she knew I was the subject of a mercy killing. But this can be done without anyone else knowing. Will you at least do me a favor, Riley?"

"Just name it, Dad."

"I want you to make contact with this group and see if they'll help me. The phone number's on a piece of paper in my billfold. It's in the top drawer of the bureau over there. All I'm asking is to give them a call and find out what you can."

A long moment passed as father and son communicated only with their eyes.

"Okay, Dad. I'll do it. Now, why don't you get some rest?"

~~~

Riley had returned to his dormitory at the St. Peter's campus across town. In the loneliness of his room, he struggled to find an answer to his dilemma. While he loved his dad dearly, he didn't know if he could be a party to expediting his death. The church doctrine that he knew so well was unequivocally opposed to euthanasia. And so was he—at least he had been until this point. Dr. Brown estimated his dad could probably live for another six to nine months. During that time he would either be experiencing excruciating pain or be so drugged he wouldn't know where he was. The young priest-to-be turned to God in prayer. Finally, he decided that he loved his father too much to have the suffering last any longer than absolutely necessary. He asked God's forgiveness for what he was about to do.

After unfolding the crumpled paper, Riley dialed the barely legible phone number. Eight rings later, he listened to a gravelly voice.

"Yes. Who's calling?"

"My name is Riley Whitcomb. I'm calling on behalf of my father."

"Theodore Whitcomb?"

"Yes, that's right. He's terminally ill and needs your help."

"How did you get this number?"

The seminarian answered the question and then asked, "I have to say that this is against my principles, but my Dad wants it done. Can you assure this could be handled with complete secrecy?"

"Yes, but it's very expensive…It could run as much as a hundred thousand dollars."

Cost was not a factor in Riley's mind. Knowing that his father usually carried more than that in his savings account, he replied, "That doesn't matter. How can I have proof of your discretion?"

"That can be arranged. Would you hold on for a moment, please?"

After a lengthy pause, the voice returned to the line.

"Here's what we can do."

TWO

Detective Zachary Gerrard finally stopped reliving his last moments with Molly Starr and returned his thoughts to the present. He looked at his watch. Normally at nine o'clock he would be absorbed in a book or watching *The Practice* on TV with his daughter.

It had been three hours since the dispatcher had requested his visit to Starr's residence on Deerfield Road in a section of Dubuque known as Barrington Lakes. He and his associate, Detective Lou Davis, had arrived at about the same time.

Two squad cars blocked the street. Their flashing lights played across the front of a spacious, authentic-looking English Tudor home located in one of the city's most fashionable residential areas.

Two young women gripped each other, sobbing, on the front steps, obviously grief-stricken at the untimely death of their aunt.

A small crowd of curious onlookers had positioned themselves as close to the home's entrance as the yellow restraining tape would allow. Zack noticed as he peered out through the front window that the crowd had not dissipated since their appearance on the scene. He hoped keeping an eye out would somehow speed the arrival of the county coroner.

The whole thing reminded him of a cook waiting for the water to boil; it takes forever if you keep watching.

The diminishing evening light caused his reflection to appear on the window. It reminded him of the early stages of a Polaroid photo developing before his eyes. The fairly round face of his reflected image appeared incongruous with the reasonably trim build of a six-foot-two cop approaching middle age. A full head of hair graying at the temples surrounded a narrow nose, smaller than average mouth and prominent chin that comprised features his wife had considered handsome. While his energy level bordered on hyperactive, he had a well-worn quality with others.

~~~

Detective Zack Gerrard was spoiled. Fighting crime in Dubuque, Iowa was totally unlike his experience in Minneapolis. He didn't consider this as running down his locale of the past six months. It was just that a city of sixty thousand did not have the need or the resources of a metropolis when it came to criminal investigation. He and Lou comprised the entire Investigations Division of the Dubuque Police Department. There were no specialists for homicide, burglary, sexual abuse, et cetera. His new position also required coordination with the Iowa Division of Criminal Investigation in Des Moines for assistance with the analysis of evidence gathered at the crime scene.

While the Dubuque PD was getting a new forensic laboratory, thanks to Molly Starr, they had no sophisticated crime lab at this time. This meant working with forensic and other criminal experts nearly two hundred miles removed rather than in a building next door.

But, all in all, Gerrard loved his new community. There was no way he would go back where fond memories had soured. That was the reason he had left a job he liked with excellent potential for advancement.

~~~

The young women on the front steps were nieces who traditionally made a Sunday evening call on their aunt. They gave him and Lou their account of the past few hours. The girls had entered the home with a key Molly had entrusted to them. Hearing no response to their greeting, they began preparing dinner with groceries they had brought. They knew Molly would be home shortly. Evidently her Women's Book Club session ran a little long.

Jill recounted her experience with her sister and the two detectives. "When I made a bathroom trip I passed Molly's bedroom and, naturally, glanced in. The drapes were closed but there was enough light to at least see a shape under the covers—it had to be Aunt Molly. She appeared to be asleep with her back towards the doorway.

"I was puzzled. This wasn't the Aunt Molly I knew. When I talked to her earlier, she said nothing about being ill; plus she *never* took afternoon naps. She's not that old and has more energy than either of us.

"Anyway, I flicked on the bedroom light and went to wake her. When I nudged her shoulder, she didn't move. When nothing happened, I pulled her towards me." Jill stopped speaking, too affected by what came next.

"Jill squealed like I've never heard in my life," Chris said, taking over the story from her sister.

"When I came running, she blocked the door so I couldn't get in."

"I've never seen a look like that on anyone," Jill responded sorrowfully. "Aunt Molly's face reminded me of one of those mannequins in a horror museum. I don't think she died peacefully."

Zack inquired, "Did either of you do anything in the room, other than your turning over your aunt's body?"

"No," Jill replied, recovering enough to resume her account. "I forgot about going to the bathroom. We saw a glass and a pill bottle on her nightstand. But we didn't touch them. Chris called 911.

"Then we didn't do anything but go out to the front steps until the police arrived. They said I could use the bathroom on the lower level. I hope that was okay."

After finishing their interviews with the detective, Zack suggested the girls wait in the living room until the county coroner had reviewed the scene. He promised to keep them advised of her progress.

~~~

Zack's thoughts returned to the present as he spied Brenda Sagers, the county coroner, making her way to the front door.

If this catastrophe had happened a month earlier, Zack would have felt more confident with the county medical assistance. Brenda, who had completed her medical residency in St. Louis, was appointed coroner only a few weeks ago. For the prior forty years, Doc Crew had been the county's medical fixture. Zack had enjoyed his short association with the old guy.

Doctor Quinton Crew was the only coroner most people in Dubuque had known. Somehow he managed to keep pace with changes in technology, including being fairly well versed in forensics. People often said he had incredible energy for a man a few years beyond normal retirement and enjoyed that crusty exterior, even though he could be compassionate.

Now, though, Zack was dealing with an unknown factor. He knew that Sagers had graduated in the top half of her St. Louis University medical school class. However, though she had been exposed to the most cutting edge technology, she had no actual job experience. He couldn't help but notice that the doctor presented a well-proportioned figure and a bubbly personality. Her geeky glasses drew attention from a rather plain face.

"Detective, this is supposed to be my day off," Sagers exclaimed as she arrived in an apparent effort to draw a smile.

"I know what you're saying," Zack replied. "You may find this to be a somewhat interesting experience." In their brief acquaintance, the detective felt Brenda lacked self-confidence and masked it with humor and bravado.

Since coming to Dubuque, this was Zack's first involvement in what seemed to be a suicide. But why would a lady, who had so much wealth and took pleasure in sharing it with others, want to do herself in? His intuition told him not to necessarily accept things as they appeared. He remained suspicious.

Brenda interrupted his thoughts, "You don't say. Well, let's take a look. How disturbed is the crime scene?"

"Not too bad, really. As far as we can tell, a niece pulled the victim's body from a position on its side to its back. Other than that, she and her sister haven't disturbed anything in this wing of the house.

"There weren't any signs of forcible entry into the house and the bedroom doesn't appear to be disturbed. Our cursory examination of the body revealed no obvious wounds. We did find a pill bottle and a water glass on the victim's nightstand. It was either suicide or staged to give that impression."

"Well, lead on McDuff. Let me take a look and we'll get this over with."

~~~

Lou was already updating the Chief of Police, Scottie Baldwin, in his office. Zack overheard Lou's last few words as he entered.

"...spent his time picking puke off the bathroom floor."

Pretending not to have heard that remark, Zack warmly greeted his associates.

The chief said, "As I was saying to Lou, this is one of the most devastating deaths our city has ever experienced. Next to the Whitcomb families, Molly Starr was probably our city's greatest philanthropist.

"The mayor and the council are going to be looking for answers. Zack, do you have any specifics on the episode last night?"

As the lead investigator, Zack had intended to relate the previous night's findings. "I'm not sure what Lou has covered with you, but here's my take on the situation." He proceeded to give his report. After highlighting the investigation, Zack said, "The coroner tells us that during her cursory examination she may have identified what appeared to be a small puncture wound in the vein of her left arm. Maybe Molly was given an injection or injected herself. Brenda is going to visit with her doctor to see if there was a recent blood test, if she had a drug habit, was a diabetic, or any other possibility. There was also a very slight bruising on her right forearm and on both of her legs above the ankles. When I mentioned an autopsy might be required to determine the cause of death, the nieces consented to doing so.

"We dusted the water glass on the nightstand for prints. Then it was sent overnight to Des Moines for an analysis of any possible residue that could confirm its contents. Brenda indicated a massive dose of the type of pills from that empty pill bottle might possibly be sufficient to cause death.

"The prints on the glass belonged to the victim. The interesting thing is they weren't positioned on the glass as one would expect. I wouldn't take a drink from a glass by holding it in that manner. The print pattern could suggest someone had placed Molly's hand around the glass after she died.

"Molly's prints were the only ones found on the pill bottle. The only other unusual evidence we found was a speck of what we think was vomit on the floor of the bathroom. It appears Molly was ill, threw up in the toilet, got in bed under the covers and passed away. That should be confirmed by an examination of her stomach contents."

The chief responded, "Brenda's findings are a priority. Make certain she does nothing else until her work is complete. The entire city will be anxious to learn her findings."

~~~

Rather than call the county coroner, Zack decided to walk the two blocks to the morgue and determine what progress Brenda was making.

The front desk was vacant. Zack felt it was an early coffee break for Simone. He headed through the swinging doors to the coroner's office, which was adjacent to the corpses. He felt about as comfortable in this environment as going to the doctor for a prostate exam. And the odor of formaldehyde only further irritated his queasy stomach.

"I was about to call you, Zack. I figured old Scottie would be chomping at the bit. I've been in here since five this morning. The nieces wanted an autopsy and that's what I've been doing. I've also spoken with the victim's doctor and to forensics in Des Moines.

"Molly's doctor said she should have been as healthy as a horse. Her physical last month revealed she was in excellent condition for a forty-eight year old. There's no reason she should have had an injection for medical purposes.

"I also talked to Dale." Dr. Dale Douglas was the chief forensic scientist with the state's Criminal Investigation Division. "One of his people will finish a project in

Davenport this morning and should be here by afternoon to help complete the forensic analysis.

"One other thing, that speck in the bathroom was as you expected. It was vomit, but it didn't belong to the deceased. There was no match to the contents of Molly's stomach. Its freshness indicates it was deposited six to nine hours prior to my arrival at the scene."

Zack responded, "Maybe someone got sick because they found Molly dead or was even there when she died."

Brenda was into her findings and not the investigation. She added, "The contents of Molly's stomach included the same sedative that was marked on the pill bottle. I'm in the process of reexamining the hematology report. So far I haven't uncovered any other foreign substance in her blood. At this stage, I'd have to say she committed suicide."

"You're saying a sufficient quantity of that sedative could cause her death?"

"I'd think so. Fifteen or twenty Ambien at ten milligrams should do the job. Remember, she was a petite lady."

"What about the agony etched in her face? Would sleeping pills cause that type of reaction?"

"Not likely. But remember, 'agony' is a literary term, not a scientific one so I can't really say anything about that. Besides, damn it, Zack, I've been working my ass off and I'm tired. Let me take a nap and I'll think about it. Okay?"

"Sorry, Brenda, I'm just playing the devil's advocate. I appreciate all you've done. Please stay in touch."

For some reason Zack wasn't as confident of the suicide diagnosis as Brenda was. God, he thought, why couldn't old Quint have stuck it out one more month as coroner?

The medical update was given by Zack to the chief and his investigative partner. He didn't mention the two things that made him feel uneasy about Molly's death, the dying facial expression and the vomit.

Being a seasoned investigator with a larger exposure to homicide gave the detective an inclination to be suspicious. He hoped he wasn't being paranoid about the cause of Molly's death.

After updating his associates, he planned to dust that toilet bowl for prints and have another look at the pill bottle.

THREE

Over the millennia, water from melting glaciers had cut a wide path through rocky terrain. When the water level subsided the result was a sprawling river that separated Iowa from Illinois and Wisconsin. That geological process produced lowlands on the west side, the Iowa side, of the Mississippi River. This lowland area furnished an ideal setting for a settlement that became the city of Dubuque. Its convenient location adjacent to the waterway was essential to the town's commercial development.

Each side of the river valley was bordered by massive, rocky bluffs. These formations channeled the direction of the community's growth over the past one hundred and fifty years.

~~~

Early evening in late May was an ideal time to live in Dubuque. Zack Gerrard and his nineteen-year-old daughter were enjoying one of their infrequent times together. They had parked their bicycles and were standing on Dubuque's highest elevation, in Eagle Point Park. Kristen had just returned from finishing her freshman year at Northwestern University in Evanston. Tomorrow she would be headed to her roommate's family cottage in northern Wisconsin for a few days.

"That view is spectacular, isn't it?" Zack marveled at the site from the top of one of Dubuque's highest bluffs. Bordered by lush green trees, the wide river meandered into the distance. "I'll bet you can see for more than five miles." He squinted as he pointed to the east with his arm extended. "Over to the left is Wisconsin and there's the border with Illinois."

"Dad, you sound like a rep for the Chamber of Commerce."

"I'm still impressed with this area. You know, next week we'll have been here for six months. I guess I should say *I've* been here that long."

"I think I'll like it too, Dad. I'm just not very well acquainted yet. But this summer I'm going to get to know two of my classmates from here."

"It's been tough not having you around all the time. With Mom and you both gone, it's been an adjustment. Fortunately, I love my work and it keeps me busy. I don't even mind my moonlighting job at Alliance."

"Dad, it's terrible you have to work nights. Being a cop is a full time job in itself."

"It's only for another year or two. By then all your mom's medical bills should be paid. I appreciate the chief's willingness to let me do this. Thank God you've got nearly a full ride at Northwestern."

"The chief knows a good man when he sees one. So, how're things at the office of Dubuque's premier investigator anyway?"

"Actually, I just may be on the biggest case of my career. One of Dubuque's most prominent ladies died yesterday."

"Who's that?"

"Molly Starr. She was loaded. But she used her money for a lot of good causes. In her forties, never married and worth more than twenty million bucks. It's too bad I didn't get to know her better." Zack regretted the joke as soon as he said it.

"Nice talk, Dad! So what happened to her?"

"That's what I'm going to find out from the coroner and forensics at DCI."

"The what?"

"The state Division of Criminal Investigation."

"Oh."

"Anyway, some things have bothered me about whether this was a suicide. A forensic expert from Des Moines should be able to confirm the cause of death. I'll meet with him and the coroner in the morning. It's hard to believe anyone would harm this lady. She gave several hundred thousand dollars to local charities each year."

"If anyone can get to the bottom of this, it'll be you."

~~~

The police station was quiet as Gerrard made his way to his office on the second floor, but he noticed the chief was already at work preparing for the meeting he had called with his two homicide detectives.

Zack waved good morning as he strode to his cubicle on the other side of the secretarial pool. His was the corner office with the better view that was traditionally occupied by the lead homicide detective. It was separated from the office of his working partner, Detective Lou Davis, by a conference room where most of their planning occurred.

Zack had learned of Lou Davis' progress through the ranks of the Dubuque police department over the past eighteen years. Starting as a traffic cop, Davis had advanced to his present position of second-in-charge of investigations. Lou had the reputation of being steady and dependable. The number two detective, with short brown hair and dark eyes, was stocky with slightly slumped shoulders.

Although only about five-and-a-half feet tall, he looked like he could physically hold his own with most anyone.

Lou had told Zack his seniority on the Dubuque force entitled him to be the lead investigator. Even though he had expressed confidence in Zack's abilities, Zack had the impression that Lou would not be opposed to backstabbing. Zack had heard such comments before and yesterday's remarks behind his back to the chief only confirmed it.

Zack's office was not expansive; however, the two windows made the area seem larger and the outside light was uplifting. When faced with a difficult problem he would often swivel his desk chair to view outside and contemplate as he observed the business activity to the north and the imposing bluffs with the Fourth Street Elevator railcars climbing the steep embankment.

Despite the view, Zack's cubicle was austere. His desk, cluttered with files and unfinished reports, was accompanied by two chairs for visitors once they were cleared of document piles. There was one filing cabinet with two photos on top, partially hidden by more folders. One was a vacation photo of his daughter, his wife, who had died nearly three years before and himself. The other was Kristen's high school graduation picture. Two diplomas and one certificate were the only items to adorn the walls.

His diplomas were a Bachelor of Arts degree from the University of Wisconsin and graduation from the Minneapolis Police Academy. The certificate represented completion of a Police Academy course on forensics. There was no carpet, rugs, sofa or greenery. The décor matched his no-nonsense work persona and dedication to the job, but clearly one who loathed paperwork.

"Zack, you're wanted in the chief's office. He and Lou are ready to meet," Millie stated, in her matter of fact manner. He was glad that she was the non-excitable type so necessary in pressure situations where emotions had a tendency to surface. Millie had been handling administrative duties for a number of years. She also knew how to handle the chief when he got uptight.

"'K, Millie. I'm on my way. Say, while I'm in there, could you call Brenda Sagers for me? I'd like to see her this morning about the results of the autopsy."

"Sure thing, honey. Now you'd better get in there." Millie said "honey" often and it seemed to mean different things in different situations. Zack took it as a well-intentioned and good-humored attempt at maternal endearment.

Zack hustled in to Scottie Baldwin's office where the chief and Lou had begun to discuss Molly Starr's death.

"Zack, anything to report on Starr?"

"I'll know more soon, Chief. I'm scheduled to meet again with Brenda and DCI anytime soon."

The chief was uptight. "This death is one hell of a note. Only a few days ago we made her Citizen of the Year for her financial contributions to the police department over the past decade. And she's just made another gift to outfit our forensic equipment. Now some of that equipment could be used on her. If that isn't ironic, I don't know what is. Six months from retirement and now I get this high-profile death. I was looking forward to an uneventful last half of the year. Let's hope it was a suicide," the chief said grimly.

~~~

As soon as the detective had returned to his office his phone rang.

"Detective Gerrard, my name is Riley Whitcomb. I'm a student at St. Peter's Seminary. I've been reading about the death of Molly Starr and I have some information that might help with your investigation. I think face-to-face would be best, if that's okay with you."

"I *would* like to meet with you Mr. Whitcomb. Can I get a phone number where I can contact you? Right now I'm scheduled to meet with a state forensic expert on the case."

Zack sensed disappointment in the voice of the caller, but Whitcomb gave Zack his cell phone number and finished with, "Classes are out for the summer. You should be able to reach me anytime."

When he hung up, Zack realized his abruptness might have been interpreted by the kid as blowing him off. Well, the youngster was probably right. The lead detective had higher priorities on the case. Impatient, he phoned Brenda Sagers' private line to determine when he could meet with her and the DCI forensic man.

Brenda responded to his question, "Matt Rodgers is finishing up his report. How about we meet around noon? I can assure you Zack, we're going as fast as we can. We just don't want to overlook anything."

"Well, call as soon as you can." Jesus, he was impatient. He couldn't just sit around. He decided to phone the seminary student, but first he wanted to check out his credibility.

Zack dialed the monsignor's office at St. Peter's. Even though he had not met him, he reckoned the president of a small school would probably know if a student was a flake or not.

"I'm sorry, Monsignor Mulcahey is out of his office. This is Sheila Patterson, his administrative assistant. Can I help you?"

After introducing himself Zack inquired, "Ma'am, I wonder if you could tell me anything about one of your students, a Mr. Riley Whitcomb?"

"Riley. Oh yes, we're very proud of him. Outstanding student, very responsible. Riley helps the seminary in our recruitment efforts." Her voice resonated with confidence and authority.

"I was checking since he offered to share information of the utmost importance."

"Detective, if Riley tells you something, you can certainly believe every word of it."

"Thanks for your comments, Ms. Patterson. That really helps."

~~~

The investigator decided to adopt an apologetic tone when he finally connected with the student's cell. "Riley, sorry for being so abrupt when you called earlier. We get a number of crank calls on many of our investigations and we've already had several on the Starr case," Zack lied. "I'd like to meet with you at your earliest convenience."

"I could see you any time," Riley bubbled.

"How about right now then? Is there a coffee shop or restaurant where we could meet that's convenient for you?"

"Yeah, there's a Denny's nearby on Fifth and Locust."

"Okay, see you in a few minutes. I'll be the slightly gray-haired guy in a dark blue sport coat."

As Zack hurried to leave his office to meet the seminarian, he yelled to Millie. "Got an urgent meeting. Let the chief know I may be onto something that could help with the Starr case."

"Sure thing, honey."

~~~

It was a perfect time for a confidential meeting at Denny's. The breakfast crowd was thinning out and lunch would not be in demand for more than an hour. A slender, young man around twenty in the far booth acknowledged Zack with a wave as he entered the eatery. As Zack approached,

Riley was on his feet with his hand extended and a friendly smile on his face.

"Hello, detective. I'm Riley Whitcomb."

"Thanks for coming. Would you like some coffee while we talk?"

"A Coke'd be great."

The waitress was already on her way. "Ma'am, we'll have a Coke and an iced tea, if you please."

Then Zack pulled a legal pad from his briefcase. "Hope you don't mind if I take notes. Standard police thing. Your last name is Whitcomb, right?"

"Yes, sir."

"Any relation to Nell Whitcomb?"

"Yes, my mother."

"You're in the seminary?"

"Yes, St. Peter's; I graduate next week."

"Does that mean you'll be a priest?"

"It sure does. I've planned on it for several years."

"So what do you have for me Mr. Whitcomb?"

"At my Dad's request I encountered a situation which put me in touch with information which could relate to Ms. Starr's death."

"Hold on a second, I don't follow the connection."

"Maybe if I gave you some background it would make more sense. Have you got a little time?"

"If you can tie it in to Molly Starr's death, I'm willing to spend the day."

"Well, it shouldn't take that long."

Just then Cindy Lou returned with the drinks. After a few gulps of Coke, Riley continued.

"I come from a very strong Catholic family. A few years ago something happened to me to convince me to become a priest. The reasons aren't important to this discussion. However, it reinforces our family's commitment to living under the rules of strict Catholic doctrines. My father is terminally ill with cancer. He's suffering a great deal. In secret, he asked me to assist him in investigating the possibility of euthanasia to put him out of his misery. No one else in our family was to know about this because mercy killing is strongly opposed in the Catholic religion. Consequently, what I'm about to tell you has to be in the strictest confidence. Even Dad doesn't know I'm meeting with you. Can you assure me this will remain only between the two of us?"

"I'll try to do whatever I can. But I must advise you if anything you say is pertinent to the Starr investigation, I may have to share that info with the chief of police. Can you live with that?"

Riley frowned as he thought for a minute. Then he responded, "I guess I'll have to. Okay, here's what happened. Dad obtained a phone number of a local euthanasia group. I can't tell you how he got it. Anyway, I promised to contact this group to see if they could assist Dad and do so in complete secrecy.

"I'm sorry I'm taking so long, but I'm finally getting to the connection with Molly Starr. You see, I called the phone number Dad gave me and I was invited to a meeting to learn about euthanasia right here in Dubuque. In an unusual way they predicted Molly Starr's death. Are you still with me?"

Zack straightened his posture. "I'm all ears, Riley. Please keep going and give me as much detail as you can."

"Okay. You're going to find this hard to believe. The meeting was six nights ago at ten p.m. at the Omega Building. You know it?"

"I think so. Isn't that in the warehouse area on the south end of the old business district near the river?"

"Yeah, but it's virtually deserted now. I believe Alliance Manufacturing used to use it for storing excess inventory."

The mention of his nighttime employer struck a chord with Zack. Any involvement by them would have to be coincidental. Heck, they had warehouse space all over Dubuque.

"...dark and vacant. Detective, still with me?"

"Sorry, something you said triggered a thought. Please go on."

"I was saying it's pretty eerie opening a door someone leaves unlocked for you late at night in a deserted part of town. Anyway, I did as requested and knocked on the west door before going in. Inside, I found a large room with a table and chair all by themselves in the middle. The only light was a reading lamp on the table. I saw a handwritten note propped against a tape recorder. As you can imagine, I was feeling really uncomfortable. But I had a duty for my dad — plus my curiosity got the best of me."

Curiosity was getting the best of Zack, too. He was completely engrossed in this bizarre adventure.

Riley continued. "The note instructed me to sit down and push 'play' on the tape recorder. For at least ten or fifteen minutes I listened to a distinctive gravelly voice expound on the virtues of mercy killing even though it is considered illegal. The speaker said they practiced euthanasia strictly to relieve the suffering of the terminally ill. Their work had been conducted regularly over the past couple years. But they were committed to confidentiality and the utmost secrecy. The voice said eliminating suffering was something God would want. To substantiate their authenticity, I was told of a mercy killing that would be performed shortly. A card had been left on the table." Riley fished it out of his shirt pocket. "Here...all it says is 'MAS, Barrington Lakes.' They said if I checked the obituary section of *The Herald Tribune* in a few days, I'd find the death of someone with those initials. The day before yesterday I found a match."

Zack responded, "Molly Ann Starr lived in Barrington Lakes."

"Exactly," said Riley. "And her death can't just be a coincidence. Isn't that episode one of the most incredible things you've ever heard?"

"Boy, you can say that again," Zack remarked. He felt certain this case was not euthanasia; it had to be murder. However, at this stage he felt it was best not to share these thoughts with Riley Whitcomb. "Riley, you were smart in contacting the police. Anything else you can tell me? Like, did you keep the number?"

"Oh, I did keep the phone number of the group." He grabbed his billfold, withdrew a crumpled paper and handed it to the detective. "One other thing. The recording ended by saying because of the risk, there would be a fee for their services and it would be large— but the funds would be used for charity. They also told me to leave my phone number. They promised to review my request and call me in a week."

"Riley, since you're here I wonder if you can give me some information on a completely unrelated matter. It concerns an issue about a St. Peter's employee. At some point I'll have to discuss it with the seminary president whom I have yet to meet. Can you tell me anything about the monsignor?" Zack detested using white lies, but here he was pulling a second one on this student in the same day. Riley's barely credible story put his veracity in question in spite of Sheila Patterson's favorable comments.

"You bet," the unsuspecting student replied. "I have a spiel on the monsignor that I give to prospective students. It goes like this. Monsignor Mulcahey has been the president of St. Peter's for about six years. His scholarly background includes valedictorian at Notre Dame, Rhodes scholar and a doctorate from Cambridge. Pretty impressive, huh? Well, off the record, he can be a bit of a cold fish and likes to be in control. He's charming and politically astute. In his six years at the helm, he has reversed the fortunes of St. Peter's. Most of his energies are spent on the seminary. You can stay on his good side by just following his rules. His big weakness is collecting rare books. Wait'll you see his office. He's got more first edition classics that anyone I've ever heard of. And he likes to play bridge. Does that give you an idea what he's like?"

"Yes, thanks, Riley. It's important the two of us keep in touch about this case. Here's my card, feel free to contact me any time. My cell number is on the bottom. Thanks for talking to me. It was a pleasure meeting you."

"You too, Detective."

"Please call me Zack."

Zack reviewed his notes for a few minutes after Riley had left. He decided to keep this dubious incident to himself until he could check it out more. No sense giving Lou some far out story to banter about.

FOUR

As Zack was returning to the police station his cell phone rang.

"Hi, Brenda, are you guys finished yet?"

"That's what I'm calling about. Matt and I have wrapped things up. We've got some answers for you. If possible, Matt would like to be on the road to Des Moines tonight. Can we meet with you, Lou and the chief in your conference room soon?"

"I'll be right there. If you don't mind, why don't you call Millie and have her order lunch in for all of us. She knows what I like. I'll see you in fifteen minutes."

This could be a good day, he thought. It sounded as though they would have a cause of death for Molly and he was eager to explore leads that Riley had given him.

~~~

All the parties were assembling in the conference room when Zack arrived. Millie had ordered lunch.

Brenda introduced Matt Rodgers to the two detectives. The chief had met him previously.

"Matt will relay our findings," Brenda said with confidence. "He's the forensics expert."

The DCI man started with a rehash of background information concerning Molly's medical history, followed by the cause of death.

"A short time ago, the DCI lab called to report on the analysis of Molly's water glass residue. The glass was clean. As far as they could tell it hadn't been used.

"The sedative that had been in the pill bottle was Ambien. At ten milligrams, fifteen or more of these taken at one time could have killed her." Rodgers paused for effect. "But, while that *could* have been the cause of death, it wasn't."

The room's eyes were now riveted on the DCI man. "Brenda has already told you traces of the sedative were found in her system. But the amount she ingested was only sufficient to put her to sleep, and then only light sleep. As you suspected, Zack, Molly's prints on the glass were not consistent with someone drinking from it.

"In fact, Molly Starr's death was due to an intravenous injection of an element normally found in the body: potassium. Brenda didn't give much concern to discovering its high level, since it's a natural body substance. It is biodegradable and the excess would eventually disappear completely. My estimate is, at the time of injection, the dosage would have exceeded more than a hundred times what you would expect to see. The shock to a person's system weakens the heart and brings about an abnormal rhythm. Cardiac arrest probably occurred within a few minutes of the injection. It's not a pleasant way to go, I might add.

"The bruises on her arms and thighs, although slight, would suggest she was restrained in some manner...to hold her while the syringe was inserted. Being frail in stature, Molly was not that strong. In a struggle she could be easily controlled by two normal-sized people. Traces of cotton indicate towels could have been used to hold her down thus minimizing bruising. Did either of you detectives find white towels on the premises?"

"We didn't see any, but we'll check again," Zack said.

Matt continued, "Zack, I also concur with your conclusion regarding the vomit found in the bathroom. More than likely, it was left by one of those present at the death scene. Brenda's note about its freshness tends to confirm this theory. Questions?"

The chief asked, "Matt, are you saying that the vomit didn't match the contents of Molly's stomach?"

"Yeah, Chief, and as fresh as it was, it had to have been left there that afternoon."

Zack added, "The nieces didn't go in the bathroom so it likely belonged to the perp who simply missed it when cleaning up the rest of the mess. It was obvious the floor around the toilet had just been washed, however that speck of puke could have been easily overlooked since it was behind the stool."

After a moment of silence the chief remarked, "Matt, thanks for your help. Brenda and you are to be commended for your fine work."

Just then, Millie brought in the sandwiches and drinks and distributed them.

Being anxious to begin his two hundred mile drive to Des Moines, the forensics expert said, "If you don't mind I'll eat my lunch on the road. I'd like to get home before dark. If you think of anything else, please give me a call."

The lateness of the meal caused the four famished participants to eat hurriedly in silence, until the number two detective questioned his superior.

"Since the bathroom vomit might be that of the perp, maybe you should have dusted the toilet, Zack."

"I did...early this morning," was the response, much to Lou's visible irritation. "I found a partial print on the toilet bowl in the vicinity where you might hold on to the stool while upchucking. As expected, it didn't belong to Molly. I've placed it on file so we can eventually check it with any suspects. I also examined the empty pill bottle. If Molly was taking one Ambien nightly, there would have only been four pills available at the time of her death, based on the date printed on the label. That's consistent with Brenda finding only a trace in Molly's stomach."

It may have been egotistical, but Zack couldn't help smiling inside while he exhibited a serious face. He decided not to mention his discussion with Riley until he had confirmed a few things at St. Peter's Seminary.

~~~

Summer schedules at colleges were less hectic. Zack had no problem in arranging a meeting with St. Peter's monsignor, who was normally running in several directions at once. The detective drove up the steep hill on Loras Boulevard and turned right at Alta Vista. As he neared Kirkwood, he spotted the entrance gates of St. Peter's campus. It was a study of incongruities. The architecture was cold, but the well-manicured landscaping and lush foliage made an inviting setting. As he surveyed the seminary buildings, he recalled reading in the school's brochures that they were of Gothic design with some elements of Craftsman style. They were patterned after the buildings of the neighboring educational institution, Loras College. There were six buildings nestled in lush and towering oaks that stirred rhythmically in the gentle summer breeze.

He slowed as he noticed the signage for Clark Hall, the administration building which housed the monsignor's office. Beyond his destination stood the library and Parks Hall where classes were held and the dormitory was across the lane not far from Allee Chapel, the campus's centerpiece. The single story, cement block building, barely visible due to being shielded by trees, must have been for maintenance. As he reached the top step of Clark Hall he surmised this to be one of the city's highest points because he caught sight of the Mississippi in the distance.

Monsignor Timothy Mulcahey's administrative assistant, Sheila, was the first person the detective met. He responded to the introduction by explaining that he had talked to her about Riley Whitcomb and appreciated her assistance. Sheila directed Zack into the president's office to the visitor's chair by the desk. She reported the monsignor would return momentarily. In that brief instant Zack's trained eyes took in the splendor of the office. The most conspicuous sights were the massive antique desk and chocolate-leather chair with matching chairs for visitors and the wall-to-wall bookshelves crowded with well-cared-for, rich, leather bindings. If those were rare books as Riley had said, the accumulated value of that wall could approach Zack's lifetime compensation as a cop. Zack's panoramic sweep also took in a separate reading table and chair, a chocolate-leather sofa, antique coffee table with matching end tables, a large Persian rug, and Florentine velvet drapes girding mullioned windows. Indirect lighting further enhanced the extravagant appointments.

Zack felt a hand on his shoulder and rose to greet the room's permanent occupant. With great difficulty his concentration returned to the job at hand. As he shook hands, Zack said, "It's a pleasure to finally make your acquaintance Monsignor Mulcahey. Your office is luxurious. And that wall of books is monumental. If I worked here, I'd spend all my time on the couch reading your books."

"Please be comfortable," the monsignor said as he directed the detective to return to the chair at his desk.

"I'll have Sheila get us some coffee. Is black your preference?"

He studied the seminary leader whose slight build and short stature belied his ability to control situations as Riley had inferred. He presented a well-tailored look even though his dress was casual in keeping with the summer schedule.

"Er…yes. That would be fine," Zack replied. He hadn't been paying attention, captivated by an extraordinary rich, leather bound book on the monsignor's desk. He could not keep his eyes off that volume which had to be strategically situated for the purpose of impressing a visitor. "That's a magnificent edition of Tolstoy's *War and Peace*."

"You can pick it up. You'll notice it's a first edition."

Zack carefully examined the exquisitely tooled leather jacket and turned to the back of the title page as he commented, "It certainly is. I'd consider that a rare and expensive find."

"Right, you are."

Zack wanted to get down to business but decided on a polite segue. "I haven't been in town long, but it's been long enough to hear how well St. Peter's is doing.

"A friend of mine has long tenure with the seminary."

"Who's that, Detective Gerrard?"

"Father Will Meloy."

"Detective, he's practically our professor emeritus. Next year will be his twentieth here. He probably knows theology better than anyone in the Midwest."

"He and I go way back. He was my favorite teacher at St. Mark's in Lake Forest. Since I've been here we've socialized and played some golf.

"I appreciate your taking the time to provide me with some information. First of all, I'm checking on Riley Whitcomb. Are you acquainted with him?"

"Heavens, yes. Riley's one of our best students. He'll receive his graduation diploma this week and be ordained soon. His first job after graduation will be with the seminary. This past year he was a part-time recruiter. He did so well we're bringing him on full time."

"Monsignor, does Riley have a history of exaggeration?"

"I'm not sure I know what you mean."

"Do you know if he makes up situations or has a tendency to blow things out of proportion? Or is he a person who's looking for attention?"

"Are we talking about the same person? Riley Whitcomb is a down to earth, sincere, serious person who's always looking for ways to help others. He's practically a poster child for a student ideally suited for the priesthood."

"Riley, told me such a preposterous story, I had to confirm his credibility. He mentioned meeting with a group that advocates euthanasia. As you're aware, euthanasia is illegal even though it can be of the best intentions. We always try to check such things out." Zack didn't want to bring up the connection with Molly Starr.

"My lord, that is hard to believe. But I wouldn't doubt Riley's word. Dealing with Riley or any of his relatives is an especially delicate situation. There's something you should know about him and the other Whitcombs."

"What's that, Monsignor?"

"The Whitcombs are largely responsible for St. Peter's existence as well as its financial well-being. Riley's great grandfather, Thomas Whitcomb, was a founder of St. Peter's. He gave us our first four buildings and contributed a million dollars to start our endowment fund in 1918. The extended Whitcomb family, which includes Riley's parents and some aunts and uncles, gives us nearly a million dollars each year to operate. Now that's not for publication. But it shows you the importance of maintaining favorable relations with Riley and his relatives. Their financial support is absolutely essential to our ability to provide a quality theological education. Hopefully, you can see the importance of handling this investigation with discretion."

"I understand, Monsignor. I'll certainly keep you abreast of anything we find out."

On the return to his office Zack wondered what his partner, Lou, and the chief would think of the discovery of a euthanasia group. This was especially true if it was one that could have brought about the demise of a very healthy, wealthy patron of the community.

FIVE

Zack dialed the number. After several rings an automated voice answered. "The number you have dialed is no longer in service. Please dial the operator for assistance."

The chief and Lou were peering in through the open doorway to his office. Millie had rounded them up to learn Zack's good news. Unfortunately, it had just soured. As he slammed the phone down in disgust, they walked in, removed the piles of documents from his visitors' chairs, and seated themselves at his desk.

"Son of a gun," Zack said in exasperation. "This whole case could have been so much easier."

The chief inquired, "What're you talking about, Zack?"

"I got a lead this morning from someone who knew...*in advance*...that Molly Starr was going to die."

Zack saw eager anticipation showing on the faces of both of his associates.

"I got a call from a seminary student who was given a prediction. He'd been told an individual from the western outskirts of Dubuque with the initials 'MAS' would die a few days later. Four days later, Starr died in Barrington Lakes."

Both of the policemen wanted to hear more so Zack gave them a detailed account of his conversations with Riley and Monsignor Mulcahey.

The chief said, "My first reaction was that you were dealing with some sort of nut. But with the monsignor vouching for him, I'd tend to believe what he's telling us. If Whitcomb's info stands up, we've got a homicidal group right here in our community."

Lou added, "One thing we should do is check on the ownership of the Omega Building and have a look around."

"You want to handle that?" Zack directed his question to Lou.

"Sure," he replied. "I'll get right on it."

"For the time being we should keep the whole euthanasia thing confidential, especially any connection with Molly Starr. That make sense?"

The other two nodded in agreement.

~~~

Riley Whitcomb was in his dormitory room with his best friend and fellow student, Dan Perkins. He had just finished telling Dan about his dad's desire for a mercy killing, the euthanasia meeting with the prediction of Molly Starr's death and his meeting with the police detective.

But before Dan could respond, Riley's phone rang. After a few moments, of listening, Riley simply said, "Thank you, Marty. It wasn't unexpected," and hung up. Then he mumbled, ostensibly to Dan, but as much to himself. "I knew Dad's days were numbered. But I guess you're never prepared to lose someone so close. Oh, God, why do you always have to take the good ones first?" He rubbed his bloodshot eyes and blew his nose.

"I'm so sorry, buddy. Ted was like a second father. Why don't you lie down? I'll be back in a flash."

Dan rushed to his room across the hall and returned in an instant carrying a never-opened pint of Jim Beam. "I've been saving this for a special occasion, guess this counts though it wasn't quite what I had in mind at the time. Here take a swig." His friend passed Riley the bottle and said, "I'll join you." The two finished the contents in quick gulps but their resulting facial expressions showed they were not seasoned imbibers.

"Marty suggested I come home as soon as possible." Marty was Nell Whitcomb's long time housekeeper. "Mom's lying down. The priest and your folks should be there soon."

Riley and Dan's parents had been interconnected through close friendships for nearly all of their lives. Both families had their roots in Dubuque and their social and business ties virtually melded them into one large clan.

Riley and Dan were uncannily alike in many ways. Although Riley was a year older, the two were similar in physical appearance, mannerisms, beliefs, and goals in life, so much so that many took them for brothers. Both had short blond hair, blue eyes and slender builds. They could have been mistaken for one another, even though Riley was two inches taller.

As Dan drove Riley across town to his home the two became more philosophical. "Riley, I don't know what else you could have done for your dad under the circumstances."

"Yeah, I'm just sorry he suffered so much. That euthanasia group is doing the right thing. I don't care what the pope says about mercy killing. I think there's a place for it and even though the Church isn't in favor of it I'm going to support it any way I can when I become a priest."

"Still, you did the right thing by talking to the police."

Riley's mind drifted to thoughts of the euthanasia group. Maybe he could join them. After his ordination next week, his full time employment with the seminary assured he would remain in the area. There'd be plenty of opportunity to contact them when he worked as a recruiter for St. Peter's. The more Riley contemplated this matter, the greater was his impatience to discover more about the euthanasia group.

~~~

"Hi babe, I'm home. I'm going out to dinner with Will." It was Friday evening and Zack had the night off from his Alliance security job. He would have preferred spending it with Kristen. It was her last night home for a few days, but she had arranged to be with her friends. Well, it probably wasn't any different for other families in similar situations; the kids wanted to be with their peers rather than stuffy, boring parents. At least they could share some one-on-one over breakfast at Guido's in the morning before her roommate's ride arrived.

"Hi ya, Dad. Be sure and say 'hi' for me. I haven't seen him in a long time. I promise I won't be out late, so we can have a nice breakfast in the morning." Zack received a quick peck on the cheek as Kristen hurried out the door.

As Zack drove to Father Will's he reflected on his long relationship with the professor. Father Will Meloy had been Zack's favorite teacher at St. Mark's High School in Lake Forest, Illinois, twenty-five years before. They had kept up regular contact over the years. Christmas letters. Birthdays. Will had presided over his wedding with Joan. And as the godfather, he was there for Kristen's christening. A couple of times Joan and he had even journeyed from their home in Minneapolis to visit Will in Dubuque. Will encouraged them to move to the Iowa community. However, opportunities for advancement tied Zack to the Minneapolis PD.

When Joan passed away from breast cancer three years ago, Zack wanted to leave the city. Memories of Joan and his good times in Minneapolis were still painful.

In fact, he couldn't wait to move. But he had pledged to his dying wife he would make certain that Kristen remained in the same high school. In her senior year Zack began looking for a police job in some other community. Timing can mean a great deal in life and Will took advantage of that by mentioning an opening in the Dubuque department. Zack applied and was hired as the lead detective on their force.

With his arrival in Dubuque, Zack managed to get together with Will once or twice a month. He thought of Will's life, what little he knew. Will seemed such a private person. He loved to talk about anything except his own life, always managing to change the subject when it came to himself. Nevertheless, Zack had maintained enough contact through the years to be familiar with Will's interests and activities. However, he recalled only one time when Will ventured into his own life's story to any extent. It was when he had stayed over after Kristen's christening. The two of them had been alone, drinking and philosophizing. The event with Zack's daughter had reawakened Will's thoughts of his earlier life. Will had recalled how he was drawn to the priesthood because of his family's misfortunes. His father had left home when Will was about ten. The family had little money so Will worked whenever he wasn't in school. His younger brother had something called Guillain-Barre syndrome, an autoimmune disease that damaged motor and sensory nerves.

Church charities helped the family survive his brother's medical bills. Will never forgot that and as a result dedicated himself to God, which eventually led to the priesthood. Miraculously, Will's brother remained alive. His mother continued to visit the younger brother every day at a special home for the suffering. Will had even mentioned his mother's plan to relocate his brother where the cost of his maintenance could be more reasonable. Zack knew that Will sent money home to his mother whenever possible.

Zack assumed that the financial drain continued to this day. It was a subject he never broached with Will though, whose stoicism and pride would allow no further discussion of the matter. If it weren't for that one night's exchange, Zack would not even have been aware of Will's secret plight. The friendship came with the unspoken agreement to never revisit Will's private turf.

It was with this thought that Zack approached the western outskirts of Dubuque where Will lived. He traveled by the fairgrounds on the Old Highway Road. Once virtually in the country, this area was now surrounded by new residential developments. Will's acre of ground, accompanied by good landscaping, provided privacy for the two-story frame dwelling with an attached workshop.

Zack returned to the present as he swerved down the winding driveway to his friend's home. He popped his lean frame out of the Toyota with an energy level still high for a person in the early forties. Before he could reach the front steps his friend was out the door.

Will's bulky physique gave the appearance of a former NFL linebacker. From a distance, his slight balding looked like a skin colored beanie. Except for a few barely noticeable red veins on his bulbous nose that Zack assumed was associated with alcohol consumption, Will's wrinkle-free countenance belied his mid-fifties age. The friendly face vouched for his tenderheartedness and compassion.

"Good evening, my boy, great to see you," Will said.

They simultaneously exchanged the greeting the two had first employed nearly a quarter of a century ago—a partially extended arm with a thumbs-up accompanied by a wink. Zack reflected upon how that gesture had originally come about: Will had been handing back the final test results in his theology class. Seeing the "A" grade, Zack impulsively balled a fist and raised the thumb in Will's direction as he winked. The proud teacher responded instinctively in the same manner. Ever since then, it was a silent communication of friendship between the two.

"Hello, Will, glad you could join me."

"Wouldn't miss it for the world. Man, am I hungry. What could be better than all the catfish you can eat and a few brewskies during happy hour?"

Will squeezed his massive body into the front passenger seat of the Toyota. The seat cushions were compressed to their thinnest level yet. "Will, you look like a grizzly bear being stuffed into a model car."

"If you think *this* is snug, just wait 'til our trip back when I've got a half-dozen catfish under my belt."

"You're the connoisseur, buddy. If you say this place is good, that's all the convincing I need. But you know I'm not much of a fish-eater. Reckon they'll have steak?"

"I guarantee this is the most incredible deep fried catfish ever served. If you aren't totally satisfied I'll pop for the whole bill. Twenty-five bucks will cover the total cost for both of our all-you-can-eat meals and *still* leave room for a generous tip.

"And, Zack, I'll bet there isn't one person in ten in the city who knows this place. It's just beyond the Maquoketa Caves Park. Don't worry about a map, I'll give directions as we go. Entire trip should only take about forty minutes by the back roads.

"Bet the majority of the customers are hog and cattle feeders. But they swear there's no better fish. The place started with catfish from their own private lake. It's become so popular the fish is now shipped in — fresh. I hear they get thousands of pounds, one truckload right after another."

The Toyota wound its way through hilly, isolated back roads. The patterned fields reminded Zack of a quilt he had on his bed when he was a boy. For several minutes the fellow travelers silently enjoyed the early summer beauty as the sun reddened and began its slide behind the tree-lined meadows.

"Spectacular, eh Zack?" Will finally noted. "I always marvel at the beauty man concocted with God's help," Massive oaks cast shadows that spattered fields of knee-high corn; precise rows of soybeans seemed woven with the contours of the rolling cropland.

"Bet you're ready to celebrate the end of another school year, Will."

"It's been a good one, but I do need a break. Did you know next year'll be my *thirtieth* teaching? Ten in high school and twenty here at St. Peter's. Hard to believe I'm now considered the old fart on the faculty!

"Zack, now that you've lived here for half a year, you getting to feel at home?" Will continued.

"Haven't given that much thought. Everyone makes me feel comfortable in Dubuque. I love the community; love my job. But, Will, when I take time to reflect I feel this big hole in my life. I didn't mean to get so serious. Guess I still grieve for Joan. It's doubly hard with Kristen leaving the nest. Thank goodness you're around. Tonight we're going to your favorite place for dinner. I can't help but think of my favorite place, Houston's, back in Minneapolis. It unleashes all sorts of memories. That's where I took Joan on our first date. I'd been investigating a burglary at Zale's jewelry store, where Joan worked when I met her. Took more than a month to figure out it was an inside job. During that time I interviewed her several more times than necessary because I liked being with her. Finally, I got up the nerve to ask her out for dinner at Houston's. On one of our dates there, about four months later, I asked her to marry me. We always went back there for special occasions. I'm afraid there'll never be another one like her, Will.

"Kristen was very close to her mom; but she seems to have been able to overcome the sorrow. Keeps encouraging me to do the same. She even suggested we could go out on a double date! Can you beat that? I can't imagine parking in some romantic setting and watching my own daughter in the rear, necking with some oversexed teenager."

Will released a hearty laugh. Then, just as quickly, switched moods. "Not to change the subject…well, yes, to change the subject, frankly—how's the job going?"

"I feel I'm contributing more each day. The chief is great to work for. I just wish I could get Lou to get over his problem with me. He tries to cover it, but I know he burns inside about having to report to me when he's got the seniority."

"How about that Molly Starr case? Anything you can publicly report?"

"Well, I've met with the coroner and one of the state's forensic experts, but it's premature to draw many conclusions." Zack had always believed in the confidentiality of ongoing investigations, even with close friends. However, he figured he could say a few things about Molly, since some of the findings had leaked outside the police station.

"Between you and me this looks more like a homicide than a suicide. It seems she died of a drug-induced cardiac arrest." Zack knew he should not tell anything about the euthanasia aspect of the case.

After traversing the Maquoketa Caves State Park, they reached the crest of a hill. Zack slowed to a crawl as the situation seemed like reaching the highest point on a roller coaster. The other side of the hill declined so severely, all he could see was the blood-red sky. After a few more yards he remarked in amazement, "Holy cow, is that where we're going?" He was looking out of his side window because the front of the car revealed only horizon.

"That's why they close this place in the winter," Will replied. "I've been on ski slopes that aren't this steep."

"I wonder if we shouldn't have come earlier. Looks as though there's more than a hundred cars down there." With a little imagination Zack could envision a miniature house made of white playing cards surrounded on two sides by a multitude of Legos representing cars with pans of water to the left and back forming the private lake.

"Zack, Friday night fish fries are the most popular time here. People start signing up for tables by three o'clock even though it doesn't open until five. Just means we'll have time for a few extra beers."

The conversation was light during the three-beers-apiece cocktail hour. Will bought a round for some parishioners he knew at All Saints. The topic over catfish was one of Will's favorites: the hapless Chicago Cubs and their current nine game losing streak.

The Toyota had barely exited the parking lot when Will opted for some shut-eye. Zack's mood had mellowed and he enjoyed the peace and quiet of a short trip home.

"Okay, Will. This is your stop."

"Er...ah...oh. Guess I overdid it on both the beers and the dinner. But I enjoyed the quality time with you, Zack."

"Me, too, Will. Let's play some golf one of these days."

Will struggled to pry himself out of the car. Zack did not drive off until Will had stumbled into his home and turned on a light.

SIX

The combination of bright sun and recovery from the previous evening caused Father Will Meloy to don his sunglasses. Regardless, he was in festive spirits as he strode to the administration building of St. Peter's Seminary. The fragrance of the freshly mown grass reminded him of his newfound golf addiction. Later in the day, he planned to hit some shag balls at the Bunker Hill course. Somehow, he had to adjust his swing to eliminate that darn slice.

This was Will's second-happiest day of the school year. He would conduct his last class of the semester after a short meeting with the monsignor. His happiest day of the year was always his first day of teaching in the fall.

Father Will reflected on his only remaining work responsibility after today, which was the grading of final exams. This year's class of scholastic achievers would make that a pleasurable task. He might even resort to Father O'Dea's preposterous prank. His fondly remembered former teacher jokingly bragged about the "stair step method" of grading, whereby he simply tossed the final exams down a stairwell and those landing on the highest steps got the highest grades.

The only blemish the theology professor anticipated on his good mood today was about to occur. As the resident historian, he needed to verify the monsignor's memory regarding the seminary's history in preparation for a visit by Cardinal Clancy. The monsignor had assured him that proud days would soon arrive for Dubuque's Catholics.

"Hi, Father Meloy, the monsignor is expecting you and he has a mutual friend in there with him," said Sheila. "Your hazelnut coffee is still brewing. I'll bring it in to you in a minute." Although she was the assistant to the president, no duty was too trivial for this attractive matron.

Will tapped politely on the open door as he entered the luxurious office of the seminary president.

"Good morning, professor," the monsignor said as he peered studiously over his Gucci reading glasses. His minuscule mustache complemented a frail physique. But Will considered the force of his personality more than compensated for his undernourished five-foot-four-inch frame. "Cliff and I were discussing Ted Whitcomb's funeral. You hate to see such a fine man pass away so prematurely. He'll be sorely missed."

And so will his money, reflected Will. He quickly asked the Lord for forgiveness. That was a tacky thought.

"It was a good turnout," Will responded, and your eulogy was magnificent." He walked towards the monsignor's other visitor to shake his hand. "Hello, Cliff, how's everything with the city's leading physician?"

"Can't complain, Father. The monsignor and I were just talking about the big weekend ahead for the Church."

"Oh, you mean Riley's special ordination?"

"No," the doctor responded, "I was actually thinking about the Brackett House dedication."

"Yes," the monsignor said, "It's not every day we host both a cardinal and the archbishop. Archbishop O'Donnell says the cardinal is extremely impressed with the Brackett House's programs for the disenfranchised elderly. Evidently, he'll be making an important announcement about our achievements."

"That should bode well for the two of you, since you both serve on that board," Will replied.

The monsignor responded, "And for everyone involved in this important new venture. Well, Cliff, thanks for updating me on the Brackett dedication plans. Let me know if I can do anything else to prepare for the big event." With a courteous farewell, Dr. Brown excused himself.

"Will, I appreciate your taking time to play tutor concerning the seminary's history. I plan to give Cardinal Clancy a campus tour prior to Riley Whitcomb's ordination. Then I'll take him and Archbishop O'Donnell to the reception. How about if you join the three of us for breakfast the next morning since you'll be in the receiving line for Riley? Then we can go together to the Brackett House dedication."

"Sounds good to me," Will said appreciatively. He looked forward to renewing his acquaintance with the cardinal.

Sheila arrived with Will's favorite coffee and he inhaled the aroma of the hazelnut blend with evident pleasure.

Will proceeded to review the school's history with the monsignor. His final comment confirmed the strategy the monsignor had planned for the cardinal. "I think your approach to emphasize the role played by the Whitcomb family makes sense. Not only does the Whitcomb money keep us operating, Riley's ordination is really the main reason for the cardinal's visit."

Will left for his class with confidence that the monsignor was prepared to make the positive impression everyone expected.

~~~

The two detectives met in their conference room to exchange information. It concerned the Omega Building where Riley

Whitcomb had learned of the clandestine euthanasia efforts and its tenant, Alliance.

Lou spoke first. "I met with Byron Tway, owner of the Omega warehouse. Says he seldom visits the place. Since it's still under a long-term lease to Alliance he suggested I contact Chris Lazorno, one of their foremen, who has ready access to it.

"Chris was very cooperative and he met me at the building so I could have a look around. Seems that most of the time the facility is idle. Some of the products Alliance has been subcontracted for are stored there. Ground floor doubles as a meeting room where equipment manufacturers send their people to learn how to use those products.

"I went through all three floors of the building. Outside of boxed inventory, all I saw was a stack of tables and chairs on the main floor that are used for demonstrations. Chris left for lunch while I examined the furniture. After a half hour I got tired of dusting for prints. I found enough different ones to account for half the people in town!"

"I guess we shouldn't have hoped for much," Zack said. "But it doesn't rule *out* the possibility of being used as Whitcomb suggested, does it?"

Zack did not wait for a response. "I did discover one other thing about Alliance's connection, Lou. With my night job at the company I hear all the rumors, and, interestingly, there's been a good deal of talk about Molly Starr. Apparently she had enemies in both labor and management of the company. That shocked me. Here's a woman who's donated so much to local charities but who's detested by so many at Alliance. My supervisor told me there was a scare that she and some of what they call her do-gooder friends were trying to put Alliance out of business."

"Why the heck would anyone do that?" Lou asked.

"PCBs it turns out. Seems the feds were cracking down on the company for polluting Rock Creek to the point where it was a danger to local homeowners. We need to follow up on this, Lou. I think I'll get us an appointment with the CEO."

~~~

At ten in the evening, most seminary students were either cramming for tomorrow's final exams or preparing for bed. Not Riley Whitcomb. He was wide-awake and ready to make his move.

A severe thunderstorm was bombarding most of the region. In its wake was a path of darkness. Riley reckoned the electrical blackout was the result of a lightning strike on the electrical substation. He also reckoned it was fortuitous for him since it would provide cover for his mission.

With an umbrella in one hand and his flashlight in the other he dashed for his car. During a pause in the downpour he inhaled the fresh ozone aroma, reminding him of the days when his mom would hang his bed sheets out to dry.

There was no traffic. At Dodge Street he could see a fire truck with its lights flashing near one of the revered buildings on the national register. He continued east and south until he caught sight of the Omega Building.

Since the momentous meeting where he had learned of local euthanasia efforts he'd been thinking of how he could make contact with the group. They must have read of his father's death because they had not called him. He tried the phone number where he first had reached them and found it had been disconnected. His only option was to hope they would be having another meeting at the building he had visited. Under the circumstances, he anticipated some difficulty in convincing them he wanted to assist them.

Nearly every day since that first encounter he had driven by this place. There had never been any activity and the two ground floor doors were locked. The only other access he could imagine was to reach the roof of the single story building adjacent on the north and to enter Omega's second floor through a window. There were no windows on the first floor, so there was no way from ground level to determine if lights were on in the building.

Tonight Riley planned to scale the facility next door to determine if Omega was accessible from there. Possibly he would be lucky, see a light, and find a meeting in progress.

Storm clouds parted to reveal a full moon whose illumination cast swaying shadows of a nearby oak tree on the south exterior, the only movement in the area.

His Nike's were silent as he plotted a track around the building from the east, backside. He kept his flashlight dark for fear of attracting attention. As he rounded a corner he jolted to a halt. Directly in front of him was a massive form, so close he could easily reach out and make contact. The hairs on the back of his neck stood at attention. An instinctive reaction caused him to jerk on his flashlight and aim it in the face of the intruder.

"Boy, you scared the heck out of me," Riley blurted. "Have you seen my Sparky?" It came out almost as if he planned it. What else could he use as an excuse?

The badge on the barrel-chested security guard flashed with the light. The expression on his face indicated he was equally surprised.

With as much casualness as his courage would permit, Riley commented, "Darn dog was spooked by the lightning and took off. This is usually his stomping ground during the daytime, so it's the first place I looked."

The obviously relieved guard replied, "Lucky I didn't whack you. You frightened the hell out of me, too. Right now I've got to hit the head and check my pants. I think you scared the piss out of me."

The seminary student exhaled in relief. He watched the security guard depart in a bowlegged march as if he were a two-year old, attempting to minimize chaffing his thighs. No use pressing his luck tonight. He'd be back again soon.

SEVEN

Before Zack would venture into the lion's den of Alliance's chief executive officer he wanted to be prepared. Herbert J. Pratt had a reputation as an intimidating hard ass.

In the detective's experience, every small town had someone who kept tabs on everything worth knowing about, usually someone at the local paper. In Dubuque, it was Hank Ryan, senior editor at the *Herald Tribune*. Accordingly, Zack made an appointment. He had previously met this locus of all-things-noteworthy socially, but doubted the editor would recall it.

Zack was shown promptly into Ryan's office, observing that it was on the other end of the spectrum from that of the monsignor. Glass windows comprised two inner walls of the smallish cubicle devoid of furniture except for two chairs opposite the editor's desk. Newspapers were stacked along the walls giving the impression of a total disregard for organization. The occupant was not attempting to impress visitors.

Partially hidden behind a desk strewn with more newspapers came a voluminous, deep voice. "'Morning, Zack. Nice of you to drop by. Say, how is that Kristen of yours enjoying Northwestern?"

The detective knew he had come to the right place.

His first impression of the diminutive white-haired gentleman in a white starched shirt with suspenders and a dated tie was that he looked about the age of the newspaper, which was in its seventieth year.

"Hello, Mr. Ryan. Kristen loves the school and she's doing fine, thanks."

"Just put those papers on the floor and have a seat."

"Mr. Ryan, the…"

"Please call me, Hank," he interrupted.

"Well, Hank, the chief holds you in high regard. He suggested if I wanted the unvarnished truth I should call on you. And that's why I'm here this morning."

"Coming from him, that's quite a compliment. What can I do for you, Detective?"

"Hank, as you probably know, we're in the midst of investigating Molly Starr's death."

"A catastrophe! That's what it is, real tragedy for the community."

"Initially, we found it hard to believe she would have been murdered. Didn't seem to have an enemy in the world. Now we discover one organization in town that couldn't be happier that she's gone."

Before he could go further the editor interrupted, "Alliance Manufacturing."

"Correct. And apparently the sentiment goes from the top to the bottom of the company. Can you help me understand why?"

"Son, it's all about money and jobs. Molly and some of her well-intentioned, environmental activist friends nearly put Alliance out of business and cost hundreds their jobs. Molly always was an active proponent of a clean environment. I mean, who doesn't want that? But for some time she publicly chastised the company for being the biggest polluter in eastern Iowa. Now, manufacturing plastic parts causes an enormous waste disposal problem. For years they were dumping tons of pollutants in Rock Creek, which, as you know, flows into the Mississippi. Molly got all worked up about it and organized a picketing of their operation. Not only was it embarrassing to the management of the company, it resulted in some *astronomical* fines! They would've had to file for Chapter 11 if the governor himself hadn't stepped in to negotiate a loan guarantee program to cover the huge cost of waste disposal.

"Can't say Molly didn't have balls! Completely disregarded security measures to protect her from threats she was getting."

"Hasn't Herb Pratt been especially vocal about his feelings for her?"

"You're right there. But Herb's way too smart to get tangled up in any murder plot."

When Zack left the editor he visualized the hatred that could have come from many at Alliance. He supposed it was possible that the hate could have triggered something that resulted in Molly's death.

~~~

Riley Whitcomb didn't like to give up easily. That evening, shortly after ten o'clock, he made another trip to the Omega Building. He parked a block and a half away and walked up Salina Street along the west side to his destination. There was no traffic and he saw only one person a half block ahead going in the same direction.

This time he was more cautious as he casually strolled past the front of the building on the opposite side of the street. He spotted the security guard on a coffee break at Winkies, directly across the street.

He could see that the roof of the one story building directly to the north of Omega was easily accessible.

Effortlessly scaling the back of the building with the assistance of a large metal trash bin, in less than two minutes he was peering into one of the second-floor windows. He could see a beam of light streaming from the main level through an opening on the second floor.

With his elbow wrapped in his jacket he tapped the previously cracked window glass. Almost noiselessly the shards fell out from the point of contact. After removing a large piece, Riley reached inside to undo the rotating lock situated on top of the lower pane and entered quickly.

Carefully he made his way to the source of the light beam with only one misstep causing the smallest of squeaks on the ancient flooring.

Something was happening on the floor below. By carefully balancing on the beam supports of something that resembled a delivery chute he was close enough to hear conversation, but not able to view the participants. At this angle he could see only a small area of the old floor below. The intermittent droning of a noisy fan had its good and bad points. It covered any slight sound he might make but it also made listening more difficult. From time to time, he heard snippets of chatter and it appeared that most of the discussion was by a leader who had a gravelly voice.

He'd recognize that manner of speech anywhere! It had the same distinctive rasping sound he had heard on the recorder from his first visit.

Others in the session below did not speak nearly as often. Riley strained to hear the leader's words. "…next appointment…month…condition has worsened…Chandler…terminally ill patient…advanced diabetes…despondent…meds not working…no hope left…could help out on this?…ninth…I'll proceed…newspaper…house." The significance of what was being said brought out goose pimples on his sweaty arms.

Meanwhile, he was getting a cramp in his left leg from trying to remain perfectly still. And he found that any movement he made to restore circulation produced a creak in the floor. Suddenly, the conversation stopped and Riley went rigid, afraid to even breathe. The tenseness in his muscles felt like minutes had passed. Then, he noticed a movement of shadows. A flash of gray material disturbed his view of the floor below and then another movement of the same color. He filed the light medium gray color into his memory. Apparently the meeting was breaking up. Could it have been caused by the sound of his inadvertent movement?

Riley stayed as motionless as possible. In spite of cramping in both legs, he remained in the same awkward position for several more minutes after the light in the room below went off. Then he tried inching back to his entry point. He remained there for what seemed like an interminable period until he was sure the coast was clear.

By the time he returned to his dorm, the clock registered five after midnight…but it felt like he'd been gone for twice that long.

Unable to sleep, he tapped on Dan's door. His friend was slow in responding but gave a groggy invitation to come in.

After hearing of Riley's second experience with the euthanasia group, Dan held the same opinion that he had before: "Riley, I think you should go back to the police. You now have solid evidence that could help them to expose this group."

"You're right, Dan. I'm sure they're planning another killing. I'm calling Gerrard first thing tomorrow"

~~~

"Thanks for coming right down, Riley. I can't wait to hear this new information on our euthanasia friends," Zack said.

"Here's what happened late last night," Riley proceeded to relate his most recent encounter in detail. "The background noise made it difficult to understand. The conversation I heard was in choppy fragments. But there was no question they were planning another event. It's a terminally ill patient who is suffering and wants help right away. The details were hard to follow, but I specifically remember a few words that seemed important."

Riley took a crumpled piece of paper from his pants pocket and read: "Chandler, ninth, newspaper and house."

"As soon as I got to my room I wrote them down so I wouldn't forget. I didn't sleep much last night, kept mulling over what I heard."

Zack broke in, "Riley, you took one heck of a chance there. As much as we appreciate your efforts there's no sense getting killed yourself. You'd be smart to stick to saving souls and leave the warehouse adventures to the cops. Don't get me wrong, this is crucial info…I just don't want to open a new case with your name on it."

Whitcomb was not to be deterred though. "There's one other thing I could add about last night. My view into the room was limited to a small part of the floor. So I couldn't see anyone clearly, but I *did* get a glimpse of a couple of the people's clothing as they left. It happened so fast and I wasn't prepared, but I believe two of them were dressed in the exact same kind of gray. That seemed strange to me."

"Good observation. Now listen, Riley, I didn't want to say anything earlier, but we think this group is performing murders. Their operation may have been originally geared for euthanasia, but other killings could also be on their agenda."

In a way, the seminarian had anticipated this. He feared the secret group was doing something other than deeds of compassion but had so wanted to be part of a something that could bring peace to the suffering, terminally ill.

"You've been a great deal of help," Zack continued. "Based on your report, I consider this group—or whatever it is—to be extremely dangerous, especially if they knew they were being overheard. So, like I said for your own safety, I'd recommend you cool your spying and just keep us posted on anything that comes your way."

As Riley left, Zack considered the wealth of information he had just received from this amateur sleuth. As much as he appreciated having the data, he knew that further Hardy Boy antics like this could not only cause Whitcomb's own premature demise…it could, at some point, start to interfere with his own police work.

EIGHT

The investigative trio of Zack, Lou and the chief were in the conference room between Zack and Lou's office. Zack had completed his report of his most recent discussion with Riley Whitcomb. He approached the blackboard where he had previously written information pertaining to this case. Prior to today, under the Molly Starr headline, was listed "euthanasia group," "Riley Whitcomb," "Omega Building" and "Alliance Manufacturing." This morning he had added under Riley's second meeting the notations, "Chandler," "ninth," "newspaper," and "house," and "two dressed in same color."

Before anyone arrived Zack had been contemplating the words he had chalked. Once they were seated he said, "The only sense I can make of the four new words is that something could happen to a Chandler on the ninth. Maybe it will be in the paper. Who knows at what house?"

Lou commented, "The two-who-dressed-alike could be a coincidence or it could be some sort of uniform."

The chief was thinking out loud. "It seems as though we need more information before we can make any sense out of it. In the meantime, we need to concentrate on Molly Starr. What are our plans, Zack?"

"Lou has more of her relatives to interview and I'll be following up on her business and social contacts."

~~~

Later in the day Zack and Lou conferred.

"I haven't had much luck with the relatives, Zack," Lou confessed. "I talked to Molly's only sister, a nephew, a niece and the two nieces who were at the crime scene. Doesn't appear to be anything extraordinary to report. Everyone's got an alibi. The last remaining relative, another nephew, will be returning to town in a few days. I'm hoping that interview will give us something."

"Lou, as far as what her friends and business associates told me, Molly didn't have an enemy in the world. But I'll qualify that in a moment. Most of her time was spent making gifts to charities. So I decided to check with the one person in town who keeps tabs on everything that's important in the community, Hank Ryan, the *Herald*'s senior editor. He mentioned Molly's unpopularity with Alliance, same as I heard from the rumor mill." Zack related the specifics of what he had learned.

"I guess I do recall reading efforts to stop Alliance's pollution now that you bring it up. Forgot Molly was the instigator of that confrontation."

"Well, you can hear more about it firsthand if you want to come with me to meet with Alliance's chairman, Herb Pratt. I made an appointment for oh-eight-hundred tomorrow."

"Okay Zack, should be interesting. I don't live far from their headquarters. How about I meet you there?"

"I'll see you then."

~~~

The detectives were shown into the chief executive's office punctually at eight o'clock.

"Good morning, gentlemen. I have a good suspicion as to why you're here. Molly Starr, right?" Herb Pratt asked.

"Right you are, sir," Zack opened for the pair. "I realize this seems far-fetched but we have to check out all the possibilities, especially where Ms. Starr might have had an unfriendly relationship."

"Unfriendly, you say. It was damn hostile! She nearly bankrupted us and that would have caused hundreds of layoffs. She wouldn't listen to reason. Thank God the governor came to our rescue. I must say, outside of our situation, she did many fine things for the community. But she just wouldn't see the big picture. We provide a lot of jobs for Dubuque people."

Zack did not back off his questioning. Maybe this guy was used to intimidation, but it wouldn't work with him.

"Mr. Pratt, I'll just come out point blank and ask: Can you think of anyone in your company whose animosity might have got the best of them, any hotheads?"

"Hell no, Detective. No one around here's that stupid. I'll admit we weren't sad to see her go from a business aspect. But you can put any involvement in our murdering her to rest. We're law-abiding citizens around here. Well, except for one little dumping incident."

The chief got a chuckle out of Pratt's remarks when he learned about them later. "'A little dumping' he said. Forty or fifty thousand tons of pollutants seems like more than a little to me. Heck, that schmuck's lucky he wasn't thrown in prison. I know he thinks he's God, but committing murder, that seems hard to believe."

~~~

It was the tenth of the month when Zack flipped through the *Herald Tribune*. This morning brought back memories of the hearty morning breakfasts prepared by Joan. He appreciated Kristen's effort to rise early and prepare his meal and it was nice to have her back from her trip. She certainly meant well, so he wasn't about to complain about the burnt toast and hard eggs. But he had to inwardly snicker. How would her future husband react to such culinary treatment?

An item in the paper jumped out at him. "Babe, you're not going to believe this! Remember when I told you about this Whitcomb character meeting a group that practices euthanasia? This confirms what they told him. Someone named Chandler Logan died yesterday, the ninth, just as predicted. The obituary says he died of complications related to advanced diabetes. I'll bet you another piece of burnt toast his demise was premature."

"Dad, are you saying you're going to find another victim with a needle mark?"

"That's exactly what I'm saying."

~~~

His early arrival at work found the chief working at his desk. He alternated bites of donut with sips of coffee as he reviewed reports from the night shift. When he saw Zack he barked out, "Bring your coffee and come on in. In case you're wondering, I've already read it."

Zack knew what he meant. "Just as advertised, huh? Think we should have an autopsy?"

The chief replied, "Yeah, maybe you should talk to Harry. The body's at William's Mortuary. I'm sure Harry could delay the embalming process 'til you can get him a court order. I'll have Millie get Polly Larkin in the DA's office to prepare it for you. If Chandler Logan was murdered, I'm going to ask the DA to temporarily transfer Polly over here to help on the investigations. Understand she's a real whiz."

Zack made his way to the conference room where he contemplated the chalkboard. He wanted to temporarily transfer his thoughts from Chandler Logan to the Molly Starr case. He studied the written clues hoping something he had missed would suddenly be revealed.

"Good morning, honey."

Zack realized Millie was in her maternal mode.

"While you were with the chief," she said, "Riley Whitcomb called to inform you about an obituary in this morning's newspaper. Said this had to be the 'Chandler' he told you about. Also, Ms. Larkin will soon be here with an order for the judge. The chief asks that you accompany her to the judge to emphasize the urgency of an autopsy on Logan. In the meantime, I've brought Polly's employment file. She'll be attached to the detective unit immediately. She might not win a beauty contest, but she's plenty smart and tough as nails. Not only are we getting our own legal counsel, she's also considered a whiz on the computer."

Ignoring the less considerate portion of Millie's well-intentioned intel, Zack focused on the folder entitled "Myrtle P. Larkin." "No wonder she goes by 'Polly.' Probably named after a rich relative. 'Thirty-one years old, married, B.A. in computer science from Iowa State, law degree from University of Iowa, employed by Dubuque County as an assistant district attorney.' She had been in her present position for six years. If she was as good as she sounded, she'd be ready to move on shortly."

Lou had joined Zack in the conference room when the chief stopped by with their new assistant. She was not nearly as bad a looker as Millie had intimated.

Zack considered her to be taller than average and what some people called big-boned, but the longhaired blond, blue-eyed attorney had a well-constructed figure and a face he would definitely call handsome. In the peculiar vocabulary of Zack Gerrard, that might be somewhat pretty or attractive, or maybe so-so. If you removed the studious glasses and downsized the nose she might make the "definitely pretty" list.

"Gentlemen, I'd like you to meet your new associate, Ms. Larkin."

When called by that term, the men knew enough to stand up and act accordingly. Lou was first to respond. "I think we've already had the pleasure. I'm the one who provided the evidence so you could put Anthony Scolara away."

"Certainly, Detective Davis, it's nice to see you again."

"Please call me Lou. And this is our lead investigator, Zachary Gerrard."

"It's nice to meet you, Ms. Larkin. You can call me Zack."

"I will, if you call me Polly. I'm not fond of my given name, 'Myrtle.' But I'll say when my namesake passed away, her thoughtfulness provided the down payment on our new home."

Zack liked her immediately. She'd add some panache and cohesiveness to the investigative team.

~~~

The Dubuque County Courthouse was only a block from the police department. Accompanying Polly to the meeting she had scheduled with Judge Hardin, he was pleased the judge was available.

"I'm still not used to this heat so early in the morning," Zack said. Weather like this seldom happened in Minneapolis.

"Humidity. Regardless of the temperature it can never be as hot as the judge's chambers if you rile him up. And I'm speaking from six years' experience," Polly assured her companion.

They were greeted by the judge's assistant as they entered the judicial area. Lila was consistently calm and polite, the antithesis of her boss, Judge Samuel Hardin. "Good morning to both of you. The judge is at your disposal, although he was only expecting you, Ms. Larkin." She escorted them to the judge's chambers.

"*Je...sus Cur...ie...st*! What's the big deal, bringing the lead detective with you?" The scrawny-framed jurist with unruly white hair appeared less intimidating in his shirtsleeves and reading glasses.

"Your honor," replied the detective. "I came along to reinforce the urgency of this matter."

"Hell, Gerrard, that's all Ms. Larkin would have had to say! I believe everything she tells me." He said, in her direction, with a wink and a twinkle in his eye, "Right, Ms. Larkin?"

"I would only hope so, your honor," she replied.

Zack took over. "If you don't mind, sir, I'd like to give you some background. We have reason to believe there's an organized effort of murder-for-hire within the city. Our first discovery was associated with the Molly Starr homicide. A reliable source indicated he knew in advance of the killing, though not in form he could do anything about. She died of an overdose administered by injection. We believe that another person, Chandler Logan, who passed away yesterday died in the same manner. The information came once again from our reliable source."

"Detective, I'd like to make an appointment with this guru. If he's that good at prognostication, maybe he can tell me if I'm going to get reelected this fall."

Zack said, "Your honor, an immediate autopsy of Mr. Logan is extremely important to determine if he died in the same manner as Molly Starr. If that's the case, it'll go a long way to proving this murder-for-hire group is operating."

"Okay, let's give it a shot. Ms. Larkin, if you come back in an hour I should have the order prepared."

~~~

That night Zack received a call on his police cell phone. The call had to be important.

"Zack, this is Brenda. I've finished Logan's autopsy and you were right."

"Brenda, before you say any more, may I come down? There's something else we need to discuss."

"Sure, take your time. I'm just having a sandwich. All that cutting gives me an appetite."

"If I did that, Brenda, I wouldn't be able to eat for a week. See you in a couple of minutes."

The county coroner still had the remnants of a corn beef sandwich on her plate. Some were even attached to her lab coat. The french fries were gone, but not the pickles. Zack remembered being told she disliked them because they reminded her of some part of the human anatomy. Zack didn't care to know what that referred to.

"Mr. Logan died of an overdose, but the substance was different this time. He was injected with enough morphine to kill an elephant. From the general state of his health, it was probably a good thing he passed away. Advanced diabetes affected his circulation and was causing his kidneys to fail. In addition, he had ulcers in his duodenum and his heart was damaged to the point where it was probably less than two-thirds efficient. He was facing one problem after another. It sure didn't make for much quality of life. I wouldn't think he'd want to continue living. He was already on morphine. So at least you have to give the killer credit for injecting a substance that was compatible with his situation."

"Brenda, we have reason to believe there may be more deaths than Chandler Logan and Molly Starr. There were possibly a number of killings of the euthanasia variety within the past couple of years. That might mean terminally ill people were dying prematurely. Our department would like to know if the area physicians have a sense that any of the terminally-ill have been passing away much earlier than expected."

"Your timing couldn't be better, Zack. Most of the area doctors will be attending a county physicians meeting tomorrow night. I'll poll them and give you the results day after tomorrow."

"That'd be terrific. I'll look forward to hearing from you."

NINE

After a day's detective work, Zack was at Alliance Manufacturing, ready to relieve his partner who had served as a guard for three decades. The old-timer's head jerked back as Zack entered the guardhouse.

"Fred, I think you've been sleeping on the job."

"Hey, Marshal, I wouldn't do that!" The longtime security guard who was now semi-retired loved to call the detective by the jokey nickname he had given him when Zack started at Alliance. Fred's personality alternated from fun loving to crotchety, depending upon the hour of the work schedule. Zack was fortunate that the two could split a shift. Usually Fred worked the earlier half from two to six p.m. and Zack was on duty for the four hours after that.

Since the death of his wife a couple of months ago, the veteran guard never seemed to be in a hurry. He was lonely and, quite often, he would keep Zack company for the first half-hour of his stint.

As the two shared the guardhouse Fred ate the sandwich he had brought along. "In your thirty years on this job I'll bet you've gotten to know most of the union people," Zack said.

"Most of 'em. Company benefits are so good there's not much turnover."

"You know Chris Lazorno?"

Fred stopped munching and gave his co-worker a squint out of the corner of his eye. Slowly he said, "Yeah, I know him. Ya gotta be careful 'round him. He's a trouble maker."

"What do you mean? I haven't noticed much in the way of problems around here."

"He's the top dog of a gang. Must be five or six of 'em. Closer than warts on a hog. Chris is their leader. What I hear, they spend a lotta time together. Probably doin' no good."

"What kind of trouble has he been in?"

"He's smart enuf' to start somethun' and sit back while his buddies carry through. When they all heard 'bout the pollution problem he riled 'em up at that goody two shoes, Molly Starr. I know that bunch's happy she's gone. We all are. Nobody wanted to lose their job."

The detective was amazed. The animosity towards the environmental activist-slash-philanthropist ran deep.

~~~

Zack was tired. How long could he keep up the pace of two jobs when his main one was becoming so all-consuming? He continually thought about the Starr investigation. Sometimes he was actually too tired to sleep. But not tonight—he was asleep as soon as he hit the bed.

He'd rather take a sledgehammer in the gut. The doctor just told them she was dying. The cancer that was in remission was back and this time there was no hope. They prayed together. She kept a bold face and wouldn't discuss it. He knew she was ticking off the days on her internal calendar. He pretended not to think about it. They planned so many activities to keep their minds off of the fact that it would be her last year. Her last Christmas. Her last month. Her...

Startled, he jerked up. He was sweating profusely. Zack still had nightmares about Joan's death. She was everything he could have asked for in a partner. He longed for her. What was there for him without her? He must have slept. The clock claimed five-thirty. It was time to get up.

~~~

The second day of round-the-clock surveillance of the Omega Building was no different than the previous one, thought Sergeant Hugh Murphy. This was getting damn boring.

Around ten p.m., during his four-till midnight shift, he was able to dash across the street to Winkies to appropriate two donuts and a coffee to-go. He wondered why cops were so fanatic about coffee and donuts. When he retired in another three years he planned to cash in on that addiction by opening a coffee shop next door to the police station. He figured the business couldn't fail, plus he could remain in the loop for police scuttlebutt.

To avoid unnecessary suspicion, Murphy was dressed in dark plain casual clothes. He knew none of the coffee shop regulars would recognize him.

As luck would have it, his trip to relieve himself and stock up on calories and caffeine corresponded to the moment when a swath of light flashed from the opened door to the targeted building. Darkness returned in an instant. Evidently someone had entered, turned on a light, and closed the door. Hugh told Winkies' lone employee to keep the change as he briskly headed back to the scene. Gosh darn it, he said to himself, he didn't have time to wait for the one dollar and twenty cents change he had coming. Fat chance he could list *that* on his expense account.

The surveillance team had concealed a ladder to the roof of the adjacent structure as well as a propped open window for easy access. A few panels of plywood covered with carpeting permitted noiseless entry to the opening in the ceiling that Riley Whitcomb must have used to view the main floor below, now occupied by Sgt. Murphy.

The sounds he heard were chopped phrases interrupted by the intermittent drone of the air conditioner. Occasional low laughter came from people at ease with one another. He could hear the periodic hiss of a beverage can being opened.

During the course of the next hour, he heard some comments that conceivably could be relevant to the Starr investigation, which he noted on the pad he brought along. He relied on the tape recorder concealed under the table to catch anything of value that his ears missed.

As the congenial session came to a close, the participants were briefly in view as they rearranged their chairs. Murphy noted at least three of the group wore the same gray apparel. Could this be the gray clothing that Riley Whitcomb had alluded to?

The uninvited watcher tiptoed out of the Omega Building's second floor onto the roof of the adjacent facility. He raced down the ladder and approached the corner of the building in time to see the backs of five of the participants head for a camper and SUV in the parking lot across the street. Hugh identified the last member who was locking the door. It was the Alliance foreman, Chris Lazorno.

~~~

By seven the next morning, Sgt. Hugh Murphy was reporting to Lou in his office. The detective made notes as the sergeant reeled off the phrases he had recorded the night before.

"I think that's all the pertinent stuff, Lou. I'm leaving you the tape recording of their meeting. I've listened to it twice and only came up with a couple of things I missed. I added those to my notes. Between the outbursts of folks having a good time and that dang air conditioner, the recorder had difficulty catching everything. Maybe you'll hear something I overlooked," the sergeant mumbled, exhausted.

"Good job, Murph. Why don't you take the rest of the day off and catch a few Zs."

~~~

After listening to the tape recording, Lou added his impressions to Sgt. Murphy's observations. The sixty-plus minutes of camaraderie had been boiled down to less than a dozen comments relevant to the Starr case. Statements included: "good riddance to that do-gooder, Starr," "don't screw with our job security," "let's make plans soon for our next outing," and "that should bring in some big bucks."

TEN

Zack followed the last bite of his Egg McMuffin with a swig of black coffee. His Toyota made good time as most of the traffic was going in the opposite direction, toward downtown. He was in a hurry to arrive unannounced at the Chandler Logan residence. Sometimes, he believed, surprise took suspects off-guard enough to not be prepared with pat answers for his questions. It was before eight that morning when he rang the doorbell.

He imagined Logan's spouse would be well into her seventies. So he was taken aback to be confronted by an attractive woman of about thirty, wrapped in a robe that must have been thrown on in a hurry. The openness at the neck left little to be imagined. After an embarrassing glance he noticed her hair was disheveled and she was shoeless.

"I'm sorry to bother you so early in the morning, miss. I'm Detective Gerrard from the Dubuque Police Department and I was hoping to talk with Mrs. Chandler Logan."

"She's not here right now. My mom took her to the hospital late last night. I'm her granddaughter, Sandy."

He showed her his identity card as he said, "Sandy, I had wanted to ask your grandmother some questions about her husband's death."

"Well, sir, that's why she's not here. She was really depressed after Grandpa's death and Mom was afraid she'd commit suicide. They called me to care for her animals while Mom took her to the hospital last night."

"Do you think she felt guilty because of the way he died?"

"I'm sure of it."

"Sandy, we know how he died. That's why I'm here."

"Why would police come when he died of diabetes?"

"He was put to sleep by someone who gave him an overdose of morphine."

"Omigod, you're saying somebody killed him!"

"That's right and I'm here to find out who did it."

"I know the doctor said he needed something for his suffering. Grandpa just took what he was supposed to."

"The county coroner feels differently. I'm told he had enough morphine in his system to kill an elephant."

"I've got to sit down. C'mon in, there's coffee in the kitchen."

Zack followed the granddaughter to the back of the house where he found the kitchen a pigsty. Dirty plates were piled in the sink and on the counter. Newspapers and magazines had been flung across the dining table and chairs. The place reeked of coffee and stale cigarette smoke. Sandy rinsed two of the unwashed cups. "Would you like cream or sugar?"

"I think I'd better pass; I had a large Starbucks on the way over here. Thanks anyway."

As she poured her own drink Sandy looked out the window. "It's such a nice day. I love this weather."

It was obvious to the detective his subject didn't want to talk about the murder of her grandfather.

"Miss," Zack said, "I know this is unpleasant, but I have to get to the bottom of this. It's going to be necessary for us to formally question your mother and grandmother about this. However, anything you feel comfortable telling me now might make for less unpleasantness when I bring them in. Before you say anything, though, I want to apprise you of your rights." Zack began the recitation, "You have the right to remain silent…"

Sandy brought her coffee to the kitchen table. Tears began to well in her eyes. Before sitting, she grabbed a few tissues and used one to blow her nose. It became apparent from her actions that the police would have no trouble in developing a strong case of complicity against her mother and grandmother. "I don't need an attorney. I just want to do whatever I can to make it better for Mom and Grandma. If your questioning got too bad, Grandma could have a stroke. If I tell you what I know, will it help their case?"

"It certainly won't hurt," the detective said with compassion. After a momentary pause he continued. "Do your relatives know who caused your grandpa's death?"

"Let me start by telling you why Grandma went to the hospital. Knowing she helped decide on ending Grandpa's misery made her feel so guilty that she got very depressed. Mom took her to the emergency room because she was worried she'd commit suicide. Of course, Grandma knew the end was near. Grandpa'd suffered so much. And when he took the medication, it was so powerful he was just out of it. But it was driving Grandma crazy. He begged them to let him go peacefully. The doctor inserted an apparatus so Grandpa could give himself small doses of morphine to help with the pain. But the doctor said he couldn't do any more to hurry up his death. We all thought we were doing him a favor by arranging for a mercy killing."

"Maybe you were, but according to the law, what happened was still illegal. Were you here when it happened?"

"No, but I know what took place. Mom said a nice lady came and gave him a shot in the arm. It wasn't long before he slipped into a coma and then passed away shortly after."

"Did your Mom say anything else?" Zack inquired.

"Only that they had one heck of a time raising the money. But she said it would be worth it. His pain would be over and the medical bills would finally stop."

"I'll bet that cost a lot."

"Both Mom and Grandma had to sell their cars and I don't know what else. I think Mom said it cost twenty-five thousand dollars!"

"It's not for me to say whether your grandfather was better off or not...but what your mother and grandmother did was murder."

"Oh God, you can't send them to prison!"

"You've done them a favor by admitting what happened. But they definitely are accomplices to a crime. Even though you grandfather was going to die, he was the victim of a mercy killing. Best thing your mother and grandmother can do now is sit down and talk to us and someone from the district attorney's office. By cooperating they can certainly help their cause with the court.

"What hospital did they go to?"

"Finley."

"Finley Hospital. That's on Grandview, right?"

"Yeah."

"What're their names?"

"Grandma's is Alma Mae Chandler and Mom's is Louise Dunn."

"Because your grandmother is in poor health we'll try to be careful with her. Sergeant Jan Skinner will check with the doctor first and then inform them a trip to the police department is necessary. She'll bring them down and, if all goes according to plan, we should be able to bring them home no later than the middle of the afternoon."

On his way back to the station Zack wondered what he would have done differently in their situation. He was fast becoming a believer that euthanasia had a place in the law. It would have certainly been easier on his wife. God, he missed her. She had given him the best eighteen years of his life.

~~~

A little over an hour later, Sergeant Skinner notified Zack that the two ladies had arrived for their scheduled meeting. Alma Mae, Chandler's wife, and Louise Dunn, his daughter, were standing directly behind Sgt. Skinner looking solemn. With a combination of pleasantness and official police conduct, Zack greeted the two. They cowered as their faces showed forced smiles. He escorted them to the conference room where both Lou and Polly were waiting. Zack began the inquiry.

"Ladies, we extend our sympathy for the loss of Mr. Logan. I've taken the liberty of having Ms. Larkin, representing the D.A.'s office, sit in. Since we have reason to treat you as accomplices in this death you may want to have your attorney present."

"Mr. Gerrard, I'm the daughter and will do most of the talking. This has been extremely difficult for Mom. She's now on medication. You can count on our cooperation. We need not have an attorney here."

"In that case, Mrs. Dunn I'll advise you of your rights in this situation." He did so.

"Thank you for being so understanding with my daughter, Detective," Mrs. Dunn said. "What we did may have been wrong, but what were we supposed to do? Can't you understand Dad's complications were killing Mom not to mention bankrupting her. Dad knew this and wanted a way out."

"Mrs. Dunn, could you tell me how your father died?"

The two suspects looked at one another for a moment. The mother was sobbing uncontrollably. Finally, she gathered herself together and nodded to the daughter as if to say, "It's okay…tell them what happened."

"A nice lady came to the folk's house. I was there with them. She was very professional, like a nurse. She gave Dad a shot in the arm. We held Dad's hands and talked for a few minutes. Then he nodded off and slipped into a coma. After a shudder he passed away." As Louise looked at her mother, both were tearful.

Zack inquired, "How did you find someone to do this?"

"Sandy learned of it from Brockton Starr. She and her husband have been close friends of his ever since high school."

The mother's grief was uncontrollable. Louise pleaded with the detectives. "Mom is not doing well at all. Is there any way we could continue this discussion tomorrow? If she's still bad, I'll talk to you alone. We want to get this over with as much as you do."

Lou responded, "I understand Mrs. Dunn." He turned to his associates, "Is that okay with the two of you?"

They both nodded in agreement.

"Let's do the same time and the same place tomorrow. We'll see you then."

Polly assisted the ladies out of the conference room.

Zack turned to his partner with a look of disgust. "Brockton Starr is the key to this whole thing, Lou. Why in the hell can't you get him in here to talk to us?"

"I've been trying. He should be back in town any time. I'll get right on it."

~~~

Only a couple of minutes after the lead detective returned to his office, Lou burst in.

"Brockton's finally back! He'll be in to see us at two this afternoon."

"Thank God." The relief on Zack's face was obvious.

"The other thing is we may have a lead on who's involved in the mercy-killing group." Lou informed Zack of Murph's good fortune from the previous night's surveillance of Chris Lazorno and his buddies at the Omega Building.

Zack replied, "I uncovered some interesting info on Lazorno last night, too. Here's what my fellow security worker had to say about him." Zack told the story.

"It sure seems like Chris could be the leader of the mercy-killing group. Shouldn't we be bringing him in for questioning?"

"Yeah, let's do it. Between him and Brockton Starr we should finally be making some headway on this case."

Lou added, "I hope Brockton's well rested. He may never have another good night's sleep."

~~~

Polly made another trip to the courthouse, as planned. This was not foreign territory as she had worked in the building for nearly six years.

"Hello, Rita. Hi, Rickey. How's things? I'm here on a different mission today. Could you run a copy of Molly Starr's will?" While Rita made the copies, Polly engaged in friendly conversation with Rickey. He loved golf nearly as much as Polly's husband. In fact, the two had competed for the city championship the previous year. As she left with the documents, Rickey reminded her, "Tell Keith my new Cobra is adding twenty yards to my drives. Could be a new champ this year!"

~~~

The chief had called for an update meeting as Polly returned to the station. The four met in the conference room.

Lou was pleased to announce some progress. "Molly Star's last heir is back in town. Brockton Starr had been on a trip with his wife. He'll be in for his interview at fourteen hundred."

Polly then gave her findings. "I've reviewed Molly Starr's will but I couldn't find anything particularly unusual for someone who's accumulated more than twenty million dollars. Half the estate goes to twelve local charities. The remaining half'll be split between five nieces and nephews."

Zack reported on meetings with Chandler Logan's granddaughter and subsequently with his wife and daughter. "They've implicated Brockton Starr as a connection to the mercy-killers. We should know more after we talk to him this afternoon. I was amazed the granddaughter admitted to a twenty-five thousand dollar payment for the euthanasia service! Bet we won't be able to trace where *that* money went. Had to have been cash."

The chief added, "Since this case is so similar to Molly Starr's, I'd bet money was also paid for her death. I believe we should get a court order to search the financial transactions of any relative of Molly's who might have disbursed funds as payment for her death. Polly, are you willing to see the judge again?"

"Sure, why not."

~~~

Polly Larkin was once again in Judge Hardin's chamber. "Thank you, your honor, for seeing me so soon. Before we get to my business, I'd like to take one moment to tell you how valuable Chandler Logan's autopsy was." Polly related how proof of Logan's murder led to his granddaughter admitting a twenty-five thousand dollars payment for the mercy killing. "Judge, we have every reason to believe a payment was made for Molly Starr's murder. We therefore request authorization to review the financial accounts of her beneficiaries to search for any disbursement of funds that could have been used to pay for her killing. I would like to add, we also have some evidence in this case we haven't publicized. Although the Starr crime scene was wiped clean we found a partial print that we're confident belonged to the perpetrator." She explained the vomit speck and the print on the toilet.

"Well, Ms. Larkin, I can't just give our police department carte blanche. However, under the circumstances this request appears reasonable — as long as we limit its scope to transactions of a certain size. I'd say twenty-five thousand dollars or larger. Can you live with that?"

Polly responded, "That'd be fine with us, your honor."

"I'm aware of the immediacy required. Lila will have the order for you by noon."

~~~

With the judge's order in hand, Polly was eager to find unusual financial transactions and to do so in a hurry. There was no time for lunch today. Possibly whatever she discovered would be helpful to the detectives when they questioned Brockton Starr in a couple of hours.

With five heirs, and who-knew-how-many financial institutions to contact, she appreciated the three-phone hookup in the detective conference room. The simultaneous use of three phones caused her to chuckle as she thought of her mother's phone-junkie attraction to the telephone.

The last few minutes had made the hour and thirty-some calls worthwhile. Apollo Mortgage had ferreted out a loan that had been made to Mr. and Mrs. Brockton Starr, one of Molly's nephews. The mortgage company agreed to provide details when Polly came over.

Within twenty minutes she was standing in the lobby of Apollo Mortgage, court order in hand. The manager had copies of all the loan documents, knowing Polly would come equipped with the judge's papers.

A one hundred thousand dollar second mortgage loan had been made to Brockton Starr and his wife. What made the transaction more revealing was that the funds were disbursed in cash. Bingo! Mr. Starr received those funds ten days prior to the death of his aunt. Double bingo! A further investigation of Brockton Starr's financial accounts revealed no deposit of those funds. There was no other record of the one hundred thousand dollars; the money just disappeared.

Polly rushed back to the office to relate her good fortune to Zack and Lou. She knew they would be meeting with Mr. Starr any minute.

Lou remarked, "This puts the onus on our nouveau riche suspect. I'd say his days of freedom are as numbered as a Swiss bank account."

ELEVEN

At two o'clock Brockton Starr ambled in for his appointment—at least that's how it appeared to Zack, keeping an eye out from the conference room. Starr smiled and looked confident as he was greeted by Lou. After the two entered the conference room and introductions were made, Lou began the questioning.

"I appreciate your coming to see us about your aunt's untimely death."

Brockton replied, "I apologize for not being available sooner. My family and I've been with my wife's parents in Denver."

"I'm sure Molly's death was quite a shock to you."

"Yes, Detective, I was especially close to her."

Lou continued, "There have been some new developments concerning her death during your absence from the city. As you're probably aware, your sisters, Jill and Chris, didn't believe your aunt committed suicide. Consequently, they insisted on having an autopsy performed. Between newspaper accounts and talking with your sisters, you've probably learned we are now considering this to be a murder."

"Just shocking, terrible!" Brock replied.

Lou said, "Brock, what you may not know is that we're investigating *another* recent murder case where the circumstances are surprisingly similar to your aunt's death. Those similarities give us reason to believe that a murder-for-hire scheme is going on. And we believe it's been taking place for nearly two years. All of those deaths have been the result of drug overdoses injected into the victims.

"Just to make sure you're aware, your aunt died of cardiac arrest brought about by a massive injection of potassium. Since potassium is an element normally found in the body, it wouldn't be searched for as a lethal weapon. Although it's bio-degradable, at the time of the autopsy this substance still registered far beyond safe levels."

As Lou was speaking, Zack thought about the strategy the detectives had planned. Normally, they would conduct more of a fishing expedition with their questions and even bait him with questions alluding to his involvement. In this situation, however, they were sharing nearly all of the evidence...for two reasons: First, the facts were indisputable and; second, they needed immediate feedback on how the euthanasia group operated. They had to put an end to any other possible killings as soon as possible. Thus, they were willing to show their hand now, rather than wait to present it at trial.

Zack took over. "I have to be candid: being a relative and likely heir of a multi-millionaire naturally makes you a suspect in this investigation. So at this point we're going to advise you of your rights."

"Detective, I'm here to cooperate because I don't have anything to hide. Please, what can I tell you?"

Zack turned aggressive. "Mr. Starr, we've uncovered evidence that *could* tie you to this crime. We're not expecting you to say anything until you talk to an attorney. But we do want you to hear how compelling the evidence is against you."

"Why don't we start by getting some basic information about you," Lou said.

When it got to his employment, Brockton said, "I work for Alliance. I've been there for more than three years."

That response drew Zack's attention since another Alliance employee might possibly be part of a group that murdered Molly. Maybe Brockton Starr and Chris Lazorno were in this together.

"Lou, can I interrupt your questions for a minute with a couple of my own?"

"Sure," he responded.

"Mr. Starr, have you heard any comments about your aunt by anyone in your place of employment?"

"I know many of the people didn't like some of her outspoken opinions. She said our company was a danger to the environment. Her exaggerations could have cost many people their jobs."

"Did you ever hear of any coordinated effort to stop her from speaking out?"

"What're you saying? You think some Alliance employees were trying to silence her? You gotta be kidding!"

Lou brought up the detectives' mass murder theory with a few embellishments. "In a murder case that has similarities to your aunt's, large cash payments have been made to an organized group that commits murders, styled as mercy killings. They've received as much as a hundred grand for their work." Starr's jaw dropped perceptively. "Brockton, you received one hundred thousand dollars in cash a week before she died," Lou said. "That was the exact amount you borrowed from Apollo Mortgage on a second mortgage loan."

The color seemed to drain from Brockton Starr's face as he fidgeted. Zack could see Lou was taking more time than needed to review his notes. Smart tactic. Why hurry,

Zack thought, when you've just driven a nail in the guy's coffin.

Lou resumed. "Those funds never showed up in any of your accounts. Don't you think that's unusual? What'd you do with the money, Brockton? A family trip to Denver can't be *that* expensive."

Starr stammered some unintelligible phrases. Within a few seconds he became quiet. Then he blinked his eyes repeatedly and drummed his fingers on the tabletop. The detectives could see beads of perspiration forming on his upper lip.

"Oh, there's one other detail," Lou continued. "Did you vomit in your aunt's bathroom and then attempt to clean it up? The vomit didn't match the contents of Molly's stomach. A fingerprint was found on the outside of the stool. We're betting both belong to you!"

Starr slumped further in his chair. His body language had changed dramatically since his arrival a short time ago.

Zack's turn. "Brockton, before you say anything, just hear us out. There's no question we've got the goods on you. Sandy Gregory even told us you gave her the contact for mercy-killing so she could help her grandfather avoid his misery."

As planned, Zack decided it was time to up the ante. "Listen, you pathetic piece of shit, proving your guilt is a slam dunk! Why, we've got enough evidence on these pages I'm holding to try your case right now. But, frankly, you're small potatoes to us. We're more concerned about exposing this murder ring than we are with nailing you. So here's what we propose. It may not seem like it now but this *may* be your lucky day if you play your cards right. You're guilty and will have to pay for your crime. Our proposition is that if you give the district attorney information that results in the apprehension of the others in this murder-for-hire scheme, they *may* offer a plea bargain for a reduced sentence. Way we see it, your choice is between a few years in prison…or life. While I'm not an attorney, I would advise you to talk to one before you say anything to us."

"By the way, you're not leaving here today," Lou added. "As soon as we're finished, the officers outside the door will be placing you under arrest. You'll be permitted to phone your attorney and have him come here."

"So, Mr. Starr," Zack returned to the alternating offensive, "we'll wait to hear from you and your attorney. Any delay on your part is *not* in your best interest. We want the murderers put behind bars before they commit more. So the sooner you can get back to us, the better it's going to be for everyone."

Zack and Lou got up and headed for the door. They didn't expect a response. Their exit from the room was accompanied by the entry of two policemen who handcuffed Brockton for his trip to the county jail.

~~~

In less than two hours Brockton Starr and his attorney, Walter Richards, had requested a meeting. The two detectives met the suspect and his counsel in the interrogation room of the Dubuque police station.

The attorney began the discussion. "My client has informed me about the situation. Before we respond, could you please review the charges and the evidence against Mr. Starr?"

The detectives had anticipated that any attorney worth his salt, and Richards was certainly worth a lot of salt, would want hard evidence and not theories. Zack was prepared to handle such a presentation if it were required. He began outlining the reports of the coroner and state forensic expert as well as information regarding the Chandler Logan investigation and the records of Apollo Mortgage.

"Zack, your case is mostly circumstantial," Starr's attorney noted. "You're going to have difficulty even holding him in jail."

"Walt, let me tell you what's likely to happen to your client. We're in the midst of a goddamned rash of homicides. How do you think Brockton's jury is going to react if more killings take place when he could have done something to stop them? We want those responsible for the killings arrested and their activities closed down. We want Brockton's cooperation and we want it now. I suggest you have a heart-to-heart discussion with him. We're not going to screw around." Zack paused a moment, for effect. "Let me be perfectly clear: The DA informed me that, as the prosecuting attorney, he's willing to discuss a plea bargain involving a reduced sentence for information obtained. I was told in no uncertain terms that the offer is good for today only. They want this ring of killers shut down ASAP! If Brockton wants to fight this, good luck. He's guilty and the prosecutors will show no mercy if he doesn't cooperate. We're going to nail his ass so bad it'll never get off the cross! C'mon, Lou, let's get out of here before I show how pissed off I *really* am!"

The detectives hurried out of the interrogation room before the other parties could respond. Once they were in a private conference room with the door closed, Lou erupted. "Jesus, Zack, I didn't know you had that in you! You had Brockton shaking in his boots. If we don't hear they're willing to cooperate, I'll eat my hat."

"Showmanship, Lou, showmanship. Now let's go downstairs and get a soda to go with your hat sandwich, just in case. Maybe they'll have come around by the time we're finished."

On their way, Zack dialed his office on his cell phone. When Millie answered he asked, "Is Polly there?"

"Yes," Millie replied. "Would you like me to put her on?"

A few seconds later their new associate investigator responded. "Hi, Zack, what's up?"

"Lou and I just put the screws to Brockton Starr and we think he's about ready to confess. When he does we'll need someone from the DA's office to handle it. Could you put that hat on and be ready on a moment's notice if we need you?"

"Sure thing, I'll be standing by. Just give me a buzz."

By the time Zack hung up he was being paged.

Returning to the interrogation room, they found that Brockton had decided to speak for himself. "I'm willing to cooperate if you can assure me I won't have to spend the rest of my life in prison. Can you do that?"

"Hold on a minute, Brockton. We'll get someone here from the DA's office. You can negotiate with them."

Zack called Polly and she was on her way. In less than five minutes she arrived and was introduced to the suspect and his attorney.

Polly knew that her job was to close the deal without necessarily giving away the store and responded to Starr's concern, saying, "We've gone through this routine under similar circumstances. The leniency of the court depends directly on the assistance you provide in helping us identify whoever actually committed the murder. I *can* tell you that if you give us your best effort at revealing all you know and possibly identifying the guilty party you have my word we will do everything possible to reduce your jail time; maybe to as little as ten years." The suspect mulled it over for a minute and then glumly responded, "I guess that'll have to do."

"Before you begin I need to read you your rights," Polly said. After doing so she told him he could begin his testimony.

"This whole thing started because of a terrible financial mess, a business venture that didn't pan out. My wife and I agreed we couldn't afford to go any deeper into debt. It had to stop so I went to Aunt Molly for some help. Problem was that she had already bailed me out of two other costly situations. So, I really couldn't blame her when she turned me down.

"I was worked up to the point where I actually considered suicide. But I just couldn't do it. Then, I remembered how Grandma had handled a situation where her choices were not so good. She was caring for Grandpa Joe, who's my step-grandfather. He was terminally ill and Grandma was watching the money stream out of their life's savings. They weren't on Aunt Molly's side of the family and due to a falling out they once had, there was no way Grandma was going begging to her.

"All of a sudden Grandpa Joe died. That was a little more than a year ago, I think. I didn't know what actually caused his death until a month or two later. As far as I knew he was suffering but was expected to live for another six months to a year.

"Anyway, I was alone with Grandma one night. After I helped her move some furniture around we had a couple of drinks. It must have been in a guilty moment she told me what had happened to Grandpa. She had heard of a way to hire a mercy killer. It seemed like a blessing because Grandpa suffered so much. So Grandma found this group who helped in 'assisted suicides' when the patient was known to have no chance of recovery and the suffering was horrible.

"Grandma said she left her plea for help in a designated drop box at a UPS store. Not long after that she got a phone call saying she should send them the doctor's report on Grandpa. They promised to review the request. However, this group would not make further direct contact with her. If her request was accepted, she would be notified within two weeks through a coded message in the *Herald Tribune*, in the 'personals' section of the classifieds. The appearance of Grandpa's initials would indicate their willingness to assist. Then a few days later, a website would give specifics as to the time and date of the mercy killing. Someone would come at the designated hour and take care of the situation. Grandma was told to have fifty thousand dollars in small denomination bills at that time. When the time arrived, a lady came and gave Grandpa a shot in the arm and that was it.

"I used the same procedure for Molly. However, they told me their usual business was mercy killing, which was justified on the grounds the victim was about to die. Murders were more risky business. As a result, the fee would be substantially higher so the cost to me was a hundred thousand."

Zack and Lou looked at each other, restraining any overt expressions. Zack interrupted Starr's narrative to ask, "So, tell me if I've got this straight...you needed money, a lot of money, and you figured by killing your wealthy aunt to make it look like suicide you could inherit enough to pay the group *and* get out of debt. That about right?"

Brockton nodded. "Yeah, that's right."

Zack said, "But how could you be sure you'd even get any money from her will? What if she gave it all to her charities?"

"Well, we all had a pretty good idea that she was worth about twenty million...it was open knowledge among the nephews and nieces. And Aunt Molly had been pretty straightforward with us these last few years. She made it clear that we'd all be taken care of fairly."

Starr paused his narrative to throw up his hands. "What was I supposed to do? I was in a box! Molly was rich and I couldn't see any way out! So I got my three-digit number, checked the website and everything went according to plan. I stopped by my aunt's around noon and slipped four of her sleeping pills into her soft drink. A woman showed up about two hours later as scheduled and did the injection. I hated myself for doing it but what choice did I have, given my situation?"

Zack broke in. "Brock, did you vomit in Molly's bathroom?"

"Yeah, I got sick watching Molly's heart attack. I couldn't handle it. Oh shit, I thought I'd cleaned the mess up pretty well. "

He's a piece of work, Zack thought, a real shit. But if Brock's information was valid it could lead to the arrest of others who were far worse than this pathetic worm.

Lou wanted Brock to elaborate on a few of his statements. "I've got a couple of questions for you. Which UPS store did you use?"

"The one at the mall, the Kennedy Mall."

"How did you find their message in the *Herald Tribune*?"

"It was in the personal classified ads under the name *Chris Crim*."

"What was the name on the website?"

"*LaCree...Lacrima Christi*. It's on AOL.com."

"How'd you know the message on the *Lacrima Christi* website was for you? What'd it say?"

"Their site carries religious verses, usually a daily prayer and three bible verses. At the end of the prayer there's a series of letters and numbers. Three letters represent the initials of the intended victim and five numbers give the month, day and time the event is to take place."

In a more composed manner than she felt the situation may have deserved, Polly spoke, "Brockton, you've given us some valuable information. We'll need time to check out what you've said. If what you told us pans out, we'll honor our agreement by recommending whatever leniency can be allowed."

"I appreciate that, Ms. Larkin." Then Brockton directed his comments to the two detectives. "I know I can identify the woman who gave Aunt Molly the injection. She's in her late twenties with short dark hair and very thin. If you'd like I could work with a police artist who could draw her picture. And I'm sure I could pick her out of a lineup. "

Zack replied, "Both could be helpful but I think that'll do it for now. Possibly, one or more of us will return tomorrow if we need more information. Lou, anything else we need at this time?"

"No, Zack, that's a wrap." With as pleasant a farewell as could be made under the circumstances, the three investigators left. Their findings were going to be good news for the chief, Zack thought.

TWELVE

While Zack was making his way back to his office, Millie stopped him. "The coroner wants you to call. I put her cell phone number on your desk. Seems eager to give you some information."

As he dialed Brenda's number he hoped she had feedback from her fellow doctors. The medical examiner answered on the second ring.

"Zack, you were right! Eight physicians at last night's meeting believed some of their terminally ill patients seemed to have died prematurely. Evidently none of them had given the matter much thought. But when I brought it up, it was like a light bulb turning on. Offhand, they came up with eighteen names of patients who, on the average, very likely passed away three to six months sooner than anticipated."

"Brenda, we just got a confession for the murder of Molly Starr. Once we check out the info we may be able to come up with a list of victims of this murder-for-hire group. Then it'll be interesting to compare those names with your list. Might even be a few more than you now have. Incidentally, they seem to have a 'for-profit' branch to their operations: Molly's death netted them a cool hundred grand."

"God, I guess I got into the wrong side of the business," she laughed, with a morbid edge to her voice.

~~~

This so-called euthanasia group was a bunch of mercy-killers and busy ones at that, thought Zack. He was eager to nail the group and bring an end to what was shaping up as the worst crime spree Dubuque—maybe the state—had ever seen. Hopefully, this morning's questioning of Chris Lazorno would start that in motion. Lou had been busy into the wee hours the night before, preparing for the meeting with the Alliance foreman.

Zack hurried to the detective conference room to find Lazorno being led in to what had to be an anxiously awaiting detective. As he joined the other two, one look at Chris Lazorno told him the keeper of the keys to the Omega Building was not happy to be there.

"Chris, I think you already know Detective Gerrard," Lou said.

"Yeah, I've seen him out at the security shack."

"Thanks for coming in, Chris," Zack replied.

"I hope this doesn't take too long," the foreman said with apparent annoyance as he turned his attention to the one who arranged the meeting. "We got a demo set for ten."

Lou responded somewhat more formally, "Mr. Lazorno, we'll keep this as short as possible, but under the circumstances, I don't think that's really your top concern at the moment...we're considering you a suspect in the death of Molly Starr."

"You gotta be kidding!"

Before proceeding further, Lou gave him the Miranda warning.

"I don't have no attorney! Hell, if I need one, I'll let you know. How am I tied into the death of that wealthy bitch, anyway?"

Lou answered, "We know the Omega Building was used to tell an informant in advance that Ms. Starr was going to die."

"S'that got to do with me?"

"You control access to that building. The night before last, you and some of your associates met there to celebrate her death and talk of committing another murder."

"That's a bunch of crap and you know it!"

"Didn't your group toast to Molly Starr's death?"

"You betcha. We'd do that every chance we got."

"Didn't you talk about another outing and planning to get some more money?"

"Jeez-us. Your spy needs to have his ears checked. That was just a get-together of my buddies."

"The what?"

"Six of us high school pals were on the football team that won the state championship. Stayed close for the past ten years, all work at Alliance. Now we drink beers when we can and ride motorcycles. That ain't a crime is it?"

"What about this outing and collecting some money?"

"The *outing* as you call it is next month's motorcycle trip up to the Harley festival in Milwaukee. If you're talking about collecting money, you must mean our monthly trip to East Dubuque where we load up on lottery tickets."

Zack had no gut feeling whether this guy was on the level or just darn sly.

Lou continued his grilling. "Chris, have you ever heard of *Lacrima Christi*?"

"Sure I have."

Both detectives leaned forward in anxious anticipation.

"Well, what do you know about it?"

"*Lacrima Christi* is one of the things that ties our club together."

Lou gave Zack a glance that resonated with satisfaction and said, "Go on."

"It's our favorite Italian wine. We always drink it when we party with our wives."

Lou's expression was one of obvious disappointment. Incredulous, he asked, "Are you serious?"

"Just ask my wife. She likes it best of all."

"I need a break," Lou said, as he nudged Zack's leg under the table.

When Lou was out the door, Zack spoke. "I could use a pit stop myself. You need one, Chris?"

"No, I'm fine. But I could use a refill on my coffee."

"I'll have Millie bring it right in. Be back in a minute."

The restroom was empty except for the two detectives.

"Goddammit, Zack. I think Chris is lying. There are too many coincidences not to believe he's involved.

"I didn't get a chance to tell you, but last night I found out his son owns a computer software service business on north Washington. That means he could have set up the *Lacrima Christi* website. And the *Chris Crim* name Brockton mentioned could be an abbreviation of 'Chris Lazorno and his brothers in crime.'"

"It fits together, Lou. When we go back, go ahead and follow up on those two points. Chances are he'll have an answer for them, too. So we may have to keep him and his group under surveillance and do more digging."

By the time the detectives returned, Lou had regained his composure and proceeded as planned. Chris Lazorno was cool in denying any computer assistance from his son or any knowledge of *Chris Crim*. Before he was excused, he did leave the names of the other five members of his group.

~~~

The two detectives were joined in the conference room by the chief and Polly. They reported the good and bad news. Brockton's confession was a major breakthrough in the investigation. But they still needed to find out if Chris Lazorno and his friends were members of the murderous group. Their progress to this point raised everyone's spirits that a solution to the murders was close at hand.

"Well, we sure know more than we did a couple of days ago. You guys were on target with the murder-for-hire theory," remarked the chief.

Zack responded, "We now know their entire m.o. We just don't know any of the players, but we've got several areas to check out: *Chris Crim* at the newspaper, the UPS Store and the *Lacrima Christi* website." He wrote those names on the blackboard.

"If we analyze all of the *Chris Crim* personal ads over the past two years, that should give us information on other victims. I'll call the paper to get copies of those ads for us.

"Lou, do you want to go to the UPS store and see what you can find out about our renter, *Chris Crim*? We can get an order to get the store to identify whoever is using that drop box if need be."

Lou nodded a response but appeared to Zack to still be in a funk over the questioning of the Alliance foreman. "I'll do it," he said, "but I also want to follow up on anything associated with Chris Lazorno."

"Sounds good," the lead detective responded and then he said, "Polly, why don't you check into the *Lacrima Christi* website?"

She replied, "If we can get the names and dates of victims from the newspaper maybe we can confirm them on the website. However, could be a problem breaking into a website to retrieve their historical data. Still, there's a way to get around that."

"How's that?" Zack inquired.

"Make it legal. Get a court order to permit the search."

The chief responded, "Let's do it, Polly. Draw up another request for the judge ASAP."

"Okay, Chief."

The chief continued. "Coming up with the names of *victims* may not be too difficult. But we still need to identify the perpetrators. To do that, we need to follow the money trail.

"It so happens I recall a Christi name, tied to the Brackett House. This was before your time, Zack. This Christi group was organized to raise the initial funds for starting the Brackett House. I don't know what happened to them after they got 'The House' project going."

Zack inquired, "Chief, did you just call the Brackett House by the name 'House'?"

"Yeah, people familiar with that project usually just call it 'The House.'"

"Look at one of the words Riley gave us," Zack said as he pointed to the word 'house' on the blackboard. "This may be stretching things, but what if the word Riley heard referred to the Brackett House. Is that possible?"

The chief said, "I don't know, Zack. You may be on to something but the word 'house' covers a lot of ground. You know much about the Brackett House?"

"Not really. I've heard it mentioned around town but I never asked what it does."

"Well, the Brackett House opened its doors a little over two years ago. Caters to the needs of the elderly who are poor. In addition to basic food and shelter, they provide some healthcare, too. They pay for some minimal health insurance and most pharmacy needs. If you fall below the minimum wage level they'll actually pay for all your meds. Now, there's an awful lot of old folks in this county and a lot of them are poor. So, the House has a big appetite for regular funding. What if the need for funds is related to the money raised by murder-for-hire? Wouldn't that be ironic, killing to help the poor!

"Zack, you might want to visit the Brackett House. Poke around a bit. Maybe you can uncover something. Your best contact would either be the chief executive officer, Sister Miriam Barton, or the office manager, whatever her name is. Personally, I'd opt for the office manager, because, frankly, that Sister Miriam is an officious bitch even if she *is* a nun. I'll have Millie get the name of the office manager for you."

"Sounds good, Chief. Say, Polly, why don't you also check on *Lacrima Christi* with the state registrar? Maybe you can find something on them or any organization using Christi in its name that's been doing business around here."

~~~

When the meeting ended Polly was the last to leave. Zack hung around because he wanted to speak with her alone.

"Could I have a few minutes of your time, Polly, to talk about something before you head out?"

"Sure thing, Zack, what is it?"

"Why don't we go across the street for some coffee where we can be by ourselves."

Polly gave the detective a skeptical look as if she was about to be reprimanded. "I hope I'm doing my job okay."

"Don't worry, it's not that. You're a real asset to the team."

The two made awkward small talk as they trekked across the street to Barney's Coffee Shop. Zack pointed to a booth in the far corner, which was far enough away from two other groups to ensure privacy.

After ordering, Polly inquired, "So what's really up, Zack?"

"Polly, I'm having mixed feelings about this investigation. We need to nail whoever killed Molly Starr, but I'm reluctant to arrest those who put terminally ill people in deep suffering out of their misery."

"I know where you're coming from. I've heard some doctors sometimes hurry up death for their suffering patients during their last hours or days. While it may be humane, it's definitely illegal. Ending a life weeks or months in advance is a real problem. Where you draw the line is a tough one."

"Well, I had my dog put to sleep a couple of years ago and the vet said I was being kindhearted. I also know that my wife, Joan, wanted euthanasia during her last couple of months. It was no picnic for her. I would have been doing her a favor. I guess what I'm trying to say is, I have to uphold a law which I'm not sure I believe in."

"The state of Oregon has wrestled with this problem for some time," Polly responded. "I think they permit euthanasia under very strict conditions. If I had to bet, I'd say other states will eventually do the same thing." Polly added, "Zack, I think a lot of people agree with you. It's a fine line we walk in the legal business."

While the detective felt better hearing that he wasn't alone, it didn't solve his problem. But he didn't labor on his dilemma; the chances were his personal feelings wouldn't present a problem with enforcing the law.

~~~

Shortly after eight in the morning Polly was prepared for another session with Judge Hardin. Lila had confirmed he would be available. Zack, deciding to accompany her for moral support, made conversation as the two headed for the judge's chambers. "How've you managed to get along with that crusty old bird?"

"I just remember to be respectful, use some humor and, when necessary, show him a little leg," she responded jovially.

"What do the male attorneys do for an encore?"

"That's their problem," she replied as she continued to smile.

The pair was immediately shown into Judge Hardin's chambers. Polly handed her new request to the magistrate.

"Why don't the two of you just move in here?" the judge opened. "I see more of you than I do my court reporter."

"We're aware of that, your honor. This is a complex case with far reaching circumstances," replied the lead detective.

"Cut the crap, Gerrard. I guess I can see where this is going. Why don't the two of you take a load off? Sit down for a couple of minutes while I give this a rough run-through, in case I have some questions."

For five minutes that seemed like an eternity to Polly, the judge studied the request. Then he looked over his reading glasses and said, "Based on what you told me before and what I see here, I think I can understand its importance. Maybe I'm being overly sensitive but I definitely don't want to get caught with my tits in the wringer with voters of special interest groups like the Italians or Catholics. I'm up for reelection in a couple of months and if I lose, I'll end up spending my entire days with my wife, Amelda. Now *that* would be a fate worse than prison....Just kidding—but I do have to uphold my reputation for being a hard-ass with you guys."

Hardin finished studying the papers and said, "OK... here's the deal. I hope you get these bastards, and when you do, I'm personally going to lock 'em up and throw away the key. Ms. Larkin, if you'll stop by after lunch, the signed order will be ready for you. Now get out of here, so I can get some work done," he said, with a wry smile on his face.

~~~

When Zack returned to his office he noticed a post-it note on his desk. It said simply 'Kate O'Brien, B. H. ofc mgr,' with a phone number. He was curious to find out what role, if any, the Brackett House might play in this investigation and immediately dialed the number.

"Kate O'Brien? This is Detective Gerrard with the Dubuque Police Department. I'd like to come by to talk to you about an investigation we're conducting. Your organization might be able to give us some information."

"Certainly, Detective, my schedule is fairly flexible. I can meet with you this afternoon if you'd like."

"Fine. If it's okay, I'll come over at four-o'clock."

"That sounds good. I'll look forward to helping in any way possible."

~~~

The detectives were scheduled to complete their interrogation concerning the Chandler Logan murder. However, they learned that due to Mrs. Logan's mental state, they'd have to question Chandler's daughter, Louise Dunn, alone. Louise was on time for the ten o'clock session and appeared more at ease than the previous day.

"Thank you for coming back, Mrs. Dunn," Zack said. "Hope your mother is feeling better."

"She's heavily medicated and that seems to be helping her get her rest," Louise replied.

It was obvious from the black under her eyes that she was the one who needed some sleep, Zack thought.

"I've asked Ms. Larkin from the D.A.'s office to join us again," the detective resumed. "Before we start, I need to advise you as I did previously, of your rights under the Miranda rule."

After repeating it, Zack inquired, "Would you like to have your attorney present?"

Louise responded, "I don't think that's necessary. We've already admitted our involvement in Dad's death."

"OK, Louise, let's review some of your previous testimony, and then we have a few more things we'd like to cover."

For nearly an hour, Louise answered questions posed by Zack. Her comments corroborated what Brockton had told them. She then talked about the negotiation process with the euthanasia representative. At that point, Zack inquired, "I guess the whole procedure can be fairly costly?"

Louise remarked, "There was no way we could raise the fifty thousand dollars they originally asked for. I must say they showed some compassion when they agreed to help for twenty-five.

"Detective, what we did was wrong, both Mom and I are prepared to pay for our actions," she added.

"We'll be turning this case over to the district attorney. I'll let Ms. Larkin talk to you about that."

"Mrs. Dunn, I need you to come over to the courthouse with me for a few minutes," Polly said. "There are a few things we need to go over at the DA's office."

~~~

Late morning was generally a busy time at Kennedy Mall, still the primary shopping paradise for anyone within twenty miles. Someone was pulling out of a parking space close to the UPS store. Lou figured it must be his lucky day.

The UPS manager was easy to spot in his brown uniform. Lou explained, "We're involved in an investigation of someone known as Chris Crim and we believe he...or they...have a mail drop at this location. Is that right?"

"Yes, sir, box number 187."

"So, do you know who picks up their mail?"

"Not really, sir. A lady usually comes by once a day to check the box, but I don't know who she is. Let me ask my helper who's in the back."

The manager was only gone long enough for Lou to read one of the contemporary greeting cards available in the card rack. He had to give the store credit; they were marketing something in virtually every square foot of their space.

"Sara has seen a lady come in occasionally. But she doesn't know her either."

"Does this lady come by about the same time each day?"

"Yeah, she's generally here between two and three."

"Could you describe her?"

"I don't know how good I am at descriptions but I'd say she's in her twenties, dark hair, and skinny. She's pleasant, but very business-like. Usually nicely dressed...you know, jacket and skirt."

"That's a darn good description. We should have you on the panel at Chamber meetings when we talk about how to identify suspects. If you don't mind, we'll keep an eye out for this woman. Oh, and I'd appreciate it if you would keep this confidential."

"No problem. Glad I could help."

Lou wrote down the manager's description of the *Chris Crim* party and returned to his car. He planned to have Sergeant Janice Skinner wear plain clothes and keep this location under watch. She should like the duty, since, from what he heard, she spent most of her off-duty time shopping, he thought wryly.

THIRTEEN

Back at the office, Lou took a call from his law enforcement friend in the Chicago area. He was excited to learn what had been found about one of Chris Lazorno's close buddies, Ronald Roselli. "You've got an answer already, Johnnie? That's great!"

Johnnie Newman had been a friend ever since the two were in the police academy together twenty-five years before. Being the Skokie Chief of Police gave Newman easy access to numerous sources in the Chicago area. Obtaining information concerning Lou's inquiry had not been difficult.

Lou's friend responded, "Ronnie Roselli doesn't have a record. But he did run into trouble when he was a registered nurse at Chicago Central Hospital two years ago. Seems he was forced to resign because the hospital administrator threatened that they might be able to prove he was stealing drugs from their pharmacy. Possibly, he was selling them on the black market."

"Johnnie, I owe you big time! That's just what I was looking for."

"My pleasure, partner, I'm glad I could help. Vera says, 'hello.' Give our regards to Sally."

Ronnie Roselli, Lou thought, was not lily white. This was better than expected. Not only did he have access to drugs at Alliance where he worked in their medical department, he had the knowledge and training to administer the injections for the so-called euthanasia group. Lou believed it was likely he could get a warrant to search Roselli's premises and might possibly find evidence that would nail the bastard and that could lead to uncovering the whole murderous crew. Lou could see his career skyrocketing when word got out that he had busted the biggest crime ring ever in Dubuque. He would keep this information to himself until he had obtained the incriminating evidence on the suspect.

~~~

Prior to his appointment at the Brackett House, Zack found a brochure on the institution to look over.

> This charitable organization was founded for the benefit of Dubuque's elderly who are unable to financially care for themselves. The elderly who are eligible for assistance are subject to a stringent examination of their financial condition. If an individual's combined receipts from income and programs of assistance fall below the federal government's standards for poverty they may qualify for the Brackett House's financial assistance program for health insurance and pharmaceutical reimbursement.

Zack agreed with the chief that a tremendous cash flow would be required to sustain those benefits. And charitable contributions were the sole source of Brackett House revenue.

"The House," as it became known, had been operating for less than two years and already was in the midst of a major physical expansion. This would be another drain on contributions even though the Whitcomb family had provided a matching gift of a million dollars.

Zack was interested to learn the names of the Brackett House board of directors. In addition to the CEO, Sister Miriam Barton, and three other nuns were Monsignor Mulcahey and Dr. Clifford Brown.

As Zack's Toyota neared its destination on the south edge of the inner city, he noted that it bordered a seldom-used railroad docking area. It nestled between the towering bluffs more than two hundred feet high to the west and the Mississippi River a block to the east.

There were two large structures situated on this city block. The newly built Brackett House employed the same architectural design as the older Julien Hotel. Both were covered in red brick with contrasting white paned windows and cement windowsills.

The Julien Hotel had been the city's first skyscraper. The seven-story building with its fifty-four rooms had been impeccably refurbished and its coffee shop was still considered one of the better places for breakfast.

The Brackett House sat on the northwest corner of this city lot. Its construction had led to an upgrading of an otherwise blighted urban blighted area. Directly across the street a retail strip mall was nearing completion.

From his angle of approach Zack could view the expansion that was underway. The back half of the existing two-story building had been replaced by plastic sheeting in preparation for the major addition.

As Zack entered the facility, an attractive woman with auburn hair and a warm smile greeted him. Her short skirt revealed legs that complimented her slim figure.

"Hi there, can you direct me to Kate O'Brien?" Zack asked.

"I certainly can. *I'm* Kate O'Brien! But please call me Kate," she said as she extended her hand. Zack sensed both genuineness and confidence in her easy mannerisms.

He responded with the firm-but-not-too-firm handshake he usually reserved for persons of the opposite sex, even as he found himself momentarily mesmerized by the intensity of her green eyes.

"I'm Zack Gerrard of the Dubuque PD. I'm grateful for your taking a few minutes to assist us. We're gathering information concerning Molly Starr." He thought, why not use this as a roundabout way to get what he was really after: getting info concerning large cash donations paid to 'The House.' He also realized he was immediately attracted to this good-looking woman who was probably ten years his junior. It had been a long time since he felt those vibes. Well, back to business. She was already responding to his question.

"...great supporter of our cause. We were so sorry to learn of her passing. What specifically did you have in mind?"

"We know of her generosity to the Brackett House and several other charitable organizations. We're just making routine inquiries into individuals or organizations with which she had financial ties."

"Ms. Starr was one of our best supporters and promoters."

Zack switched gears. "By the way, congratulations on the terrific job 'The House' is doing for the community. Do you think I could get a brief tour of the place?"

"Sure, Zack...Is it all right if I call you by your first name?"

"Please do, Kate," he responded in as friendly a manner as he could manage.

He followed her throughout the Brackett House feeling rather like a well-trained Weimaraner. She continued, "Please excuse the mess. We're roping off the new areas under construction in preparation for our dedication by the cardinal next Monday. I know it looks premature to have a dedication when we're ninety days from completion, but the cardinal doesn't get to Dubuque very often. He's going to conduct Riley Whitcomb's ordination and we're riding on his coattails, so to speak."

"It's funny you should mention Riley's name. I just met him a week ago. What do you know of him and his family?"

"They're all terrific, although I've never met Riley, personally. From what I hear, he's been dedicated to becoming a priest for some time. The Church needs more good men like him. And his family's been wonderful to us. If it wasn't for their financial support we wouldn't be where we are today!"

She continued to lead Zack through a maze of ribboned pathways erected to keep the public from the dangers of construction. "We've been making tremendous progress since I came on board nearly two years ago, if I may say so myself. Of course, 'The House' was just becoming operational at that time so I can't take any of the credit…though I was just recently promoted to office manager!"

"Well, congratulations. I'm sure the promotion was well deserved." Zack had a thought that she seemed willing enough to talk about operations. Maybe she could shed some light on their financial success. "I realize it's near closing time. Is there any possibility I could take a little more of your time, say, over a Coke?"

"Sure, that sounds fine. Just give me a minute to grab my purse from my office."

He couldn't keep his eyes off her as she walked away. He was concentrating on her entrancing gait when a nun walked by with a smiling glance that showed she was reading his mind. He was slightly embarrassed.

Within ten minutes, they had ambled across the parking lot and were enjoying their Cokes in the café at the Julien Hotel.

"My son's with his grandparents tonight. They're taking him to see the Dodgers play. The three of them are crazy about baseball. Not me. It's too slow. I tell my friends it's about as exciting as watching paint dry. Please don't tell anyone I said that."

Zack inquired, "Does your husband enjoy baseball?"

"He did. But unfortunately he's gone. He was killed in a motorcycle accident eight months ago. He was the last person you would expect to be attracted to a motorcycle. I told him I'd never get on one. They're too dangerous, but he wouldn't listen."

"I'm very sorry. Please excuse me for bringing it up." Zack was sorry he had asked that question, but for some reason he was pleased to learn she was unattached.

After a moment of uneasy silence, he refocused on the Brackett House. "Kate, why do you think the House has been so successful?"

"I'd say it comes down to two things: the demographics and the funding. We have so many elderly in the area and many of them are in tough financial straits. We're providing services they can't afford. So there's no shortage of patrons!

"But what's really made it possible is the financial support of the community. Contributions have been so good and since my arrival they've been increasing by leaps and bounds, especially during this last year. What amazes me is the large, steady stream of donations. I don't handle the money, but I do see our bank deposits on our computer printouts."

"Kate, have there been any special fund drives or large gifts that have been publicized during the last year?"

"Well, we have an ongoing drive for our building addition of course. The Whitcomb family is matching contributions up to a million dollars and our PR policy for promoting success of the drive is to mention any contributions of ten thousand dollars or larger at board meetings. We've had only a couple to report this year. Both were under twenty thousand."

Zack's hope for the connection with *Lacrima* funds was dashed. "Would you know if either a twenty-five thousand or a one hundred thousand donation might have been received in the past two weeks?"

"I'm sure I'd know about that. I usually hear of the large donations the day they're received. I'd say neither of those amounts has come in."

"Kate, the reason I ask is that large donations to an institution may figure in on a current investigation. Who handles your donations and their deposit to the bank?"

"Sister Renee does and if she can't, it's done by Sister Miriam."

"Do you see whether the funds received are by cash or check?"

"No, that's outside of my area of responsibility. However, I do see the data on the printouts."

"How would you feel about sharing those printouts with us? Before you answer that, I need to tell you that this has to be confidential. You couldn't even inform your boss, Sister Miriam, about it."

"Wow, I feel I'm being put on the spot. I don't want to do anything that could cost me my job. Sister Miriam has placed a great deal of trust in me. I guess I'd have to have more proof of the police's need for it."

Zack was consoling. "I understand completely. Let me see what I can do. It was a pleasure to meet you, Kate, and thank you for taking so much time with me. I hope our next meeting will be under more pleasant circumstances."

"That sounds good, Zack. It was nice meeting you, too. Thanks for the Coke."

Was it his imagination or did Zack catch a subtly flirtatious look from Kate O'Brien as she turned to go?

~~~

The detective squad and the chief met in the conference room near the end of the business day. Zack hoped Lou and Polly's afternoons were more productive than his. He was the first to report on his visit with the Brackett House office manager.

"When I went to my appointment at the Brackett House my intuition told me it could possibly be the depository for *Lacrima Christi*. But I wasn't so positive after talking to the office manager. Apparently, there have been no gifts this year over twenty thousand dollars, but I have to admit she was reluctant to reveal much else. However, she might be persuaded to cooperate if we gave her a good enough reason."

The chief said, "Zack, her comments may not mean much. *Lacrima* gets its money in cash. And donors to the Brackett House would certainly make their contributions in the form of a check to provide a record for the IRS. But maybe *Lacrima* is smart enough to dribble the money in. Do you think she'd give us the House's computer printouts over the past two years? If we were able to show that a large cumulative amount of cash was deposited, that could help implicate them as a receiver of the murder funds."

"Might take a legal order, Chief. If they were getting illicit funds, they're hardly likely to want to just let everyone have a look at their books! But I'll see if I can get the office manager in to talk with you. At least that should emphasize the importance of this matter," Zack replied.

Lou then took the floor for his report. "The UPS store turned out to be a good lead," he said. "We've already found a *Chris Crim* representative who picks up their mail. The store manager told me someone checks the drop box every day, usually it's the same person at about the same time in the afternoon. I had Skinner carry out surveillance in plain clothes. She spotted the suspect a short time ago and managed to follow her to the First State Bank. After stops at the cleaners, drug store and supermarket, Skinner lost her trail. However, she did get the license plate number of her car, which she's checking out now. We can probably find her again, if we have to, by making another trip to the UPS store.

"In the meantime, I'm also making some headway with the Lazorno group. Chris's son, Mike, certainly has the knowledge to establish and maintain a website. He went through the entire procedure with me when I posed as an owner of a new business. There's also a chance that one of Chris's buddies has medical knowledge and training that could be used for the murders. But I need to follow up further, it's too early to know if this has any potential."

Polly updated the others on her contact with the state Registrar's office. "No record of any *Lacrima Christi* registration. However, there was a corporate entity founded in Dubuque about four years ago by the name of *Casa del Christi*. It also operated under the names CDC and CDC, Inc. But that organization is no longer in existence. For the past two years, they have not submitted their annual renewals to the state. Their records did confirm CDC was a charitable corporation, established solely for the purpose of acquiring funding to start the Brackett House. When that goal was achieved, the corporation was dissolved.

"The founders of the *Casa del Christi* were Miriam Barton, Clifford Brown and Arnold Greene. I did some checking on the three of them. Two continue to have ties with the Brackett House. Sister Miriam Barton has been the House's only chief executive officer. Dr. Brown, a family physician, is a member of the House's board of directors. Arnold Greene was a distinguished attorney, who retired from practice more than five years ago. Interestingly, I discovered he suffered from an incurable illness for several months before his death"

"Isn't that something," mused Zack aloud. "He may have passed away about the time the *Lacrima Christi* group began their string of murders."

"Maybe he was their first victim," Lou said grimly.

FOURTEEN

"I don't think anybody's home. We've rung the bell, knocked and inspected the perimeter. No sign of life. I say we pick the lock and enter. What do you think, Murph?"

"You've got the search warrant, right?"

"Right," Lou said. He had one, but he had considered going in even if he didn't have a warrant. He was confident he had a handle on solving the biggest killing caper to hit the city and he wanted credit for uncovering it. If his intuition was correct, as it usually was, he was about to discover a wealth of data that would incriminate Ronnie Roselli. Lazorno's friend had to be part of *Lacrima*. He had the skill to give an injection as well as having access to the necessary drugs. Lou was going to be the cop who brought him down.

"Well, let's go for it," Murphy responded.

In less than two minutes the police had picked the lock on the back door and were standing in the kitchen of Ronnie and Daisy Roselli. "Murph, I'll take the main floor, you check the upstairs."

Each policeman took his designated area and began a thorough exploration. Twenty minutes later, Sergeant Murphy returned to the main floor. He shook his head negatively at the detective's query and said, "I'll check the basement and garage while you finish up here, Lou."

Lou was intrigued to find that Ronnie's wife was also a nurse. He found her framed nursing degree displayed on the den wall above a photo of the couple decked out in their nurse's garb. The photo of Mrs. Roselli's matched Brockton's description of the woman who had injected Molly Starr with the deadly dose right down to the skinny figure with dark hair. Dammit, she's the one. Everything fit together. The circumstantial evidence was piling up on Chris and his buddies.

"How's it going down there, Murph?" Lou called to his partner in the basement.

"Place is as clean as a whistle. Haven't found a darn thing."

"Maybe we'd better wrap it up for the night. We can always come back. Before we go let me show you something in the den."

Lou led Murphy to the den where he pointed out Daisy's photo and explained how she matched the description of Molly's killer according to the nephew.

"Murph, the odds are getting better that this couple was involved in Molly's and, more than likely, the other murders. Not only does the wife fit the description of Molly's murderer, the couple has the knowledge, training, and access to the chemicals used for injections."

"Could be a case against them, Lou. You know what you're doing."

~~~

Lou couldn't wait until the next day to give Zack the good news of his discovery. His late night call to the lead detective's residence was answered by a groggy voice.

"Ah. Yeah. What's up, Lou?"

"Guess what, boss. We've uncovered the killers!"

"You...what? What do you mean?"

At the end of the report Lou said, "The broom closet by the back door contained incriminating evidence. In the back of the top shelf I found syringes and six vials of unknown substances. I overnighted that stuff to Matt, the DCI forensic expert in Des Moines, for examination."

In spite of his not being lucid, Zack's response carried some amazement, "That's fantastic Lou, but why don't we keep it to ourselves until we receive the forensics report."

~~~

The Chamber of Commerce luncheon at the Julien Hotel was well attended. At these monthly meetings, speakers were invited to share their expertise on a subject of interest to the community's businesses. Today's presentation by Chief of Police Scottie Baldwin dealt with advances in security systems.

To show his support, Zack decided to attend. While his arrival was tardy there were still a few seats available near the head table. As he approached he noticed two empty chairs. He took the one next to the Brackett House manager, Kate O'Brien.

"Kate, it's nice to see you again."

She smiled warmly, as she said, "Hi, Detective!"

The policeman greeted the other three guests at the table and took his seat. As he did so, he glanced at the chief who sat next to the speaker's stand. He had already begun eating. When they made eye contact, Zack grinned, in a show of support for his boss's forthcoming presentation. The chief responded with a friendly look that combined a wry smile and an arching of his eyebrows which the detective interpreted as "I knew you'd manage to sit by an attractive female."

At moments during the lunch, Zack made small talk with Kate. While they spoke of current trivialities, his mind was focused on the charming personality and attractiveness of this woman.

~~~

After the chief ended his talk and Chamber members began to depart, Kate and Zack were the only ones remaining at their table. Zack turned to the business at hand: obtaining information on Brackett House's large cash receipts. Before he broached the subject though, he realized there was a dilemma. If the House was the depository for the illegal euthanasia funds, Kate could be part of the mercy killings as well as Molly Starr's murder. On the other hand, this was his only entrée into the House books that could be entirely confidential. If the police had to obtain a court order to get access to the accounting records, the criminal group could be forewarned and possibly driven further underground. Zack's reliance on intuition in his police work had served him well over the years; it would have to serve now.

"Kate, have you given any more thought to providing us with Brackett House deposit information?"

"Actually, Detective, I've tried to *not* think about it. I really don't want to jeopardize my job. And I am loyal to the House and my co-workers.

It was obvious to Zack that the tone of her voice, which had been warm and friendly, was now cool. At least, she didn't tell him to get lost.

"Tell you what, would you at least consider discussing it with Chief Baldwin?...to get our side of the story."

"I...I guess I could do that."

"Good. How about coming to my office at headquarters about eleven tomorrow morning and the three of us can talk about it?"

"Okay, I'll do it. I'll try to keep an open mind."

"Great. Thanks, Kate. I'll see you then."

~~~

Zack decided to wait for the chief who was saying goodbye to the Chamber president.

"Great presentation, boss."

"Thanks, Zack. Say, I couldn't help noticing how chummy you were with our lead on the House's deposit records."

"Yeah, just softening her up. She's hesitant but agreed to come see us tomorrow morning. I'm sure you can convince her to cooperate once she understands the importance of this situation."

"You know, Zack, it's not a good idea to fraternize with anyone involved in our investigations. She could very well be a part of this whole damn murder scheme."

"I know where you're coming from Chief. And I realize I'm sticking my neck out, but I have a strong feeling she isn't aware of this euthanasia group. In fact, she could be at risk if the House *is* part of the mercy killing ring."

~~~

As Kate was returning to work she mulled over her conversation with Zack. She was in a bind. If the police's suppositions about the House channeling money for mercy killings were wrong, she'd have cleared her co-workers by letting the cops review the books. But this could cost her job if Sister Miriam got wind of secretly handing over House records. However, if the House *were* a conduit for illegal money, she'd have done her civic duty in helping solve a crime.

She thought, *how did I get in this predicament? That darn detective. He is awfully good looking, though. Have I been mourning John's death long enough? I told him to never get a stupid motorcycle. I'll bet Zack, who has a more dangerous job, would never do anything like that. He's actually pretty charming and kind of cute. But he certainly needs help with his dress. How could anyone wear plaids and stripes together?*

~~~

Zack knew his best source for learning more about whoever placed the *Chris Crim* classified ads was the *Herald Tribune*'s Hank Ryan. Zack appeared at the editor's office at the appointed time.

"I'm here again, Hank, on the Molly Starr case. It appears the use of your classifieds by a certain advertiser could be crucial to the investigation. We need to review every one of their ads over the past two years. Is there any way I can get copies as soon as possible?"

"No problem, Zack, we've got all that on the computer, so it's fairly easy to retrieve. What's the name of the classified advertiser?"

"It's *Chris Crim*." Zack spelled the words for clarification.

"If we had them by three p.m., would that be soon enough?"

"Fantastic. I'll pick it up then."

~~~

Zack's next stop was to see Riley Whitcomb. He wanted to keep him somewhat abreast of the investigation…at least to the point where he could expect a call if Riley came up with anything even remotely related. A phone call to St. Peter's indicated Riley would be in his office all day. Zack left word he would be over shortly.

As Zack made the short drive to the campus on the bluffs above, he was in a mildly euphoric state. Another major breakthrough in the case had been achieved and all progress had stemmed from Riley's contributions.

The first person Zack encountered when he entered Clark Hall was Monsignor Mulcahey. He wanted to share the good news.

"Sir, your associate may have chosen the wrong profession."

"Hello, Detective. I'm sorry I'm not following what you're saying."

"I'm referring to Riley Whitcomb. He's a first class detective. On a couple of occasions Riley has provided us with crucial information on the Molly Starr investigation that has led to an arrest. I came to congratulate him on his contributions. Without his assistance, we wouldn't have made any progress in the case. The chief considered presenting him with a special commendation but was concerned the publicity might not be good for his safety."

"I'm pleased to know St. Peter's is performing its civic duty. Riley's in his office. I'm sure he'll be happy to learn how helpful he's been."

"Nice seeing you, Monsignor. I'll go in and give him the word."

As Zack was about to turn towards Riley's office, he felt a friendly slap on the back.

"Hiya, Zack," said the priest-detective.

"I was just coming to see you. Have a minute?"

"Sure, come on in and have a seat." He motioned to an empty client's chair in his office.

"Riley, we've made terrific progress on the Molly Starr and Chandler Logan cases, thanks to you."

"I called you about the Chandler name when I saw it in the obituaries. You were out, but I left a note with your secretary."

"Yeah, thanks. Great minds must think alike. For some reason I was drawn to the obituaries myself that morning.

I must have been subconsciously thinking about those fragments of conversation you overheard at the Omega Building. You had mentioned Chandler and the ninth. Right?"

"Yeah."

"Well, Chandler Logan was murdered on that date in the same manner as Molly Starr. We have solid leads on those who requested the killings. Hopefully, the interrogations will reveal the culprits who actually performed the murders. It appears this group calls itself *Lacrima Christi*. Ever heard that name before, Riley?"

"Can't say that I have."

"Well, without your tips we probably wouldn't be to first base. But we're also concerned for your safety if your involvement leaked out. So, please be careful...and you might check with us before doing any more detective work. The last thing we want is a dead hero.

"Molly's murder may have been tied to Alliance Manufacturing," he continued. "She was on the top of their hate list because of her leadership in stopping the pollution they caused. Correcting the problem nearly bankrupted the company and could have cost hundreds their jobs.

"When they became a prime suspect I thought of their gray work uniforms. Possibly that was the gray you caught sight of when you spied on the group at the Omega Building." As Zack was speaking he pulled a shirt and pants from the bag he had brought with him. "Do these look familiar?" he asked.

Without hesitation Riley responded, "No, that's not what I saw. I'm certain the fabric was darker gray and didn't have a sheen to it. Zack, that material is so etched in my mind, I'd recognize it in an instant."

Son of a gun, the investigator thought. He was sure the disappointment on his face was easy to spot.

After a momentary pause, Riley said encouragingly, "I might be able to give you some other help though, Zack. *Lacrima Christi* is Latin for 'tears of Christ.' There may be a way to find out more about this group. Let's go to the library."

"Great, what are we going to do, search for a bunch of criers?" the detective replied with friendly sarcasm.

~~~

Riley led the way up to the second floor, turned left and charged to the end of the stacks. St. Peter's library was like a mausoleum during the summer. There wasn't one person in the entire facility. No students. No faculty. Not even a librarian. Must be on break, Zack thought.

A right turn brought them to a section relegated to history of the Church. On the next to the bottom shelf was a dusty, leather-bound volume with the title so faded it was unreadable. The student lugged it to a study desk at the end of the aisle. Riley hefted the book on top of a shelf at the back of the desk, which allowed them both to read from a standing position.

After perusing the index at the back of the edition, Riley turned to a section relating to the Church during the Renaissance. He searched in a chapter dealing with sixteenth-century Pope Leo X. With eager anticipation, the two saw, buried in the text, the words *Lacrima Christi*. Then Riley flipped back to the beginning of the chapter and both stood side-by-side with their attention glued to the yellowed pages. Zack read the first section:

A MEDICI BECOMES HEAD OF THE CHURCH

A replacement was needed for the recently deceased Pope Julius II. Five cardinals loyal to Lorenzo de' Medici conspired to elect Lorenzo's son as the new pope even though he had never been a priest.

Giovanni, the thirty-seven year old son, was a papal legate of Pope Julius II. In this capacity he was known by most of the cardinals. This undertaking to influence choosing a pope was evidence of the Medici family's economic power in the early sixteenth century. The promise to share in that power and wealth motivated the five prominent cardinals.

Their unofficial polling of the other cardinals indicated only two candidates had sufficient support to be elected. Cardinal Bibbiena had slightly greater backing than Giovanni. Marsilio Baglioni of Florence, the leader of Medici's five loyal cardinals, suggested the elimination of Cardinal Bibbiena. Their conspiracy resulted in the bribing of Bibbiena's physician to poison his patient with a drug that might not be detected. Within a short time the deed was completed. A week later Giovanni became Pope Leo X. Four days after that, he was ordained a priest.

At a victory celebration, the five cardinals vowed to maintain their secrecy. They also agreed to continue the sect for the purpose of vigilance against enemies of the Church. They decided upon the name 'The Order of Lacrima Christi.' If this phrase were ever passed to one another it would be the signal to reconvene.

"They had the audacity to use Christ's name as if their actions were in service of the Lord!" Riley exclaimed in visible distress.

"Let's go someplace where we can talk about this," Zack suggested.

"There's a coffee shop downstairs," said Riley.

Each seemed lost in their thoughts as they made their way to the coffee and donuts. The two settled in a booth farthest from the only other people in the cafeteria.

After inhaling a donut, Riley said, "The present day *Lacrima Christi* has to be patterned after the old Lacrima order. Both were set up for what they thought were noble causes. Today's group started in the business of euthanasia for the terminally ill. They're even using the same concept of doing away with people in an undetectable manner."

The detective added, "But this group is also in business to make money! It seems to me they got greedy and decided more could be made in the murder-for-hire business." Zack knew it was premature to talk about Lou's lead of Chris Lazorno and his co-workers. "Thanks again for your help, Riley. Gotta run."

FIFTEEN

Promptly at eleven o'clock Millie tapped on Zack's office door. She smiled as she raised her eyebrows. "I've got someone who'd like to see you. She's, um, quite a looker; shall I close your drapes before I bring her in?"

Millie observed from the sudden color in Zack's cheeks that her comment had the intended effect as he managed a reply, "No, but thanks for the thought."

"Hello, Kate! I'm very grateful that you came down; let's go over to the chief's office." Her eyes followed the direction he pointed and, as she looked away, Zack gave her the once-over. She looked just as incredible as she had yesterday.

At their destination, the chief employed his well-practiced charm. "So nice to meet you, Ms. O'Brien. Zack and I appreciate your taking the time to listen to what we have to say. We realize this is a very unusual request. Let me get right to it: We have reason to believe there's a possibility that funds collected from a certain criminal activity are being channeled through the Brackett House."

Kate didn't speak, though the look of astonishment on her face suggested she might have difficulty believing it. Her attention was riveted on the chief.

"Ms. O'Brien, I don't want to imply the House *itself* is involved in anything illegal. But to confirm or disconfirm the suspected activities we need to scrutinize deposit activity over the past two years. With your assistance we would like to keep this part of the investigation confidential. We don't want guilty parties, if indeed, that turns out to be the case, to be forewarned."

Zack softened the request by saying, "Kate, if you're uncomfortable with helping us, just say 'no.' We realize we're putting you on the spot. But you should know there's a good chance your help could put an end to an activity that's literally killing people."

After a moment's contemplation Kate responded, "I'm overwhelmed. I like to think I'm a law-abiding citizen and I certainly want to do my civic duty. I just don't want to be a part of something that would betray the trust of my employers and that could potentially jeopardize my job. What if I turned over the organization's private documents and it turns out there's nothing there! That would certainly seem disloyal to my boss. I love what I'm doing…not to mention it would be very hard to replace the pay."

The response by Zack was compassionate. "Kate, we understand your position completely. Why don't you think about it and give me a buzz…say by tomorrow morning. I wish we could say more about the crime we're investigating, but it's essential for all this to be confidential at this time."

"I understand. And, rest assured, I won't mention our conversation to anybody. It was a pleasure meeting you, Chief Baldwin. I'll call Zack with my decision soon."

"It was my pleasure, ma'am. Thanks for listening to us."

Zack said, "Kate, let me walk you out."

Everyone's eyes were on them—mostly on the Brackett House office manager—as they left the chief's office. As they headed downstairs, Zack said, in what he hoped was a tone of empathy, "Gee, Kate, I didn't mean to put your feet to the coals right away. We wouldn't even be approaching you unless we felt your help was critical to solving this major crime. And I can assure you this is possibly the biggest crime in our city's history. That's why it's best for you to not know any more details about our investigation."

"I can imagine it's pretty important for you to have gone to these lengths!" Kate paused before finally declaring, "I guess it's silly to delay any more. You need information and if it turns out you're wrong, I'll just have cleared some innocent people. But if you're *right*, then the truth needs to come out and it won't matter that I had to go behind some backs. I don't exactly know why, but I trust you, so I'm in."

"I'm sure by tomorrow afternoon I can have a copy of the computer printout showing our deposits for you. It will list the dates and deposit amounts for the last two years." She then added, her face changing from serious to a look that was new for Zack, "I just want you to know, this is going to cost you another soda!"

"I'll bet the chief will pop for both our drinks. How about if we meet after work at the Julien?"

"Okay, I'll see you then…and bring your wallet. I get pretty thirsty after a day of sleuthing."

~~~

"Lou, this is Matt. Took a look at the evidence you sent me and I've got some data," said the forensics expert, calling from his Des Moines office.

"Great, Matt. Put it in layman's terms, OK?"

"In this case that won't be difficult. First off, there weren't prints on *anything*. Second, everything you sent can be purchased from most pharmacies or hardware stores. Third, the box of syringes is new. Finally, the six vials held a variety of substances. Two contained potassium and the other three, without being technical, were various poisons and pesticides that could be used for rodent and insect control. However, large doses of any one of these items could be lethal within an hour or less."

Lou couldn't wait to give Zack the news right away. Millie said he had stepped away for a few moments and would return soon. He knew that was her code phrase for saying he'd gone to take a leak.

As the lead detective was returning to his office he met Sergeant Hugh Murphy in the hall.

"Congratulations, Murph. You and Lou did one heck of a job the other night."

"You talking about our search of the Roselli home?"

"Yeah, if the evidence checks out, we may have a solid case against him."

"Whattya mean?"

"The syringes and six vials. If the evidence checks out, it should make prosecution a lot easier."

~~~

Detective Gerrard's comments were a surprise to Sergeant Murphy. *What vials? What syringes!*

"Hang up the damn phone, Lou!" Murph said as he slammed the veteran detective's office door shut. "What the hell's going on?"

"What're you talking about?"

"When did we find that evidence? The syringes? The six vials of whatever it was?"

"Calm down, Murph. We're heroes. We've got the goods on the biggest killers this town has ever seen!"

"Lou…what we found the other night was a bunch of circumstantial evidence. And that's it! I don't know a thing about finding some goddamned needles and poisons. You didn't mention anything to me. When we left there in a hurry you weren't carrying out one fucking thing!" Sergeant Murphy knew his blood pressure was on the rise.

"Listen, Murph. You and I both know Roselli and his wife are the likely killers. Well, the syringes and vials just make it an easier case against them. It'll be a faster trial, cost the taxpayers a lot less and the murderers will be behind bars sooner. That's a fact!"

"That's a fact, my ass! Lou, you'd better come clean and do it before this thing goes too far. I'm not going to be a party to this kind of shit. I've never fabricated evidence in all of my thirty years on the force. If you don't fess up right away, I'm going to have a talk with the chief."

"You can't do that!"

"Wanna try me? I suggest you and I go into Zack's office right now and straighten this out. He's a reasonable man. We nip this in the bud, nobody else needs to know about it."

Lou said nothing. His stare was not focused and he shook his head.

"You've got two choices, Lou. Either you're going with me to see Zack right now or I'm going to see the chief alone."

Before Lou could respond the sergeant had opened the door and stomped out.

Lou hollered, "Hold on, Murph. Let's go see Zack."

~~~

Each day since his arrival in Dubuque, Zack's desk and other empty spaces became more cluttered with files and papers. The detective likened it to out-of-control weeds with no Round Up to stop them. At this rate, his stacking space would be maxed out before his one-year anniversary. He was considering requisitioning another table or file when he heard a tap at his opened door. A red-faced cop and a sheepish looking dick were seeking admittance.

"Come in, guys," Zack exclaimed. "Just dump those files on the floor."

Murphy seemed to calm down as he closed the door and stated, "Zack, we need to talk about something." The sergeant summarized events of the Roselli household search, after which Zack asked to be left alone with Lou. Murph didn't need to know any more; he got up and closed the door on the way out.

Leaning forward and gripping his desk the lead detective gave a hard stare at his assistant seated only a few feet from him. "Jesus Christ, Lou, what were you thinking?"

Lou looked at the floor, evading eye contact, "Zack, this has been building ever since you came on the scene. You know I deserved to be the lead detective. I've got seniority and I know what I'm doing."

"This time you didn't."

"I wanted to make a name for myself. People were going to remember I solved the biggest crime ever to hit this town."

"Someday, Lou, you'll appreciate what Murph just did for you. Fortunately, we can stop this before anyone is the wiser. Since the chief's been out of town, he's not aware of this incident. No one needs to know what happened."

The junior detective nodded as he continued to avoid his superior's gaze.

"You're going to have to get over not being the detective in charge. My God, Lou, I thought we were a team. I don't withhold anything from you and I expect you to do the same. This case is bigger than either of us. There'll be plenty of glory to go around if we ever solve it…I should say *when* we solve it. But if you ever pull another stunt like this, you'll be spending your time in the ass-mowing section of the unemployment line."

"I'm really sorry, Zack. It'll never happen again. Just tell me what you want me to do and I'll do it. But if you don't mind, I'd still like to pursue the Lazorno and Roselli angle, if that's okay."

"Fine. Check with Sergeant Skinner and let me know where we stand with that *Chris Crim* woman who goes to the UPS store. And shut the door on your way out."

Zack sighed with relief as he realized the good fortune of uncovering Lou's deception at an early stage. If word had seeped out about planting evidence, they would have been the laughingstock of law enforcement, not to mention a potential lawsuit. He jotted a post-it note for his briefcase: "Murph...bottle of Canadian Club."

~~~

It was a perfect afternoon for a jog. A cold front had brought relief from the humid nineties. And though it was now only eighty, it didn't take Riley long to work up a sweat. Recently he had given up obsessing about the euthanasia people, which had now apparently been identified as *Lacrima Christi*. But his recent session with Detective Gerrard brought those thoughts back to the forefront as he trotted past Missy's Bagels. Her acclaimed baked goods frequently drew him in this direction and was nearly past the outdoor tables with the deep yellow umbrellas when something caught his eye. On the far end of Missy's patio he stopped and pretended to take a breather. As he mock-stretched, a glance over his shoulder zeroed in on the dark gray attire of a middle-aged nun seated alone reading a book.

No doubt about it: her outfit was made of the material he had seen looking down from the second floor of the Omega Building. This was what the alleged *Lacrima* members had been wearing. Were the nuns somehow involved in this mess? How could that be? The subject of his attention must have felt his stare as she looked up from her book and gave Riley a pleasant smile. What the heck, I'm going to talk to her.

"I couldn't help but notice what you're reading. My mom raves about Mary Higgins Clark. I think she's read everyone of her books."

"I feel the same way. I'm sure I'm one of her bigger fans, too."

Observing the neck chain holding a silver crucifix, Riley inquired. "You're a nun, aren't you?"

"Yes, I am."

"Well, we seem to be in the same business. In a few days I graduate from St. Peter's and will be ordained."

She smiled warmly, "Welcome to the club. My name is Sister Katherine. What's yours?"

"Riley. Riley Whitcomb. I suppose I'm going to have to say 'Father Whitcomb' soon."

The nun laughed without artificiality.

Riley continued, "I was taken by your habit. I'm not familiar with that style, but it's a smart, modest professional look."

"Oh, thanks. It's our brand new summer wardrobe."

"I see you have 'FA' monogrammed on your sleeve."

"That's our one allowable luxury, if you can call it that. It stands for our order, the 'Fallen Angels.'"

"Well, it's very appropriately stylish, Sister."

"Why thank you, Father-to-be! If you're ever in the neighborhood and fully dressed, stop by over there. It's where I work, the Brackett House." She smiled modestly as she pointed across the street. "I'll offer you a cup of coffee."

"And I'll take you up on that. Nice meeting you, Sister."

As Riley resumed his jogging he couldn't wait to phone Zack about his finding.

SIXTEEN

In the early afternoon Zack reviewed the data from the *Herald Tribune* with Polly. They each had their own copy of the *Chris Crim* personal classified ads.

"I count twenty-six of these classified ads, going back twenty months," Polly remarked.

"Those guys sure have been busy. What a gold mine this is," said Zack. "Now, all we have to do is check against the obits. With the dates and initials from these ads we should be able to confirm each death with the obituary listings."

"I'll be glad to go to the *Trib* to check that out," Polly volunteered. "Then I can compare the information to the *Lacrima* website."

~~~

On the bluff at St. Peter's, Father Will Meloy hurried to Clark Hall to complete his last task of the school year: turning in the final grades for the semester to the administrative assistant.

"Afternoon, Monsignor. I was looking for Sheila to give her my grades."

"Hi, Will. She's at the post office. Why don't you just leave them on her desk. They should be pretty safe for the next twenty minutes. Say, do you have a moment?"

"Certainly," Will spoke with only a modicum of sincerity.

"I promise, it'll only be a minute. I thought you'd be interested to know one of your prize students is collecting civic honors, too!"

"Huh?"

"The word at the Dubuque PD is that Riley Whitcomb is a detective extraordinaire."

"How'd this happen?"

"He's evidently been the key to solving that Molly Starr suicide, which turns out, actually, to be murder. Detective Gerrard said a suspect is already under arrest, thanks to our 'Father Columbo.'"

"Well, I'll have to congratulate him. Thanks for the news, Monsignor. If you'll excuse me, I've got to rush. I've got an appointment to make some divots at Bunker Hill."

~~~

Near the end of the day, Zack heard from the Brackett House office manager.

"Zack, that was actually a pretty easy task you gave me. I have copies of the deposit printouts you asked for. Just to make sure I didn't miss anything, I ran copies of the general checking account and the building account as well as the business' savings account. Shall I meet you at the Julien in a little bit?"

"That sounds good. I'll see you in fifteen!"

When he arrived, Kate was anxiously waiting in the lobby. "Hi, Zack. I've got the data you requested. I know I'm doing the right thing by helping, but I can't help feeling a little like a criminal myself for sneaking this out. But if any money went through the till at the House it would have to show up in one of these three accounts."

"That's perfect. We'll keep this information classified. Now, do you have time for a Coke?"

"I know that's what I promised, but something's come up. My mom called a few minutes ago. Dad's doctor believes he's had a recurrence of his cancer and I think I need to be there to console him. I hope you understand...I'd sure be up for a rain-check, though."

"I can do that. I hope your dad's situation isn't too bad."

"We were hoping it was being kept under control but now I'm not so optimistic. Anyway, thanks for your concern."

"Take care. I'll keep in touch."

~~~

Riley Whitcomb and Dan, his best friend and classmate who lived across the hall, had traveled across the river to Galena for their favorite pizza. Antonio's, less than twenty miles from the seminary, was the latest craze and they were there in time to beat the rush. Even then, it took two beers before their names were called for a table.

"My treat tonight, Dan. I'm ready to start celebrating my ordination."

"Two more days! I suppose I'm going to have to start calling you 'Father.'"

"Either that or 'Detective.' In my mind I'm still on the case. I plan to keep my eye out for activity in the Omega Building or anything else that seems related."

"The info you passed on must've done some good."

"Well, it's given them a start on their search for that euthanasia group-turned-murderers-for-hire. Detective Gerrard is convinced they're involved in several killings. He brought me up to date, today." Riley proceeded to convey the general drift of the investigation without revealing any of the group's names.

"Holy cow, Riley, you'd better be careful."

Whitcomb used the server's interruption to change the subject.

"Dan, I wanted you to join me tonight to let you know I'm finally comfortable with becoming a priest. You know how my decision six years ago was made in sort of a hurry. I had hoped it would make amends for letting my family down."

"Yeah, I remember. In true Whitcomb style, you and your family faced the problem head on. You also kept it quiet."

"It was the way I got thrown into parenthood, though, that haunted me. It was hard accepting I had a son I'd never know or even see. I kept wondering where he was or what he looked like. He must be in kindergarten by now."

"You can't keep beating yourself up, Riley. You made a mistake. I'm just glad you've been able to put it behind you at last."

"It's ironic, celibacy is no longer a problem for me. That one night in high school ended my sexual desire. One time and she got pregnant! What're the odds? It's ridiculous, my sister and her husband have been trying for three years to have a baby. Dad was the only one who knew what the settlement was, her new name, and where she moved to…and he took that to the grave with him."

"I'm sure they were well taken care of. Let's toast to getting over the hump."

They both roared at Dan's double entendre.

~~~

Father Will, accompanied by Dr. Clifford Brown, interrupted their joviality.

"Hey guys," Will said. "It sounds like you've been in the sauce. The doc and I were just talking about you, Riley. Ready for Sunday's ordination?"

"Absolutely. You're still going to be there to help me get ready, aren't you?"

"You bet. C'mon over for a drink tomorrow night and we can iron out the details."

"Okay, I'll be there. What time?"

"If you come around six, I'll grill out."

"Great, see you then."

After Dr. Brown's regards to the younger two, they left for their table.

Dan spoke. "I wish you could lend me some of the great rapport you have with Professor Will. I've got him this fall for a tough course, 'Early Years of the Church.'"

"You'll do fine, Dan. But if you like, I'll give you my class notes. Father Will has really been a big influence on my making it to the priesthood."

~~~

An hour later, the two were on Highway 20 heading back to Dubuque. A steep grade accompanied by a sharp curve brought a two-ton truck with blinding headlights onto the no passing center line. Riley reacted well as he momentarily swerved onto the road's shoulder to avoid a collision.

"Boy," he said, "this has to be the worst stretch of road within fifty miles."

"You can say that again," Dan replied.

Fifteen minutes later, they exited the bridge over the Mississippi and entered the Dubuque downtown bypass. Riley had an idea. "How about swinging by the warehouse district?"

"Omega Building, right?"

"You got it. I doubt anyone is there. I just have to satisfy my curiosity."

Three turns and two minutes later, they slowly cruised by the intended destination. There was no sign of light or any vehicles in the vicinity.

"I've been doing this regularly. I haven't noticed a light on in there since I spent time in the ceiling. Who knows, maybe they don't meet anymore. Or maybe they meet someplace else."

"Come on, Riley, let's head back. I'm bushed and I'm not in the mood to get a bunch of murderers ticked off at me, either."

~~~

Saturday mornings at the police station were normally quiet, especially on the second floor. However, this morning the two detectives were anxiously poring over Polly's findings. She had compiled a form comparing the dates of deaths, *Chris Crim* ads and website messages.

Polly announced, "The ads appeared on the average five days prior to the dates of death. And the website messages were usually two days before the deaths. When you consider these timing differences there was a ninety-six per cent correlation with twenty-six deaths over the past twenty months."

"Now, let me tell you two about the Brackett House deposits," Zack said. "*Lacrima* was collecting twenty-five, fifty, or one hundred grand at a crack. But I can't find those specific amounts going into *any* of the House's three bank accounts. However, I *can* tell you most of their deposits are in cash. That's pretty unusual because givers typically want a bank record of their donations, not to mention they're not crazy about carting around that much green. Now, remember that Kate, the office manager, said all gifts of ten thousand dollars or larger are reported at the House board meetings. So my interpretation of the deposit information is that someone is splitting up the cash payments and dribbling it into the various accounts, thus avoiding the ten thousand dollar reporting threshold. I don't know why else they would be getting so much cash. Seems to me that we could build a case that *Lacrima Christi* is laundering its funds through the House on this basis.

"And here's another interesting tie. Yesterday, our seminarian-sleuth Riley Whitcomb told me he'd found a perfect match for the gray attire he saw when he spied on the *Lacrima* group at Omega. Interestingly, it was a nun from the Fallen Angels convent. And guess what? Sister Gray Suit works at the Brackett House!"

"That confirms what Sergeant Skinner discovered," Lou said. "The lady she tailed from the UPS store and then lost was driving a vehicle registered to the Fallen Angels."

"On another matter," Lou continued, "Skinner and I are running into dead ends on Lazorno, Roselli and their friends."

"Lou, how about if you two follow up on the UPS nun. Go talk to her and, if necessary, bring her in for questioning," Zack concluded.

The lead detective moved to the blackboard and added the words "Brackett House" and "Fallen Angels convent." As he did so he said, "Maybe we've found a home for *Lacrima Christi*."

~~~

Over at a nearly deserted O'Donnell's tavern south of town, a meeting of a different sort was taking place. *Lacrima Christi* was in session, minus two of its members, huddled around a table.

"We're here because the word on the street is they've learned our name and where we usually meet," said the gravelly voiced leader. "What's even worse we're accused of murdering Molly Starr. Not her mercy killing, but her murder!"

"Dear Lord," a second member gasped. "We agreed our work would strictly be limited to mercy killing. We all know the merit of helping the suffering."

A third commented, "So, you're telling us we were bamboozled?"

"Exactly," proclaimed the leader. "We let Brockton Starr deceive us. He assured us Molly was terminally ill. Her medical records he sent us were bogus. Brockton was greedy, looking for an inheritance. Thanks to him, we're now guilty of something we never intended—outright murder."

"What are we going to do?" said the third one.

"We should discontinue operations. If we lay low they may not be able to find us," the second one commented.

The leader said, "The problem is we can't afford to do that. We need the money. Our efforts have been well planned from the start. We just have to be extra careful from now on. Let's have a show of hands for temporarily stopping with the thought of resuming only if the right situation comes along."

Everyone raised their hands, one more slowly than the other two.

SEVENTEEN

Two members of the police department and a nun were in serious discussion in the reception room of the Fallen Angels convent, a facility pleasant, if meager, in its furnishings. The normally quiet waiting area was even less active on weekends. There was no need to speak about delicate matters in a low voice.

Sergeant Janice Skinner was questioning the young, slender nun with short, dark hair.

"Sister Renee, we have an interest in mail that has been sent to Box 187 at the UPS store in Kennedy Mall."

Lou detected a subtle note of discomfort on the nun's face. The sergeant continued, "The UPS manager did not know who had access to the box, but did describe the person who usually checked its contents and, you, Sister, fit his description. I kept the box under surveillance and followed you to this location where the receptionist identified you."

"Well, it's true, I *am* the one who usually picks up that mail," the nun responded. "Is there a problem?"

"There could be. We have reason to believe it is being used for correspondence related to illegal activities."

"Oh my! Of course I'm only the errand person around this place."

"I see. What do you do with the mail you pick up at that box?"

"I deposit it in the largest mail slot over there," Sister Renee said as she pointed to a wall full of mail slots in the hall adjacent to the reception desk. "I really don't know what happens to it after that."

The detective walked over to examine the object of discussion. When he returned he inquired, "Sister, how long have you been putting mail in that slot?"

"Ever since I joined the order, about two years ago."

"The slot is marked *Chris Crim*. Do you know who that is?"

"I'm sorry but, no, I don't. We have a sister named Chris, but her last name is Jackson. I don't know any Crim."

"Sergeant, do you have any other questions for the sister?"

"I can't think of any right now."

He closed the meeting by saying, "Thank you for your time, Sister. If we think of anything else we may contact you again."

As the cops were en route to their car, the detective asked, "Did you notice her eyes when we asked some of the questions?"

"Yeah," the sergeant responded, "she wouldn't look directly at us, would she?"

"Nope. I think she knows more than she said. We'll have to keep an eye on her."

~~~

As soon as he returned home, Zack called out, "Hey, Kristen, what've you got going tonight?" He hoped they might spend some quality time together.

"Dad, we girls are going to take in the new Antonio Banderas movie. Like to come along?"

"Thanks, but no thanks."

"I could fix you up with a date," Kristen said with a giggle. "How about that Kate lady?"

"I'd like to, but it's probably not a good idea. She's involved in a current investigation."

"Hey, I've got an idea. I'll bet you'd see lots of people you know at the Summer Regatta."

"You mean that boat show near the harbor downtown?"

"Yeah. It's where all the old folks hang out."

"Gee, thanks a lot."

The more Zack thought about his daughter's suggestion, however, the more he liked it. Several of the guys on the force had mentioned that it was a popular event...and it sure beat staying home alone watching TV.

~~~

Riley appreciated the invitation to be with his favorite professor the night before ordination. While driving to Father Meloy's home he reflected on their association this past year. Riley had been in two of the professor's smaller classes, one concerning Church history and the other on ethics. It provided an opportunity for the two to become well acquainted. They'd often continue their discussions over coffee in the seminary cafeteria. A couple of times, one of which was the St. Patrick's celebration, Father Meloy took his "of age" students to Murphy's Bar. Riley felt that the professor's counseling was particularly helpful these last months when Riley's father was suffering so much with cancer. The student and teacher spent hours debating the value of euthanasia. Riley had become a strong proponent of mercy killing. While Father Meloy argued the Church position, Riley suspected that Father Will personally felt there was a place for it.

The professor's home was easy to get to. Riley had become acquainted with this part of the town's outskirts in high school when he had gone with his buddies to guzzle beer without fear of being caught. Now, as he strode from his car to the white two-story farmhouse, Riley inhaled the fragrance of the periwinkle lilacs bordering the driveway. The clean country air was a welcome relief from the city.

"Evening, laddie. I saw you driving up." Riley had always wondered about the authenticity of the professor's brogue. He loved to talk about his Irish heritage even though the last three generations of his family had been born on American sod.

Father Meloy opened the front door and invited his young friend to enter. A glance at the living room décor already made Riley feel comfortable. A well-worn easy chair was positioned for TV viewing. A grouping of memorabilia adorned one wall. This included a prominently displayed old family photo showing a teenage version of the professor with what had to be his younger brother and mother—all three resembled one another. However, the younger brother had the appearance of Downs-Syndrome. Across the room from a fireplace sat an overstuffed brown leather davenport that looked cozy although clearly it had seen better days. An end table was loaded with books that were partially hidden by a copy of the *Sporting News*, revealing the headline "Cubs Lose Eleventh in a Row."

"Father, I see you're still following the world's leading lost cause."

"Yes, I'm afraid I'm one of the diminishing faithful. I say a prayer for them every night of the season. Guess that doesn't say much for my connections with the Almighty. Let's go sit on the back porch."

As they walked through the kitchen Riley spotted an unopened bottle of Sebastian merlot on the counter.

"I've got Coors Light in the fridge if you prefer that." Riley nodded as Father Meloy continued, "I'll grab one for you. After the first, you're obliged to help yourself."

The professor snatched the wine he had opened and a glass and headed to the back door. "Why don't you bring that tray of cheese and crackers and make yourself at home, Riley. I'm going to start the grill." The professor stacked the briquettes in the Weber grill, doused it with some fire-starter and threw in a match. "Hope you like brats and beans."

Will settled in his rattan chair within easy reach of the snacks. The two were facing the last rays of sunlight as the burnt orange orb slid behind a forest of oaks creating a shimmering glow along its silhouette. "This is my favorite time of day, Riley. With a glass of wine, just like the Lord drank, I can watch His visual masterpiece at work. I'm glad you could come over, bet you're looking forward to tomorrow."

"Father, it's been my dream for a long time. I'm grateful you're helping me prepare. I'll probably be plenty nervous."

"I know everything'll go fine, always does. Haven't lost a seminarian yet! One thing you need to do, now that you're joining the club, is start calling me by my first name."

"Okay, Will."

As the fire burned down to coals, the two discussed the procedures for next day's ordination to be conducted by Cardinal Clancy and Archbishop O'Donnell. They also talked about the reception at the Stonegate Country Club. Riley wanted Will to take his dad's place in the receiving line alongside his mother.

Later during their meal Will remarked, "The monsignor tells me you continue to do a fine job of recruiting and, in addition, you've become St. Peter's number one detective.

Said you've actually uncovered some nefarious group that practices euthanasia without a license." His light chuckle served to acknowledge his wordplay while signaling his awareness of the illegality.

"Will, you know from our talks that I'm a supporter of euthanasia. The group you're referring to convinced me that the activity can be compatible with being a Catholic. But I did find out later that the euthanasia group predicted the death of Molly Starr, which turned out to be a murder rather than a mercy killing. I can't condone that in any way. Who knows, there could have been other murders, as well! I just did my duty and reported the matter to the police. I figure they're now hot on the trail of *Lacrima Christi*." The name of the secret organization slipped out before Riley knew it.

"*Lacrima Christi*?" The Father abruptly leaned forward in his student's direction. "I'm not familiar with this outfit."

"I don't know much about them either. I guess that's what they call themselves." Riley knew the four beers had loosened his tongue. *Oh what the heck*, he thought. *As long as I've opened the subject I might as well see what I can learn.*

"Say, Will, not to switch subjects, but do you know much about the Fallen Angels convent?"

"They've been around a long time. Why do you ask?"

"I know it sounds bizarre, but I'm actually wondering if they could possibly be involved in these murders....or at least some of them."

"I'd say that's highly unlikely. From what I hear they're afraid to learn what Larry's Pest Control finds on their premises," Will erupted with a hearty laugh at his own joke.

Eventually, the conversation turned to current events on campus and the Cubs. Riley excused himself early so he would be well rested for the next day's events.

On his return to the dorm, Riley was thankful for the opportunity to unwind. The five beers assured he would sleep well on his last night as a layperson.

~~~

Not wanting to be one of the first at the Summer Regatta, Zack waited until about eight-thirty to make his appearance. A slight breeze had blown away the day's humidity making the temperature of eighty very pleasant. As Zack headed towards the river's edge near the harbor, the myriad reflected lights from a hundred boats made the water shimmer, reminding him of a lighted, mirrored sphere rotating over a dark dance floor.

The boating event was well attended and soon enough he found some of his cronies from the department. Making sure to be polite and appear interested in their small talk of office politics, his eyes kept a continual scan of the crowd…for a figure with auburn hair and emerald green eyes.

He spotted Kate at the same instant she noticed him. A wide smile formed on his face as he approached her.

"Good evening, Detective. I'd like to introduce you to my date for the evening."

A lump in his stomach accompanied the drop in Zack's jaw. It was then a figure emerged from around the food stand.

"Kate, you said ketchup and mustard both, right?"

"That's right. Sister Renee, I'd like you to meet the city's number one investigator."

It was obvious she relished her joke as the detective's glum look was replaced by a broad smile, as he realized what had occurred.

After the three had observed the intricate maneuvers of a boat brigade, Sister Renee excused herself to find a port-a-john. Zack took advantage of this opportunity.

"Can I give you a ride home tonight?"

"Gee, I don't know if I should ditch my date. That isn't very polite," she said teasingly, "...but she *did* drive."

Upon hearing the plan on her return, Renee looked relieved. "It's just as well. I can't seem to shake my migraine."

Another hour of meeting each other's friends was enough for the two. They were ready to leave, especially Zack.

As they departed, Kate asked, "Aren't you going to ask for directions to my house?"

"Heck, no. I wouldn't be much of a detective if I didn't already know where you live."

Zack was in no hurry to exceed any speed limits and, consequently, drove as leisurely as he could to extend their time together.

Kate responded, "Zack, you seem to know almost everything about me. All I know about you is that you work for the Dubuque PD."

"Detectives dwell in mysteries," Zack said with what he hoped was just the right tone of mystery. "But, seriously, at one time I had a personal life, now there's not much to it anymore. I'll tell you what I'll do, I'll give you a tidbit concerning my immediate family and I promise if we run into each other again I'll go into greater detail."

"Okay," she said, "whet my appetite!"

"My wife, Joan, died from the complications of breast cancer nearly three years ago. I have one daughter, Kristen, who just completed her freshman year at Northwestern University. With her in college I'm learning to be a bachelor, but I haven't been very good at it. My daughter's been trying to extricate me from the grieving process and in her humble opinion; she thinks I'm about ready. In fact, you're the closest I've had to a real date since Joan passed away. Let me clarify that, though. I'm not a recluse. I've been out with women since then but the occasions were strictly for events where you're supposed to be accompanied by someone of the opposite sex. I have to say, this has been a real treat for me, to share an evening with you. I just feel a little unpracticed and rough around the edges."

"You were fine, Zack. I had a great time."

"Likewise."

By this time the car was in Kate's drive and the engine had been turned off.

"If you've got a minute, I'd like you to meet my parents who babysat this evening. Dad's only exposure to cops has been on the wrong end of many a speeding ticket. I'd like to show him one who's *not* after him."

Zack met Ralph and Nora. Nicky, Kate's three-year-old, had gone to bed. The father appeared surprisingly healthy and the mother was clearly the source of Kate's genes for good looks. In fact, Zack thought, Nora could almost have passed for an older sister.

When Kate ushered Zack to the door she said, "Sometime I hope I get to hear the rest of your story."

EIGHTEEN

Riley Whitcomb's post-ordination party was in full swing when Zack arrived at the Stonegate Country Club. He complimented himself on delaying his arrival a couple hours after the scheduled start of the reception. There were still more than twenty or thirty people waiting to congratulate Riley, his mother, and Father Will, who was acting as the surrogate father.

Zack reckoned there were more than five hundred at the event, including dignitaries such as Governor Grant, Senator Hall and Congressman O'Neal.

While he waited for the receiving line to dwindle, Zack helped himself to a few hors d'oeuvres and champagne, since Sunday was his day off. Some of the crowd encircled Cardinal Clancy and Archbishop O'Donnell who were highly visible in their celebratory regalia. Zack noted many familiar faces but only a few with whom he felt enough at ease to make small talk.

"Zack, over here for a minute," the chief requested. "You know my wife, Eileen, and Judge Hardin, but I don't think you've met the judge's wife, Amelda."

"Pleasure to make your acquaintance, ma'am. I've heard so many nice things about you from the judge."

"From Samuel? You've got to be kidding. But I will say this, the old goat holds you in high regard."

"Thanks for trying, Gerrard," said the judge. "Scottie tells me you're doing a fine job on the Molly Starr investigation. Let's hope you can wrap it up soon."

"Thanks, your honor." After some polite talk Zack saw that the line of people wishing Riley well was down to four. He caught Father Will's eye as he stood at the end of the reception line and flashed him the thumbs up sign that was their private way of acknowledging one another. As Will returned the gesture, Zack took his leave from the four. By the time the detective reached the receiving line the last two guests had finished paying their respects.

"Congratulations on your ordination, Riley…er, I should say *Father* Whitcomb," Zack said.

"Thanks, Zack. It's going to take a while to get used to that title. You know Father Meloy. I'd like you to meet my mother. Mom, this is Detective Gerrard. Detective, my mother, Nell."

"It's a great pleasure to meet you Mrs. Whitcomb. I want you to know how much help your son has been in a recent investigation."

"He's told me a little about it. I'm glad he's been of some assistance."

Will entered the conversation. "Zack, why don't we let these two sit for a moment. You can get me a drink while I tell you about the ordination."

When they were by themselves, Father Will described the elaborate ceremony in which Riley had been invested into the ministry. Not long after, an elegant sit-down dinner was served and the festivities continued until almost midnight.

Possibly, in Zack's admittedly limited familiarity, this was the social event of the decade for the good citizens of Dubuque. He doubted it would even put a dent in Nell Whitcomb's checking account.

To the best of his knowledge, the only Catholic celebrity absent from the notable event was the Brackett House CEO, Sister Miriam. The word was she was busy preparing for the Brackett House dedication to be held the following morning.

~~~

Over at Brackett House at that moment, in fact, the two nuns were almost done sprucing up the large second floor room that was a combination office for the office manager, that also housed a library and file storage. As part of the expansion project the back of the room had been knocked out and was temporarily enclosed by plastic sheeting.

"Miriam, you should feel very satisfied. Just think, tomorrow the House's contributions will be recognized by Cardinal Clancy himself. I'm sure you never expected such a thing in your wildest dreams," said Sister Katherine.

"You're right there, Katherine. I wish Dad were around to share this with me." The mention of Miriam's father brought back recollections buried deep within her and her speech sounded as if she was in a trance.

"Dad would have been so proud, but not the rest of my family. The others never gave me any credit for what I could do.

"After years of struggling, the furniture business finally turned the corner. When Dad died, Mom and my two brothers kept me out of the business. Heck, my being college valedictorian meant nothing to them. They took the store right down the drain. I know I could have made the darn thing work.

"Their petty jealousies and arrogance hardened me against men. And that brief romantic entanglement was the icing on the cake. The jerk couldn't wait until we were married to have sex. Well, I'm living proof you don't have to be a man to succeed.

"Thank the Lord for the Church. The nuns gave me security and a way to keep distance from men. It took a long time to find the Fallen Angels, but since then it couldn't have been better. I'm proud of being Mother Superior and a CEO. It's comforting to know I built the Brackett House into something that's the envy of every bishop in the archdiocese."

Sister Katherine responded, "God has been good, Sister. If you'll excuse me for a minute, I have to check a few things on the main floor."

~~~

Sister Miriam was seated on the floor next to the plastic sheeting which had once been the back of the facility but was now open and overlooking the expansion on the floor below. Through the transparent plastic she could see the uncompleted kitchen and recreation area. From this vantage point the conglomeration of pipes and framing resembled a pincushion…or was it a porcupine? In either case at this stage of construction it was foreboding. She thought: *The new kitchen and recreation hall should be completed in the next three months. Soon this framing and these exposed pipes will be transformed into a greatly expanded operation for the needy and elderly people of Dubuque. Thank the Lord for Lacrima Christi! It's made so much goodness possible. It would be tragic if Brockton Starr's deception spoiled the whole thing.*

As Sister Katherine came back, Sister Miriam's thoughts returned to the present.

"Miriam, as far as I can tell, everything's in order for tomorrow's dedication. Shall we call it a day?"

NINETEEN

After being gently poked by Dan, Riley stirred. His head felt as though the pain would never end.

"Riley, best get up if you're hungry; kitchen closes for breakfast in fifteen minutes."

Riley stirred some more. He exhaled, telling himself to clear his mind. He had difficulty focusing on the crucifix on the wall above his bed. Then his eyes navigated his surroundings, as if they were unfamiliar. His Spartan room consisted of a desk, chair, a small rug on the tiled floor and the bed upon which he was immovably sprawled at the moment. In the middle of it all, stood a compassionate Dan Perkins. Riley marveled at how much he and his best friend of nearly twenty years looked alike.

Dan continued, "I think you did too much celebrating last night Father Whitcomb. Don't you want to go to the Brackett House dedication?"

"It'd be nice, but I promised Sheila I'd report in to help with a massive mailing. Anyway I had the stage last night, the Brackett House deserves the limelight today. Do you realize I've never been there? I just never got over that way."

"Let's go to breakfast. I've been holding off until you got up and I'm famished."

~~~

This must be what people mean when they say some place looks like a zoo, Zack mused.

A large crowd had gathered for the eleven o'clock dedication on land that was no longer considered the seedy part of town. Zack was smart in walking the four blocks from his office to the dedication. He couldn't have gotten any closer by driving. The heat was beginning to be noticeable as the time neared. However, the detective's thoughts were not on the clear blue sky and the gentle breeze. He was thinking of seeing the House office manager. *My God, I'm acting like a teenager.* And it felt good! He hadn't been in this frame of mind for nearly four years, before Joan's health started to deteriorate.

A few hundred people had already congregated around the temporary podium near the new addition's entrance. He immediately spotted the walk of a confident female who delivered brochures to the dignitaries on stage. As the event was about to commence she happened to see him and gave a friendly smile accompanied by a wink.

Soon, Kate managed to circle behind the growing crowd and greet Zack. "I'm glad you could come."

"Hi. I didn't realize this was going to be such a big event."

"I just got word from Sister Miriam that the cardinal is going to make a surprise announcement regarding our successful operation. I've got to get back in case anything is needed. Maybe I'll see you later?"

After preliminary remarks by the mayor and the chamber of commerce president, the House's CEO, Sister Miriam, introduced the distinguished guests Cardinal Clancy and Archbishop O'Donnell.

The cardinal came to the podium. "It's an honor for Archbishop O'Donnell and me to be with you today to formally dedicate this fine addition to the Brackett House. While completion may be a few months away, it certainly isn't premature to recognize the outstanding contributions the House has already made to the economically disadvantaged elderly. We know of no other charitable institution that provides this group of people with food, lodging, health care and medical prescriptions. Your innovative leadership deserves to be known and duplicated throughout the country. And you may be interested to learn that Pope John Paul has personally been following your progress. In fact he has asked me to present you with his proclamation of outstanding achievement. At this time, I would like Sister Miriam Barton to come forward and receive this document."

The loud and lengthy applause was accompanied by the clicking of several cameras. "Sister, I take this opportunity to invite you to share your wonderful program with our country's Catholic leaders at the Annual Bishops' Conference this November. Congratulations, Sister. I also would like to present something just for you. This is a personal letter of appreciation to you from the pope."

Sister Miriam felt weak-kneed as she accompanied the cardinal to the new entrance where they cut the red ribbon to formalize the dedication of the House's new addition. The building was open for tours in spite of the uncompleted portion that was cordoned off. Monsignor Mulcahey, Dr. Brown and the other board members were on hand to direct the public through the maze.

Zack managed to hang around until the crowd had thinned out before he approached Kate.

"Congratulations on a fantastic day. You should feel great about the cardinal's announcement," Zack said.

"We were expecting some good news. But that was unreal! Sister Miriam is on cloud nine. Of course all the rest of us are enthused, too. Even our cleanup won't seem that bad, now."

"When you're through you could probably stand a break. Would you be interested in having a bite to eat?"

"That sounds great. The folks are taking care of Nicky and don't expect me to pick him up 'till his bedtime. Besides, you said I was entitled to more than a Coke. Only problem is it'll be two or three hours before I can get away."

"The timing's perfect. I've got some leads to work on and then I need to spend time at the office. Here's my private cell phone number. Why don't you give me a call when you know what time you'll be leaving? I'll be glad to come by and pick you up."

"Okay, I'll do that, probably around five."

~~~

The activity at the Brackett House late that afternoon was much different than earlier in the day. It appeared to the nuns as though a bomb had been set off in the place. Debris was everywhere—discarded coffee cups, crumpled programs of the event and the paraphernalia protecting construction accounted for most of the eyesore. Normally the staffers would not appreciate being relegated to clean up. However, today they did not seem to mind. The dignitaries and visitors were gone, but they had left in their wake a feeling of euphoria. Everyone was in good spirits as a result of Cardinal Clancy's announcement.

Later, Miriam and Katherine relived the accolades of the day in the privacy of the chief executive's office. Both would have been exhausted if it weren't for the adrenaline rush of the day. Sister Katherine had her sensible shoes off and was massaging her nylon-covered feet as she listened to an overjoyed Sister Miriam expound with a priceless piece of paper in each hand.

Sister Miriam said, "Katherine, I never thought I'd experience a day like today. We're the darling charitable project of the entire Catholic Church! Just think about it. We'll be showing all the archdioceses our program at the Bishops' Conference. This'll put the Brackett House on the lips of the country's Catholic leaders. And I'll always cherish my letter from Pope John Paul."

"You deserve it, Miriam. You made this all possible."

Sister Miriam appeared to be in a trance of elation as she spoke her thoughts out loud. "It makes me think all our efforts have been worthwhile. This couldn't have happened without *Lacrima Christi*. I'm certain our other members are as elated as we are. This honor calls up Christ's tears all right. They're tears of joy. We're relieving the suffering of those about to die and using their money to help the elderly who can't help themselves." She smiled deviously as she concluded, "I guess that's one part of the equation we'll have to continue keeping secret from the bishops. They wouldn't appreciate how we raised the money for our program. Well, we did help people out of their misery…most of them, anyway."

~~~

By the time Zack returned to the Brackett House, its appearance had been returned to normal. Outside of a few cars in the parking lot, he thought the place looked deserted. As the Toyota neared the entrance the woman with the confident walk hurried toward him. He jumped out to open the car door for her.

"Hi," he said, "where would you like to go?"

"They have great sandwiches at Woody's up by the locks. Barbeque is their specialty."

"Wonderful. We might as well get there by the river route."

In spite of the demanding day with the public, Kate felt fresh and bubbly. She was sharing the good feelings that had circulated throughout the Brackett House. It wasn't long before they were seated at the restaurant with a great view of the river. Two private boats were making their way through the locks to the upper portion of the waterway.

"Kate, thanks again for providing us with the House's deposit info. Even though we're still massaging the data, we believe our hunch about the House being the channel for illegal funds appears correct. Let me repeat, there's no wrongdoing on the part of the Brackett House. It has to do with where those deposits came from."

"I know I did the right thing. But now, I'm ready for the rest of *your* story. Give me more details about the life of lead detective, Zachary Gerrard!"

"I guess that's only fair since I promised to do so. What would you like to know?"

"Why don't you tell me about your family and how you got to Dubuque?"

"Okay. I'm afraid I can't give you the three-hour version without my photo scrapbook. For the time being will you settle for the five minute overview?"

Her friendly smile was accompanied by a nod.

Zack highlighted his youth, schooling, police work in Minneapolis, his wife and her bout with cancer, concluding by saying, "I couldn't stand to stay in Minneapolis. The memories were too strong. But I did stay until Kristen completed high school as I promised Joan.

"Relocating here came on advice from a friend who lives in Dubuque."

"Who's this friend?"

"Father Will Meloy. You know him?"

"I've met him, but that's about it. I hear he's a really nice guy. He's a professor at St. Peter's, isn't he?"

"Yeah. He's one heck of a guy. Very social and outgoing, and through him I've met a lot of people here. Once in a while we play golf but that's been about the extent of my social activities.

"I have to tell you losing my wife was a tremendous blow to me. Since her death I've only had a few dates. As I said the other day, it was, generally, when I had a social obligation that seemed to call for it. I know it sounds stupid. My daughter says I can't get over the grieving. She's threatened to line me up with a date if I didn't do it myself. Well, now she knows I've broken the ice.

"But enough about me. Tell me about Nicky and your parents."

"Nicky's nearly four, going on fourteen. Actually, he's well behaved and has been a godsend for my sanity since I lost Mark. My folks came from about twenty miles south of here. Sold their farm about ten years ago. Since then, Dad's been a cattle buyer for Swanson's. I'm really concerned about his cancer, though. I may have to take him to the University Hospital in Iowa City for more tests."

Zack thought the barbequed pork sandwiches were outstanding. He'd have to take Kristen here before she returned to school.

As they returned to the House where Kate left her car, Zack was impressed with how at ease he felt around her. He'd been worried how he would react to the whole dating process. Truly, it was far better than he'd expected.

TWENTY

The two detectives and Polly were in the chief's office expecting a tirade. Millie had warned them that he was on the warpath: his demeanor confirmed it. Without any morning greeting he said, "Late last night I got a call from the mayor. He wanted to know what progress had been made on the Molly Starr case. I told him we had a confession from an accomplice who was at the crime scene but did not directly take part in the murder. I said we couldn't divulge that individual's name at this time because the accessory was cooperating in leading us to the killer. I further explained that maintaining his confidentiality was essential to not letting the perpetrator know of our progress in the investigation. The mayor blew his cork. He wants a guilty party's name published. He's getting heat because he thinks we're not going fast enough on the investigation. I tried cooling him down by suggesting that the arrest of the perpetrator was imminent." The chief held open his arms: "So?"

Zack knew what that meant. Somehow, some breakthrough had to take place as soon as possible.

The chief continued. "This morning I phoned Hank Ryan to ask for his cooperation in keeping a lid on this thing. Told him the *Herald* would be the first to know when the case broke. Hank's been around the block, so I think we can count on his help. In the meantime, the mayor is mighty pissed. He'll be more so if we don't nail somebody soon!"

It was evident the chief felt pressured. His face began to redden as he said, "This investigation has hit a stone wall. Hell, our only suspect is a freakin' nun! We've got to do something now and in a way that won't drive the freakin' killers underground. We can't count on *Lacrima Christi* making any mistake that could divulge their identity. In our current situation I only know of one way to move that fast: a sting operation. I'm thinking we could request euthanasia assistance for a supposedly terminally ill patient. *Lacrima* sped up their process to accommodate Chandler Logan; maybe they'd do it again. Why don't you three think about this? Let's meet again in a few hours after you've had a chance to mull it over. If you think it's feasible, we'll need a victim for the sting. But whoever we pick has to be someone we can trust implicitly."

~~~

Three hours later the group reconvened with unanimity to proceed with the sting. After much discussion a basic plan was developed. The only missing ingredient was selecting the proper couple to pull off the scheme. The parties would have to be people who were not well known in the community, convincing in their roles and willing to accept the possibility of danger. There would be no pay for this hazardous duty and this combination of qualifications would not be easy to find.

Polly spoke, "Chief, I know fewer people in this community than you or Lou do. But as we were developing a profile for the ideal participants, I thought of a couple who might just fit the bill. They're new to the community, did some acting in college and might actually enjoy the challenge."

"Who'd that be?" the chief inquired.

"Evelyn and Bob Watters. They've only lived here about four months. I got to know them in college when we were in dramatics. Both are talented actors and Evelyn thrives on playing tough roles."

"It sounds like they meet the criteria. Why don't you talk to them and see if they'd be willing to come in and discuss the matter?"

"The timing is good, chief, they're both school teachers. They're on summer break and their schedules are pretty flexible. I'll keep you all posted on what I can work out. There's a chance, if they're interested, that they could come in right away."

~~~

Zack was amazed at Polly's resourcefulness. She had advised him and the two others that the Watters could come near the end of the day. Just before five o'clock Evelyn and Bob Watters joined the investigative group. After Polly's introductions and the chief's call for pizza, Evelyn and Bob were informed of the *Lacrima* situation. Within two hours a plan was concocted to snare at least one of the killers into the police net and contingencies were developed. The chief, being familiar with most of the medical community, agreed to try to convince Bob Watters' physician and pharmacist to prepare the necessary documentation to support a diagnosis of the late stages of colon cancer. During their planning, the chief had phoned Bob's doctor and found that, in addition to his assistance, he could have fictitious records prepared by the oncology department at the University Hospital in Iowa City. The group also helped Evelyn prepare a request for euthanasia assistance from *Lacrima*. The plea would be for urgency since Bob's suffering was so unbearable. Evelyn then handwrote the petition and it was agreed she would place it in the *Chris Crim* drop box that evening.

~~~

Punctually at seven, Zack was on Kate's doorstep. He had already driven around the block three times afraid to be either early or late. A nearby church bell chimed the hour as he knocked on the front door. Now that's being punctual, he congratulated himself.

"You look fantastic!"

"Why, thank you, sir." As they walked to the car, Kate continued, "Have you been to the new Luigi's in Galena before? I hear the chef they got is fantastic."

Zack opened the car door for Kate. "Was there once. I took Kristen for her nineteenth birthday…I only go for special occasions."

~~~

Galena's main business district was a length of four blocks sandwiched between steep bluffs and the Galena River. The narrow streets with parallel parking on both sides could accommodate only the width of one vehicle. Zack felt the odds of locating an available parking space between nine in the morning and nine at night were slim. Fortunately, he found a space around the corner in the same block as the restaurant. *An omen of good things to come?*

A distinctive green and white-striped awning marked their destination. As they entered the restaurant the notable aromas rekindled Zack's memory of his mother's delectable spaghetti sauce. He was pleased with himself for making reservations there. A good restaurant here usually meant a wait, even with a table reserved.

It took a moment to adjust to the dimly lit interior. Indirect lighting combined with the lighted candles on each cloth-covered table promoted a romantic atmosphere of elegant dining and Zack was pleased when the maitre d' took them to a cozy table in the far corner.

The meal was as advertised and conversation flowed easily. Both raved about their veal scaloppini. Zack knew he was wise in not ordering a second bottle of Licindio wine. Eventually, he also knew he'd need to talk about the case that was on both their minds, but for now...all he wanted was to drink in his date.

~~~

Zack waited until dessert to make Kate aware of the potential dangers associated with the Brackett House. He had decided to continue the plunge, based on his firm intuition and against the chief's advice, to trust this woman without reservation. Since getting to know her, her welfare had become a concern. He also convinced himself that, being on the inside, she might be in a position to further help the investigation.

"Kate, our fears concerning the House being used as a conduit for illegal funds are confirmed. Normally, I wouldn't discuss an ongoing investigation with anyone outside the department. However, because of your position at the House and the help you've given us, I feel you're entitled to hear what's been happening. I can't stress enough the importance of keeping confidential what I'm about to tell you."

"You can count on that, Zack."

"OK, our investigation has revealed that a murder-for-hire group is operating in the city." Kate sat up abruptly. The period of mellow relaxation had ended. "This sect, or whatever it might be called, seems to have started by performing euthanasia but our evidence suggests Molly Starr was simply murdered by the group. That was followed by another euthanasia murder only a week ago."

"Oh, my God!"

"I don't think you're in danger…as long as you stick to your job and carefully observe what's happening. We still don't know who's behind the killings, although we now have a name for the group—they call themselves *Lacrima Christi*. Ever heard that name?"

"No, Zack. But before I joined the Brackett House there was a group known as *Casa del Christi*. Actually, they were the forerunners of the House. They raised money to make the Brackett House dream a reality."

"Yeah, that came out in our investigation. Anyway, Kate, I'd like you to tell me immediately if you hear anything about *Lacrima Christi*. They've been very careful to protect their identity. I imagine they're almost paranoid about not letting anyone know of their existence."

"I'll definitely keep you posted."

"Kate, you have my card which includes my personal cell phone number. If you should ever need to contact me about this matter, *don't* do it from inside the House. OK?"

"Agreed. Seems it was fortunate for me that I helped you with the deposit information. If I hadn't, you might not have been aware of any House connection and I might have accidentally walked into something."

The maitre d' was now making a polite nuisance of himself to let them know he wanted to close the restaurant for the evening. All the other customers were gone.

~~~

The drive home was quiet. The *Lacrima* discussion had put a damper on an otherwise romantic evening as both were now wrapped in their thoughts of Kate's safety. Zack was convinced he had acted properly in warning her. He liked being around her and despite their short acquaintance, Zack's felt strong vibes for this woman.

As the two started to part at Kate's door, Zack found himself unable to let go of Kate's hand...and she wasn't pulling away either. He also found an arousal that he had not experienced since Joan. In fact, he didn't seem capable of taking his eyes off Kate's enchanting emerald-green eyes. Finally, he managed to extract his hand, cautioning himself against a friendly kiss on the cheek. Instead he opted for one last squeeze of her hand. *Take your time, this lady is a keeper. Oh, what the hell!* He embraced her with a feverish long kiss and Kate responded by pulling in close, all tenderness and passion.

No further exchange was needed as Zack recovered and floated back to the Toyota. The dreamlike quality he had experienced for most of the evening warmed him on his leisurely drive home.

~~~

"Where have *you* been, Dad? It's almost midnight!" Kristen exclaimed with a sarcastic grin.

"Babe, you sound just like me when I stay up waiting for you to come in. Let's go to the kitchen for some milk and cookies."

Kristen dutifully followed her father to the other room. He had given the signal he wanted to talk. She poured the milk, one medium glass and one large one.

"How many cookies would you like, six or eight?"

"Come on, Dad, you know three's enough."

Zack was well aware of the number from sharing this tradition for years. Three had been Kristen's limit since she began watching her figure.

"I'm glad you kept bugging me to go out. I had a fantastic time with the lady I had Cokes with."

"You mean Kate O'Brien? From the House? I hear she's quite the looker! Did you kiss her yet?"

Her father laughed. "Yeah. And wow!" But after a moment his dreaminess evaporated and he said, "I'm concerned about her safety, baby. Her job puts her right in the middle of one of our investigations."

"What does she have to worry about? You'll be there to protect her."

TWENTY-ONE

Arrangements having been completed with the family physician, pharmacist and the Oncology department at the University Hospital in Iowa City, the Watters were waiting for *Lacrima Christi* to make the next move. The past two days had been exciting and apprehensive for both Evelyn and Bob and they were not taking the idea of a sting operation to snare killers lightly. Both were jittery each time the phone rang.

The police were monitoring activities at the residence of the co-conspirators. They had connected the Watters' telephone to their tracing system in preparation for any incoming call for the *Lacrima* sting. Now it rang again. Since Bob was supposedly in the latter stages of his bout with cancer, Evelyn answered.

A gravelly voice inquired, "Is this Evelyn Watters?"

"Yes, it is."

"I'm calling regarding a letter you placed in Drop Box 187 at the UPS store in Kennedy Mall."

"Oh, thank heavens you called. Can you help Bob with his suffering?"

"Perhaps. How did you find out about us?"

"Through a friend of my husband's, Chandler Logan. Bob and Chandler met when they both were at St. Mary's Cancer Center. I assume you were able to help Chandler."

There was no immediate response, so Evelyn continued. "Chandler wanted to die. He told Bob he was making arrangements to end the suffering and he suggested the time might come when Bob would want to do the same thing. That's when Chandler told him how to contact you. We figured you assisted him since he passed away two weeks after that discussion."

The caller spoke, "We require proof of the need. Anything you could submit to us from your doctor or pharmacy would be helpful. If we decide to help, we want to match our treatment with his condition so the death can appear to have occurred under normal circumstances."

"I can provide whatever you need, Bob is pleading that we move fast. Each day the pain becomes more intolerable."

"We'll review the data at once. If we agree to assist, you'll be advised through the newspaper. Look for a personal classified ad in the *Herald Tribune* three or four days after you've submitted the medical reports to us. If your husband's initials appear in an ad placed by *Chris Crim*, you'll know we've decided to take on his case. The exact date and time of our assistance will appear in a website. Soon after the classified ad your husband's initials will appear on the *Lacrima* AOL.com website along with a date and time for his termination. If you move fast, that could be as early as Friday. When we arrive at the appointed hour, please have fifty thousand dollars in tens and twenties. If you have any questions, I suggest you ask them now. This will be our last conversation."

"I've written everything down. I'll drop off a copy of Bob's medical reports the first thing in the morning. I can't tell you how much we appreciate what you can do for Bob. I'll be watching the classified ads. Thanks, so much!"

Evelyn immediately phoned Polly to apprise her of the situation. Polly responded by suggesting that she and Bob should meet in the chief's office at ten the next morning.

The previous evening's conversation with *Lacrima* was replayed for the investigators with the Watters present.

The chief said, "That was a great performance, Evelyn. It looks as though we're going to have a mercy killing…and soon. We traced the call to a public phone at the Kennedy Mall. Our people were there right after your conversation but I'm afraid it was a dead end—the pay phone had been wiped clean of prints. These people are thorough. We'll requisition the cash and have it in a gym bag in case they want to see it prior to the attempt. Don't worry, Bob. Since we're sure the murder attempt will be by injection there shouldn't be any danger. Nevertheless, we'll have our best officers close at hand along with a medical team. We'll apprehend the killer before he or she can get close to you."

"God, I hope so. I wasn't planning on checking out so early in the game."

~~~

It was an ideal night for a cook out and Zack wanted to show off his culinary skills with his new gas grill.

His butcher at Maury's Market had trimmed out two beautiful beef tenderloins. Kate was picking up the other ingredients after dropping Nicky off for an all-nighter with her parents.

Kristen was going to spend the night with one of her girlfriends and that was the deciding factor in having Kate come to his place. Zack was certain their fascination was mutual. This would be the first time Kate visited his Pennsylvania Avenue apartment with a cozy fireplace and a balcony for his grill.

Zack hurriedly answered a knock on the door.

"Hi, hon," she exclaimed as she slid by him through the narrow foyer with a bottle of merlot in hand.

Zack liked the moniker. That was the first time she had called him by that name and he thought it bode well for the evening ahead.

After dinner, they watched the glowing charcoal embers dwindle as the first stars began to appear, the merlot adding to the ambiance. Zack noted that their periods of silence were amazingly comfortable.

Without a word Kate moved closer, wrapped her arms around him giving Zack a passionate but tender kiss. Then she grasped his hand and led him into the house. Zack instinctively knew the destination and he was glad she was doing the leading. His mind flashed with the question, *How long had it been since he had done what he was about to do? Too long!*

~~~

The couple slept-in the next morning. Zack easily rationalized his decision to be an hour or so late for work since he had been putting in plenty of extra hours on the investigation. Kate apparently didn't feel guilty, either.

Now acquainted with his kitchen, she decided to surprise him with a big breakfast. With no one else around she was comfortable wearing nothing more than one of his Northwestern University t-shirts, which suited Zack just fine.

Realizing he would soon be appearing dressed for work she called to the other room, "How do you like your eggs, Zack?"

"Over easy," he replied as he entered the room. "Hey, I'm jealous of my t-shirt. *I'm* the one who should be wrapped around you!" He hurried over and planted a kiss on her neck.

Sitting at the kitchen table with coffee and a large glass of juice he couldn't help but recall the last time he was in such a setting with someone dear. It was with Joan three years ago. The morning *Herald Tribune* was also at hand. *This could become habit forming.*

Kate was just serving the eggs as the back door slammed shut. In popped Kristen, sporting a large smile. She gave Kate a thorough once-over and approached with a hand extended.

"Hi, I'm Kristen. I hope you're Kate O'Brien!"

"That I am. It's nice to meet you, Kristen."

Zack could feel the crimson color pumping into his face. He grinned sheepishly as Kristen turned her attention to him.

"I invited her over for breakfast," he said as he thought, *what a dumb thing to say.*

Kristen seemed to be enjoying the discomfort she caused. She said with an impish grin to the guest, "I see you wear the same brand of t-shirt that I got for Dad."

~~~

O'Donnell's Bar was quiet except for low voices in the far corner of the room.

"I appreciate the two of you coming," said the gravelly voice. "Our numbers may be smaller but we can still handle our duties."

A second person responded, "Even though the Molly Starr homicide scared away two of our members we're still operating and making money."

"But we may not be able to do this much longer—it's getting more dangerous with the police closing in," the third added.

The gravelly voice said, "Well, this should be an easy one. Bob Watters' medicals check out. Plus his neighborhood is quiet and there's plenty of cover for coming and going. Let's get this one and call it quits for a while. Okay?"

The other two replied in unison, "Okay."

~~~

All four of them had been religiously checking the classified ads. Thus, it was no surprise when three of them simultaneously gathered in the detective conference room.

"There it is, RAW stands for Robert Allen Watters," Lou exclaimed.

"The sting is on," the chief acknowledged.

Polly added, "I'll keep my eye on the *Lacrima* website for the date and time."

Polly wasn't the only one checking the *.org* websites. Zack had become addicted to inspecting the *Lacrima* site, ending this Wednesday afternoon. *There it is*, he thought, right at the bottom of the screen of prayers and biblical verses: **RAW 6/18 @ 7**. *Tomorrow night at seven o'clock.*

Zack entered the conference room where he found Polly reviewing some papers.

"The message just came on the website," he remarked.

Polly responded, "I'll give the Watters a call. However, I'd be surprised if they aren't following this as close as we are." She picked up her cell phone and dialed. "Have you heard the news?...Good. Well hang in there. Zack says we'll get set up early in the morning before there's any activity in the neighborhood. By eight tomorrow night we should all be celebrating."

~~~

The lead detective figured he was entitled to a night out. Thank heavens Will had called. He was pleased to be invited over to his home. But as he drove to his friend's, Zack's thoughts were ever on the investigation. *Lacrima Christi* events were building to a crescendo. He hoped this tragedy was nearing its end.

Will was in good spirits, flashing the thumbs-up sign to Zack as he entered.

From the television Zack heard the last few chords of the national anthem. The crowd at Wrigley was raucous. The Cubs had won two in a row, which meant a win tonight would equal their longest winning streak of the season.

Zack knew better than to head for Will's favorite lounge chair; the davenport was plenty cozy.

After a beer, Will said, "Zack, you look uptight. Maybe another Coors would help?"

"Yeah, I'm sure it would." The detective was anxious about the sting scheduled for the following day. He knew he couldn't talk about it, but he'd sure be glad when it was over.

"Job getting to you?"

"Only this damn investigation."

"You mean the Molly Starr thing?"

"Yeah, I'm hoping there'll be something to report soon."

"You must have had a major break in the case. Huh?"

"Not yet. But, if we're lucky it could be soon."

After some silence their interest shifted to the dismal Cubs. As the game progressed Zack spotted something new on the mantel above the fireplace. The dim light made the object difficult to see, but to Zack's untrained eye the object of his attention seemed too classy for the rest of the room's décor. Less than an inning later his curiosity got the best of him. He crossed the room to inspect what turned out to be a beautiful sculpture. He said, "Will, this is new. Where'd you get it?" It was a clay sculpture of a draped woman holding a baby, sculpted in clean, contemporary lines.

"Oh, that's a Teddy."

"A what?"

"I did that in my workshop."

"I don't believe it. You mean you created this?"

"Yeah, that's what I've been doing to keep myself out of trouble. It's the first work I'm actually proud of, so I decided to display it. If you're interested, I'll show you my workshop. This Cub game is for crap anyway."

The two went outside behind the garage. Will unlocked a door and flipped on the light. "Welcome to my workshop." They entered a barren cubicle, about twelve feet square, with windows on one side. A TV was on a counter on the far wall and to the left was a floor-to-ceiling wall of cupboards. In the center of the room was a large, rugged table and chair. A hunk of what appeared to be mud was in the center of the table. It reminded Zack of a monstrous elephant turd but he decided to keep that thought to himself. Next to the giant glob was a series of fine metal tools that looked like they belonged in a dentist's office. Near them were some other unfamiliar items.

Will explained. "I needed a challenging hobby. So I've been working with an artist in Galena who's teaching me bronze sculpture. I've been doing it for less than a year."

"I don't mean to sound disrespectful but that piece on the mantel isn't bronze."

Will erupted with a guffaw. "Let me explain the process. See that clay on the table? Someday that will, God willing, become a beautiful sculpture. The clay doesn't dry out so I can work on it from time to time. When the sculpting is completed I'll cover it with a rubber substance to form a mold. Then I'll take it to a foundry where they'll use it to cast a bronze sculpture. It's an expensive process but once you have the mold you can produce a number of identical pieces. I'm not very accomplished at this stage. However, I'm encouraged. The Darnell Gallery in Davenport has seen the one on the mantel and would like to market it when the bronzes are cast. I'm calling that piece *Madonna and Child*. It was a struggle coming up with a good design. I can finally say I'm proud of that one."

"This's incredible, Will! I didn't know you were so talented."

"Really, I'm not. It just takes patience and perseverance. If it isn't right, I can keep redoing it."

"You call these 'Teddies.' Why's that?"

"Well, Zack, that's my marketing gimmick. It's my artistic logo. I'll sign each completed piece with a T on the back."

"I'd think you'd want to sign them WM since those are your initials."

"Like I said T is to attract attention."

"How did you ever come up with that?"

"I guess I never told you that story. I thought I had."

"I don't think so."

"Teddy was a name my mother gave me when I was born. My given name was William after her father, but my nickname was Teddy. You see, when I was born I weighed more than ten pounds. Mom thought I resembled a Teddy bear and that's how I got the nickname. She still calls me that.

"Well, that's enough about my secret hobby. Let's go back to the house and have another beer."

Zack left Will's home in a much more relaxed state than when he arrived. It was always enjoyable being with his friend even though he managed to keep so much to himself.

~~~

Now, as he lay in bed in a mellow state near sleep, Zack could not keep his thoughts from Kate. Last night was the first one for some time where he didn't have any nightmares about Joan. This lovely new woman in his life made him feel so comfortable. One of these days he'd have to tell her how much she meant to him.

TWENTY-TWO

The Watters' residence was ideal for surveillance. Their home was situated on gently rolling terrain in a recent development in the northwest part of the city, known as Asbury. The homes in this middle-class neighborhood were not crowded together, the streets were not busy and trees and shrubbery made for effective, stealthy monitoring.

An unmarked van containing two officers was parked in a neighbor's driveway and did not appear out of place. At the approach of the anticipated visitor, Sergeant Skinner would be able to radio her cohorts who had been concealed in the Watters' home for more than twelve hours.

Indeed, the layout of the single-story home itself seemed purpose-built for this operation. The front entryway led directly past the living room to an adjacent bedroom where Bob Watters slept. A half-bath was directly across the hall. Covert video and audio equipment had been set up in the victim's bedroom to capture every moment of the euthanasia attempt. This equipment would be monitored from the van while Detective Davis and Sergeant Murphy were secreted in the next bedroom down the hall where they could have speedy access to the would-be victim's door. Hidden with the cops were two sturdy paramedics.

The Watters' theatrical knowledge was being put to good use. Evelyn had performed miracles on Bob's face giving it the authentic appearance of being pasty and drawn. Bob enhanced the effect himself with a hand-mirror and managed to produce an upset stomach in the process.

~~~

Sister Katherine arrived at the Watters' a few minutes early after conducting her customary routine of driving around the block while scrutinizing the area. There was minimal traffic and she could see only one couple walking in the vicinity. She parked around the corner and casually approached the front door with her briefcase in hand. Katherine was not in her habit so she could have easily passed for a lawyer or insurance agent meeting a client.

"Davis, this is Skinner. Subject approaching the front door." Lou heard the message on his hand-held receiver and motioned the warning to the others in the house.

She rang the bell. It was answered after a short delay.

"Good evening, I'm here to help Mr. Watters," Sister Katherine announced quietly.

"Thank you for coming," responded Evelyn graciously. "We certainly appreciate your quick assistance. Bob has been suffering a good deal."

"This shouldn't take long. Are you both prepared for what's about to happen?"

"Yes, I think so. The two of us prayed together before he went back into a coma. He's been doing that a lot lately."

"I'm sure it's better this way. If you'll just direct me to him I'll take care of things. Before I begin I'll need to see the money."

The gym bag rested on the nearby sofa in the living room. Evelyn handed it to the practitioner. After a brief examination she said, "This looks fine. I'll leave it here by the door."

Evelyn led the solemn caller to the bedroom. The intended victim appeared unconscious as he lay prostrate under the covers, breathing laboriously through an open mouth.

The executioner cautiously positioned herself on the edge of the bed with her briefcase beside her. "He won't realize a thing. His discomfort will only be momentary as he strains to breathe." She took a vial of clear liquid from the briefcase and filled the syringe. "It's not necessary for you to watch if you don't want to."

Evelyn responded, "We've been close for so long. If you don't mind, I'd like to hold his other hand. Is that okay?"

"Sure. I'll just roll up his pajama sleeve."

Suddenly, several things happened simultaneously. Bob, unable to control his reflexes, rolled toward the nun, jerking the targeted arm out of reach from the syringe and abruptly pushing himself up. At the same time, Evelyn grabbed Sister Katherine's shoulder while two officers hurtled through the bedroom doorway. In spite of the confusion the sister reacted swiftly, as though by plan. She plunged the syringe into her own arm and immediately discharged its contents into her system. By the time the four had restrained her she was gasping for air.

The paramedics rushed in to find Sister Katherine on the floor grimacing with obvious distress.

One of them said, "She's asphyxiating."

The other replied, "I don't think we can save her." An instant later the sister lay still.

Zack, Polly and the chief arrived separately at the scene only a few moments apart. Evelyn proceeded to relate a second-by-second account of the intended murder.

The atmosphere was somber. The chief said, "Well, we've got one of 'em. It's a damn shame we couldn't question her."

Lou chimed in, "I know who she is! That's Sister Katherine. I served on the United Way board with her. She worked at the Brackett House and lives…lived at the Fallen Angels convent."

"This confirms our suspicions. At least to some extent the House and convent are tied into *Lacrima*," Zack observed.

"Let's hope you two uncover some leads at those places. My fingers are crossed that this won't drive other *Lacrima* members underground," the chief said.

Polly looked at the Watters, "You two were terrific. How're you feeling, Bob?"

Bob replied, "Relieved that it's over. That's as close as I want to get to a needle for a while!"

~~~

Back at the station, the chief and Zack commiserated over the botched attempt to catch the *Lacrima* murderer in action.

"We've got a combined sixty goddam years of police experience, Zack, and we're *still* not smart enough to know you can't use amateurs in a sting! It's not Bob's fault for panicking—hell, he was ten seconds from getting a lethal dose. But you and I should know better than to put a civilian in that position."

"Well, Chief, I guess we both got caught up in our own drama. I'm not excusing myself either, but I guess sometimes even professionals can get seduced by the prospect of an easy answer to a difficult situation."

TWENTY-THREE

Zack was at the Brackett House first thing in the morning. He didn't come to see Kate. In fact, he had forewarned her to act as though they hardly knew one another. His unannounced call on the chief executive officer, Sister Miriam, took the nun by surprise.

"Sister Miriam, my name is Zachary Gerrard, I'm a detective with the Dubuque police force. I wonder if I could have a few minutes of your time."

"Of course, Detective, what can I do for you?"

"I'm here to talk to you about Sister Katherine Small."

"She's dead, isn't she?" Tears were welling in Sister Miriam's eyes.

"Yes, I'm afraid so. Do you have some place we could discuss this in private?"

"Certainly, Officer. Let's go upstairs." The toll of pain for her best friend was evident on her face.

Zack was led to an disconcertingly luxurious room on the second floor. As he passed her office he could see Kate watching him out the corner of her eye.

"My, this is very impressive," he said. When he had seen this room during Kate's tour of the facility he associated it with a Fortune 500 company rather than a charitable organization. An imposing cherry conference table dominated the room. It was surrounded by eight plush leather chairs of a hue compatible with the table and the cherry paneling. The furniture exuded a mellow glow from indirect lighting. Along the far wall was a massive television screen surrounded by cabinetry that presumably concealed appliances and electronic equipment.

"This is our board room. Would you care for coffee or something else to drink?"

"Coffee would be great. Black's fine."

Zack continued when the coffee arrived. "The circumstances surrounding the sister's death are still confidential. I'm sure her loss means a great deal to you and the others at the Fallen Angels. It may not be the opportune moment for you to talk about her, but more information may help us unravel what took place."

Zack realized he was treading on a delicate matter. The deceased nun was a *Lacrima* member. And there was the distinct possibility that Sister Miriam was a part of that group. "What can you tell me about Sister Katherine?"

The CEO had regained her composure and took a seat across from the detective. After blowing her nose she replied almost reverently, "She was a hard-working friend. For years, before becoming a nun, she was a registered nurse in one of Chicago's largest hospitals. Sister Katherine was head of their Intensive Care Unit until she fell out of grace with the hospital administrator. She's been one of the primary reasons for our success. Her knowledge of pharmaceuticals has been critical for our ministry of serving the elderly.

"We learned of Katherine's death this morning. When she didn't come down for breakfast Sister Renee went to her room and found it empty. I called St. Mary's Hospital, where I learned she hadn't been admitted. Then I called the police. A sergeant at the front desk informed me that

Katherine had died the night before in an accident. He said that was all he could tell me at this time. I hope she didn't suffer. Can't you please tell me what happened?"

"We should be able to make the whole incident public soon. In the meantime, I wonder if you could answer a question on another matter?"

"Certainly, Detective."

"Are you aware of any local organizations that have the word Christi in their name?"

Zack noticed an almost imperceptible stiffening of her body accompanied by a coolness in her tone as she replied, "I...I don't know...Oh, yes, *Casa del Christi*. I was a member of that group along with Dr. Clifford Brown and Arnold Greene. A couple of years ago it raised funds to start the Brackett House, but it's no longer around. You must know Dr. Brown."

"Yes, I do. But I don't know Mr. Greene."

"Arnold Greene was a retired lawyer and philanthropist. He passed away nearly two years ago."

"I see. Can you think of any other groups with Christi in their name?"

Like a shot she responded, "No, I can't."

"Well, thank you for seeing me at such a sorrowful time. I'll personally make sure you're notified about Sister Katherine's death as soon as anything can be released."

With a solemn look and a nod of the head, Sister Miriam rose from her chair. "Thank you, Detective. I'm sure you can find your own way out."

As Zack exited his eyes made contact with Kate's. Neither openly acknowledged the other.

~~~

The previous night Zack had told Kate the details of the sting operation, including the Watters' convincing portrayal of the terminally ill and the bereaved spouse as well as Sister Katherine's involvement and subsequent death.

That evening, after Zack's conversation with her boss, Kate was eager to learn what had transpired.

"How'd it go?" she asked. "I've been on pins and needles all day wondering what happened."

"Your Sister Miriam is a very cool customer. She either knows nothing of *Lacrima Christi* or else she's one hell of an actress," the detective said, after relating their discussion.

"Zack, I can't believe Sister Katherine would do anything like that either. I thought I knew her so well. She seemed so concerned for the elderly. There wasn't a bigger supporter of the House."

"That may have been the problem. Is it possible she was so spellbound by the House's success that she broke the laws of both state *and* church to raise the money to keep it going? That's *my* theory."

"Off hand, that's hard to believe. But we do have a few workers who seem completely dedicated to its success," Kate replied.

"Especially when the pope himself praises their efforts."

"You mean, Sister Miriam?"

"You bet. From what you've told me, she's the House's number one supporter. In my book, that makes her also a number one suspect."

"She's just a hardnosed, dedicated businesswoman who happens to be a nun."

"Well, we're confident both the Fallen Angels and the Brackett House are connected with *Lacrima*. Everyone in those organizations has to be under suspicion," and then after a pause he teased, "except for maybe you." Zack was confident he knew his newfound love well enough to believe she could not be involved.

"Watch it, you'd *better* not include me."

The couple had been seated in Kate's living room when a muffled call came from Nicky in the bathroom. Kate raced to the scene in a flash and more choking sounds came from that direction.

A couple of moments later Kate called, "Zack, Nicky just threw up all over the place. Can you go to the closet by the back door and grab a bucket and mop?"

Zack hurried to where he had been directed, found a pail and was extracting a mop when the tip of its handle knocked a box off of one of the shelves. Zack was in shock. Between his feet he stared at an opened box that housed several syringes.

My, God, he thought, what are these doing here. *Lacrima's* method of murder was too fresh in his mind to think anything but the worst. Hurriedly, he closed the container and placed it on the shelf where he thought it had been positioned.

When he brought the pail and mop to the bathroom he saw Nicky for the first time. He had been stripped of his pajamas and Kate was running the bath.

"Don't come in Zack. It's a mess in here. While I clean up Nicky and the room, why don't you grab a beer from the fridge and relax?"

Once again Zack did as he was told. He spotted a Miller Lite on the lower shelf behind a small carton. As he removed it to seize the beer, he noticed the word "insulin" stamped on the outside of the box. His curiosity got the best of him, so he looked inside. There were five vials, two marked "insulin."

It can't be, the detective deliberated. She can't be part of *Lacrima*. How could he have been so dumb, sharing confidential information with what could well be a suspect! She had even bedded him to gain his confidence. Was this all an act?

Zack walked halfway to the bathroom and overheard Kate consoling her son. He knew he had more time to see what else he could find in the house. He began a systematic search of the cupboards. Nothing unusual showed up. A toolbox in the broom closet revealed nothing unusual, either. Next, he moved to the kitchen counter where he detected a monthly calendar. Nothing of interest was written in June's tiny squares representing the days of the month. He flipped back to May. On three days of that month the same abbreviation appeared, "LC." Next to two of them was written the numeral ten. God, is that *Lacrima Christi*? One of the dates marked "LC 10" could have coincided with Riley secretly overhearing the *Lacrima* meeting at the Omega Building. This was getting scary!

"Having fun?" Kate asked as she touched his shoulder.

The detective almost jumped out of his skin. He moved to avoid her closeness. "God, you scared me....Did you get things cleaned up?" Zack wanted to change the subject and get out of her house as soon as possible.

"Yeah, he's better. I think he's already asleep. Why don't we go back to the davenport and relax?"

"I'd like to Kate, but today has been a tough one. Besides I think your son's vomiting made me sick. Can I have a rain check?"

"Sure, hon."

He gave her a quick peck on the cheek and was out the door. He had a lot of thinking to do.

TWENTY-FOUR

The next day, Zack was enjoying a well-deserved afternoon's diversion of golf with Will. He had to get Kate off his mind. The heat and humidity combined to bake any remaining tiredness out of his system. Zack loved to walk when he played golf even though there were a multitude of hills. Will, however, was wedded to a cart.

"Hey, Will, how's everything in the forest? You've been living on the right side of the fairway all day."

"Fore," Will yelled, as his shot ricocheted out of the trees and nearly hit a golfer playing the adjacent hole.

"If you don't adjust that grip like I showed you, you're bound to stay in the woods."

Will's ball finally made it to the green. "I'm glad this is the last hole. No more playing for me until I eliminate my banana-ball slice. I'm ready for a beer. How about you?" Will appeared weary and dejected.

The two relaxed in the bar, recuperating from the heat.

"The nineteenth seems to be my best hole today," said Will.

"Will, once you fix that slice your game will be darned respectable," Zack opined.

The beer flowed easily and by the second one Will turned the conversation to Zack's work. "I've heard through the grapevine that you guys are picking on little nuns. Any truth to that?"

"That's public knowledge I guess," the detective responded. "We did catch a nun attempting to kill someone. I couldn't believe it. Actually, it was a sting operation that we set up to snare one of the mercy-killers. They're called *Lacrima Christi*. A nun would be the last person you'd expect to be involved in anything like this!

"Even though you're a good friend, I couldn't mention it earlier. Unfortunately, the nun we caught killed herself before we could question her. At least, we're finally on to *Lacrima* and now we've got plenty of suspects.

"I've told you before, Will, but I'll say it again. The hero of this investigation is Riley Whitcomb. We'd never have uncovered *Lacrima* without his assistance."

Will said, "Zack, as fascinating as this is, I've got to go. Thanks for the round of golf. Maybe by next time I'll have that slice straightened out." As he got up to leave, Zack gave Will the traditional thumbs-up and wink and got one in return.

~~~

The relaxed pace of summer in higher education was a benefit, Will thought, as he leisurely headed to campus and Clark Hall to check for any messages. It was also good politics to stay in touch with the monsignor, especially now that he was on a less hectic schedule.

The administration building looked like a tomb. No one was around. Neither Sheila, nor Riley. He did hear a low conversation coming from the monsignor's office. As Will tapped on the door the monsignor was saying good bye and hanging up the phone.

"Hello, Will. Pardon me for saying so, but you look like something the cat dragged in."

"It's pretty sticky outside. I just finished a round at Bunker Hill. Why I don't give that game up is beyond me."

"Come on in and sit down. I'll grab a couple of Cokes."

A few moments later the two were exchanging views on the cardinal's recent visit and the resulting good feedback from the community. The monsignor brought up the most astounding topic reverberating through the city.

"Will, you're always in tune with community rumors. What have you heard about Sister Katherine Small?"

"It seems she's been involved in mercy-killing, part of a secret group known as *Lacrima Christi* that practiced euthanasia-for-hire. They caught her '*in flagrante*' the other day and she...um...euthanized herself."

"That must be the group Riley made contact with."

"I know. He mentioned it to me. And Detective Gerrard continues to sing Riley's praises for uncovering this horrifying operation."

"Well, this incident could reflect poorly on the entire Church. Riley's involvement probably isn't good either."

Will ended his visit saying, "I've got to run, Monsignor. I'll let you know if I hear any more on the subject."

~~~

The monsignor left his office shortly after Will's departure and charged down the hall for Riley's office. Upon seeing the monsignor at his office door the young priest hurriedly finished his telephone conversation. Riley put a smile on his face to counteract the impatience and scowl exuded by his superior.

"Hiya, Monsignor. May I help you?"

The visitor entered the room and closed the door even though no one was within earshot.

"What have you been up to Riley? I keep hearing your name and I'm not sure it's in the best interests of this seminary."

The younger one was taken aback.

"Gee, I don't know what you're referring to. It's been a busy time for me with my father's death and my ordination…"

The seminary president interrupted, "I know you've had a lot on your mind, but I don't like the idea of you being a deputy for the Dubuque police force."

"I was only trying to help."

With a more considerate tone of voice and a conciliatory look, the monsignor said, "I'm sure you were, Riley. But this is a scholarly institution and it doesn't promote a favorable image when the word on the street is that one of our staffers is sneaking around, looking in windows and reporting to authorities."

"Gosh, I'd never want to harm St. Peter's."

"Riley, you need to concentrate on your job. You've been a good recruiter for the school and, now that you're doing it full-time, that's where we want your efforts. Have you got the picture?"

"Yes sir. But since most of the recruiting for the fall semester is done, what else can I be working on?"

"Next semester's bumper crop means we'll need more classrooms. I'd like you to study the floor plan of Parks Hall and then you and Sheila make recommendations on what rooms can be converted to classrooms. You can get the architectural plans from Mack in the maintenance building. And when you're done with that, if you're not recruiting, come see me about other duties."

Without any further word, the monsignor left.

Riley felt guilty. God, he didn't want to screw up. He couldn't think of a better job for a new priest than working for St. Peter's. As much as he understood the traditional duties of the Church's professional staff, Riley couldn't help but want to be at the forefront of the "new Church's" educational mission.

For the past two years, he'd been a part time recruiter and the results spoke for themselves. He'd brought in more new students than his predecessor. Now he could spend full-time doing what he liked best: persuade prospects that this was the premiere place to study religion. Riley knew he shouldn't do anything to make waves even though the money his family gave to the school was reason enough to keep him around. Nevertheless, he enjoyed the challenge of doing a good job.

The new priest immediately made his way to the St. Peter's maintenance building. As he hurried down the knoll and through the trees he noted how incompatible its design was compared to the other campus structures. Of course, hidden from view by the rest of the campus, its cheaper construction made good financial sense.

On his way to his destination, he remembered why he never hit it off with Mack Wright, the maintenance supervisor. The guy was an unfriendly, cold fish. Maybe it was insecurity due to working in an intellectual environment with just a high school education. But he must like what he's doing; Riley recalled that the supervisor had recently received his twenty-year pin from the seminary. Riley entered the building through one of the large garage doors and walked into a vast, well-organized area. Near the entrance were two spotless seminary vehicles, a van and a pickup. The supervisor's office was in the far corner of the building. A partially balding, tall and trim maintenance engineer with smallish wire-rim spectacles sat hunched over at his desk. He was so engrossed in paperwork that he was oblivious to the young priest's entrance.

Mack Wright looked exactly how a maintenance man should look in his blue-gray matching work shirt and cotton twill pants. He was startled by Riley's greeting. "Why hello, er.... Riley. It's Riley, isn't it?"

"Yes, sir, I'm on an errand for the monsignor. He asked me to pick up the architectural plans for Parks Hall."

"They're over there in that file." He pointed to his left and then got up to saunter over to retrieve them, cautioning Riley, "Take good care of them; this is the only set of plans we've got for that building."

"You bet. I'll have them back within a day or two. Thanks for your help."

"See ya' kid," he grunted.

~~~

"Riley...Riley Whitcomb! I'm tired of hearing that son-of-a-bitch's name. Everything was going fine until he came along."

The other member of *Lacrima Christi* responded, "That jerk's going to wish he'd never heard of us. He's going to pay big time."

The ranks of *Lacrima Christi* had been thinned. Three of the original five members were no longer involved. Two had left the group on moral grounds because of the Molly Starr murder. Then their numbers dwindled to two when Sister Katherine was lost during the police sting.

The outrage of these remaining members more than offset their small number. Retribution was the only thing on their minds. "For what happened to Katherine, we want revenge," said the gravelly voice. "Whitcomb is going to get it. We'll also do a little number on that bimbo, Evelyn Watters."

"Don't forget that detective, Gerrard. He deserves something, too," said the other. "They can't bring down *Lacrima*. Our purpose is still noble. Look at all the good we've done. The old people worship us. And, my God, even the pope is on our side!"

The plans for retaliation were completed in less than an hour. They were convinced what they had in mind would be justification for the havoc that had been wreaked upon them.

~~~

Later that night *Lacrima's* leader issued the first stage of reprisal over the phone.

"Hello, who is it?" The telephone had rudely awakened the seminary's maintenance manager from a deep sleep. At first he was in a fog, having difficulty focusing on the subject at hand. The gravelly voice jolted him to reality.

"Mack, we need your help on some sticky situations. When you're finished you'll find twenty grand in an envelope behind the paint supplies in the maintenance building. Here's what we need you to do." She proceeded to tell him.

TWENTY-FIVE

"Zack, this is Sergeant Skinner, I think you should get over here as soon as possible."

"Ugh...uh, oh, hi, Jan. What time is it, anyway?"

"A little after six. I'm at St. Peter's administration building. That's Clark Hall. I think this will be important to you."

"What's the problem?"

"It has to do with our campus sleuth, Father Riley Whitcomb. His office has been broken into and there's something you ought to see."

"Give me twenty minutes."

"Okay, in the meantime I'm going to cordon off the area, if that's all right."

When Zack arrived at the seminary parking lot adjacent to Clark Hall he saw more vehicles than he thought would normally be there at oh-six-thirty. The lead detective took the front steps two at a time. He found Riley, Sheila and the monsignor huddled in the lobby. Not far from them Sergeant Janice Skinner and a campus security guard were shielding the entrance to Riley's office.

Zack acknowledged the trio but headed directly towards Sergeant Skinner. She motioned him away from Riley's office where the two could talk confidentially.

The detective knew his associate was excited. The sergeant's speech was faster than normal. "Zack, someone broke into Father Riley's office during the night. A tornado couldn't have done more damage. The security guard and I haven't let anyone in. Riley and the two others have only seen the mess from the doorway. Let's go in there so I can show you why I called."

On the way into Riley's office Skinner introduced Zack to Norm Collins, the St. Peter's security guard. Zack inquired, "When'd you discover the break-in?"

"It was on my last round of the morning, about ten of five. Father Riley's window is partially hidden from the sidewalk by a tree but the reflection from the sun caught my attention. It was glaring off his office window in an odd sort of way. Then I noticed the reason, a large break in the window. I immediately went into Clark Hall and found this mess in Riley's office. I knew enough not to enter 'cuz I didn't want to disturb any evidence. So right away I called the police. The sergeant here arrived within a few minutes."

"Zack, I was very careful with my entry into the office," Sergeant Jan Skinner said. "I had only walked to the side of Father Riley's desk when I spotted a plastic bag in the back of that opened drawer. I didn't touch it or anything else in the room. Right away I knew you should be here to investigate."

Cabinet filing drawers had been removed and the contents strewn across the floor. The computer had been smashed. Broken CDs were everywhere. Just as disturbing, to Zack's trained eye, was the damage done to Riley's personal effects. One of his most prized possessions was a ten-year old photo of him fishing with his father. The frame and glass were broken and the photo was destroyed. His diplomas and other family pictures were in nearly as bad condition. This appeared to be an act of vandalism rather than robbery, Zack thought. His theory was reinforced when he peered in the open top desk drawer and saw what he thought was a rare gold piece. A robber would not leave such a valuable item behind.

Zack knelt down to inspect the bottom right desk drawer where Jan had mentioned seeing a plastic bag. He donned his latex gloves and with tweezers carefully extracted the bag without touching any part of the desk. It was a baggie containing white powder.

"Why don't you give Lou a call, Jan? Ask if he can come over to dust for prints. In the meantime make sure the office is cordoned off while I talk to Riley."

With that, Zack used his tweezers to place the bag of white powder in a sanitized plastic container and returned to the lobby where he found Riley. The two went to Sheila's office to speak in privacy.

"Riley, I'm sorry about your office. I need to ask you a few questions."

"Sure, Zack, go ahead."

"Have you ever used drugs?" Zack quickly added, "Before you answer that, I want you to know I'm not going to Mirandize you. Anything you say right now is strictly between you and me, off the record."

"I've never taken any drug, Zack. Not even a puff of marijuana or anything else. I was an athlete during my school years and our family would never accept anything of the sort, anyway."

"I suspected as much." Zack showed Riley the transparent plastic bag which contained a baggie of white powder. "Have you ever seen this before?"

"No, what is it?"

"My guess is that it's cocaine. Probably ten or twelve grams of it."

"Don't tell me you found that in my office."

"Yeah. It was in plain sight in your bottom right desk drawer."

Riley responded, "You think the purpose of the break-in was to plant that stuff?"

"That's exactly what I think, Father. To confirm that, I'm going to have the bag dusted for prints. But I'll need you to stop by the police station this morning so you can be fingerprinted. If your prints aren't found on the bag, you'll be off the hook. Who knows we might even pick up prints from whoever *did* plant the substance. I'll tell Skinner this is off the record. After we examine the contents I'll give you a call."

As the detective was about to leave Sheila's office, he had another thought, "Say, Riley, you have any idea who could be out to get you?"

"No. Not anyone who dislikes me that much."

"Okay, Riley. Only Skinner, you and I know about this baggie. We'll keep it that way for the time being. I'll see you at the station a little later."

~~~

By the time Riley returned from the police station, Lou had completed his examination of the office. During the noon hour, Sheila assisted the victim in returning his office to a semblance of order.

"Thanks so much for your help, Sheila."

"I think you can be back in business by tomorrow, Father. We should have a new computer for you then. In the meantime it's going to be a challenge to get your mind on work. Maybe you should ask about taking the afternoon off."

"I believe I will! Now that I have an apartment, I could work on moving my stuff out of the dorm and picking up some odds and ends from Mom."

"Good idea, Father. I'll see you in the morning."

As Riley was about to leave his phone rang.

"Hi, Riley, this is Zack. How're you doing?"

"Okay...I guess."

"Well, this'll make you feel even better: There were none of your prints on the baggie. You're off the hook...but then, I guess you knew that."

"Thank heavens. It's still nice to hear it, officially."

"The baggie was wiped clean except for one corner where we found a partial. It's not enough to do a search on. But we might be able to match it against a complete print if the opportunity presents itself. As to the contents, it was cocaine.

"Riley, I'm going to be out of town for a couple of days. I don't know if anything else'll come up but considering your early role in the *Lacrima* investigation, I want you to be very careful. If you need to contact us please call my partner, Lou Davis. I'll see you when I get back."

~~~

Zack couldn't get his mind off the possibility of Kate's involvement in *Lacrima*. Hidden syringes, insulin, and a calendar marked in several places with "LC" and some even with "LC 10" were certainly suspicious.

He had been invited over for a meal with her and Nicky at six. Fortunately, the old codger who shared a shift with him on Alliance's security duty agreed to cover for him.

Zack's stomach was nervous as he greeted Kate and formally met Nicky. His years of role-playing didn't adequately prepare him to secretly question one that he had suddenly grown to care about. Zack wanted to ease into his questions delicately.

During dinner and a discussion of Nicky's sickness, Zack saw an opportunity. "Maybe his vomiting was related to some other problem. Is he a diabetic?" he queried.

"No."

"How about you, Kate? I noticed the insulin in the refrigerator the other night."

"That. Oh, that's for Mom. She babysits so much we keep a supply for her here. She even keeps extra syringes in the broom closet."

Relief flowed through his body. Two concerns down and one to go, he thought.

"Say, before I forget Kate, do you have anything planned for the seventeenth? The department's having a company picnic."

"I don't think so." She reached behind her, grabbed the daily calendar, and gave it a cursory look. "No," she said as she handed it to him so he could see for himself. He handled the calendar clumsily so that the previous month, May, was exposed.

As he pointed to several days of that month, Zack pled ignorance saying, "Boy, you've got a lot of 'LC's' on here...whatever *that* is."

"Well, quite often it's once a week. That tells me when Lois is doing our house cleaning."

He was so relieved he started feeling guilty for ever doubting Kate. In response, though Kate would never know why, he offered to play with Nick while she cleaned up the kitchen. The boy seemed comfortable in his relation with Mom's new friend. Zack had also warmed to a situation that occasionally reminded him of Kristen at that age.

After dinner, the two talked about the vandalism at Riley's office. Kate said, "From all you tell me, Riley's such a nice guy it's hard to imagine anyone causing problems for him." She stopped for a moment to contemplate the situation and then remarked, "Is it possible his office was ransacked as a warning by *Lacrima Christi*?"

"That's been my thought, Kate. If so, it might only be the *start* of Riley's problems.

"Now though, I'm afraid I have to rush out on you. I've got an early plane to catch in the morning for that forensics conference in Dallas I told you about. I'll be back two nights from now."

They embraced at the door. It was not easy for him to leave. As he headed home he was thankful she was not part of *Lacrima*, at least as far as he could reasonably determine. And he was pleased about growing accustomed to her. He liked the idea of them being together a great deal.

As a bonus, his nightmares fled into the night.

~~~

The Marriott was an ideal place for a business meeting. By noon Zack had deplaned, checked into his room and registered for the seminar. A familiar, but slightly rounder and more tanned face gestured to him as he was about to dine alone at a nearby table in the café. He had planned to review the forensics literature he brought with him.

"Hey, Benny, how are you? Still rooting for the Vikings?"

"Can't say that I am, Zack. I'm a Cardinals' fan now that I live in Phoenix. Why don't you join me so we can talk about old times at the MMPD?"

"I haven't thought about the Minneapolis department for several months. You may not be aware, but I'm now the lead investigator in the big metropolis of Dubuque, Iowa," Zack countered facetiously.

"No kiddin'. I always took you for a big-city man."

"I was, but not anymore. There's more than enough to do and I'm enjoying the challenge."

During the meal, they brought each other up to date on their activities over the past couple of years. At one point Benny became sympathetic. "I was so sorry to learn about Joan."

"Thanks, it's been tough. There'll never be another like her. But I feel as though I can now move on." Zack didn't want to talk about Kate at this point. He especially didn't want to mention spending a night with her when she hardly gave him a chance to sleep.

~~~

The first presentation that afternoon concerned gathering DNA specimens. At the break a woman from the registration desk approached Zack. "Detective Gerrard, this message came in a couple of minutes ago."

"Why, thank you."

"What's up," inquired the always-curious Benny.

"Gotta call the office ASAP." Zack's intuition didn't like the implied urgency.

With a "Please excuse me," he rushed to the pay phone as he fished his calling card from his billfold. He was through to the chief's office in a flash.

"Zack, catch the next plane home. We just got a 'Lulu' less than an hour ago!" In the detective's short experience with Chief Baldwin, "Lulu" had been used only once by him when he described the Volkswagen driver who collided head on with a sixteen wheeler. Whatever came next would not be good. Instant concern for many people rushed through Zack's mind. Kate? Kristen? Will? "What is it, Chief?"

"Evelyn Watters is in serious condition, intensive care at St. Mary's. Zack, she was the victim of a goddamn hit-and-run!"

Zack was stunned. "Chief, you thinking what I'm thinking?"

"Yeah, damn it, *Lacrima*. Come as soon as you can." This was an order not a plea.

~~~

The flight home seemed especially long. On the way, he thought mostly of Riley's commentary on *Lacrima Christi* and the sting operation. Evelyn had been courageous in her role as the bereaved spouse. Polly must have felt guilty as hell for involving her good friend. Zack recommitted himself to doing whatever necessary to catch the rest of *Lacrima*. Until he did, there could be—*probably would be*—further reprisals from this narcissistic ring of bastards. Then his thoughts turned to Kate. She was dangerously close to *Lacrima*. He had to warn her as soon as he could. During his short layover at O'Hare he called Kate. She wasn't home, so he left an urgent message: "I'll be home later tonight. You've probably heard why. Something's happened to Evelyn Watters. Maybe you can get details from Polly. Regardless, stay home and lock the doors. I love you, baby. I'll see you soon."

Without thinking Zack had said "I love you" to someone other than those in the inner circle of his life for the past twenty years. But what was the big deal? It was so natural. Kate had to know how he felt by now. This romance had made her an important part of his life. It had sneaked up on him without much thought and he was surprised to realize he would eventually marry this woman and spend the rest of his life with her. Even with good connections at O'Hare, he didn't get to Dubuque until almost nine o'clock.

TWENTY-SIX

As soon as he deplaned at Dubuque Airport, Zack phoned Kate. She was home. She had heard his message, contacted Polly and had the doors locked. Under the circumstances she seemed calm. Zack promised to visit her as soon as he concluded his meeting with the chief who was waiting at the police station.

The second floor of the police department was like a mausoleum except for light from the chief's office.

"Sorry it took so long to get here, Chief. The sting and its repercussions were all I could think about on the trip home."

"I've been the same way. At least Evelyn's condition has stabilized. We found the vehicle that hit her. The state crime lab forensic team arrived late this afternoon. Car's now at Bob's Auto Repair. Murphy is running a check on it."

This was Zack's first opportunity to hear details of Evelyn's accident. The chief continued. "The hit-and-run happened around eleven a.m. She was returning to her car from shopping at the Target store at Dodge and Wacker. The parking lot was practically vacant when a Buick took dead aim at her. Fortunately, another shopper was on the scene to help Evelyn and ID the vehicle. Evelyn was in the emergency room within a half hour. She suffered a skull fracture and had broken bones in her ribs, pelvis and legs, enough to put her in the ICU. The various surgeries were completed a few hours ago. It's remarkable how resilient she is. Very fortunate for her...I don't think many would survive that kind of collision. The doctor is hopeful she'll eventually recover with physical therapy. Plan is to keep her in intensive care for at least a day or two.

"Zack, we've got to uncover whoever's involved in *Lacrima* as soon as possible! Until we do, more of these things could happen. Riley was lucky he wasn't personally attacked. I'm also concerned about Polly...and your paramour, Kate."

Zack responded, "This thing has to be centered on either the Fallen Angels or the Brackett House or both. In the morning we'll look into the backgrounds of everyone in those organizations. We'll especially check out Sister Renee who Sergeant Skinner identified as doing the collection at the UPS store. We'll pick her up and question her again. Is that all for this evening, Chief?"

"Yes, I think so. I'll see you in the morning. Early."

On the drive to Kate's home Zack had to smile. He recalled a proverb, "with every problem there's an opportunity." The problem brought him home early. Now he had the opportunity to snuggle up with Kate for a few hours.

~~~

His team was already in place when he arrived at his office shortly after seven. Lou and Polly agreed to investigate the backgrounds of all Fallen Angels and Brackett House personnel. Zack decided to follow up on the vehicle with the forensics team from Des Moines. Before he could leave, he received news from Sergeant Murphy. The sergeant had been successful in tracking down the ownership of the car used in the hit-and-run. The '02 Buick Limited was owned by Katz Rent-a-car in Cedar Rapids. A Mr. Wayne Oliver had rented the car two days ago for the seventy-mile trip to Dubuque. A call to his residence allowed his wife to confirm that Wayne was still in the city, at the Dubuque Inn, where he was attending a seminar.

Zack found that Oliver was still registered at the Inn and promptly called him, learning that Oliver had informed the police last evening about his rental car being stolen. They agreed to meet in the motel's coffee shop.

Zack grabbed Lou and the two headed west on Dodge Street for the appointment. As the detectives entered the café, a gentleman near the back waved to acknowledge he was their intended interviewee.

Zack got to the point immediately. "Mr. Oliver, we need a little more information regarding your stolen vehicle."

"I'm pleased to help if I can. But I don't know what I can add. I checked into the motel two days ago and didn't have an occasion to use the car until last night."

"Mr. Oliver, the front desk tells us you registered as a party of two. Is that correct?"

"Uh…yes, that's right."

Zack continued. "We were just curious. You see, we tracked you down through the rental agency. A short time ago we called your wife, who confirmed your location."

"Oh, my God." Mr. Oliver looked like he had just seen the ghost of his mother-in-law.

"Mr. Oliver, are you in town for business?"

"Well, that's what I told my wife…My secretary and I are supposed to be attending a two-day school on data processing."

Lou asked, "'Supposed' is the operative word there, right?"

"Right. Man-oh-man, I think my worst problem right now is back in Cedar Rapids."

"I hope you're right," Zack added. "That Buick you rented was involved yesterday morning in a hit-and-run."

"Oh, my God!"

"Mr. Oliver, evidently you've been busy in your room. The list of food and drink deliveries to your room suggests you and somebody must have been burning up a lot of calories. The only way you can clear yourself is to voluntarily take us to your room and hope your secretary is there. What do you say?"

"I don't think I've got much of a choice."

"You're a smart man, Mr. Oliver, at least at some things."

As they entered room 122 a mass under the covers pulled the sheets over its head.

Looking embarrassed Oliver remarked, "Betty, these are the police. They only want you to identify yourself."

She cautiously withdrew the covers enough to reveal a cute face enshrouded by rumpled brown hair. "Please excuse me for not getting up."

The two officers could not vacate room 122 fast enough. With incredible difficulty, they restrained themselves until they were enclosed in the squad car. Neither one had roared with so much laughter in a long time.

Two blocks later, Lou had settled himself down enough to comment, "Wait 'til the boys downtown hear about this!"

Zack appreciated the temporary relief from stress and worry.

~~~

The state crime lab's forensic team had thoroughly examined the hit-and-run vehicle by the time they arrived. Even though the car had been wiped clean, two partial fingerprints had been found along with one dark brown hair. A fragment of Evelyn's clothing had been embedded in the car's grill.

Zack left for the hospital to pay his respects to Evelyn. Since she was still in intensive care, where visitors other than family were not permitted, Zack asked one of the nurses if he could see Evelyn's husband, Bob, in the waiting room.

Bob's upbeat mood was transparent, but Zack thought he looked as though he needed to sleep for twenty-four hours.

"Thanks for coming, Zack. Evelyn is doing remarkably well. Right now she's pretty doped up due to the medication. She should be moved out of the ICU by tomorrow and the doctors hope she'll recover within four to six months after some extensive physical therapy."

"I'm so sorry about what happened. I can assure you we'll be working around the clock to bring in the bastard that hit her. I just came from a meeting with forensics. We've got some good leads which I'm hopeful will result in an arrest." Zack couldn't help using half-truths to paint a picture brighter than the reality he knew. He figured Bob was smart enough to realize that.

Bob said, "Polly's been so supportive. She was here all last night consoling me. I never thought we were volunteering for such perilous duty."

"Well," responded Zack, "I think it shows how desperate this group is. We're hoping our continued pressure will force them into the open real soon.

"Bob, I'm thankful Evelyn is doing so well. If we can do anything for the two of you, please let me know. I'll keep you informed of our progress as much as I'm allowed."

As he left the hospital, Zack thanked the Lord for seeing Evelyn through this horrible event. He could hardly wait to nail the scum who was responsible.

~~~

St. Mary's Hospital was not far from St. Peter's campus. Zack decided to pay a call on the monsignor. Was this seminary president somehow involved with *Lacrima Christi*? He had ties with the Brackett House. He was on its board of directors and helped with the funding to get it started. How could he afford all those expensive rare books in his office? That had to cost a fortune. Could they be funded by mercy killings? As long as he was close by, it wouldn't hurt to see what crumbs might fall off the Monsignor Timothy Mulcahey's plate.

He was in luck. The monsignor was in. When he peered in the office, the seminary president was on the phone but waved Zack into a chair by the desk.

The detective let his eyes wonder around the spectacular setting. It wouldn't matter how frequently he came here, he would continue to be impressed with the décor. He wasn't totally surprised to see a new collectable book residing on the desk. The monsignor's hand movement invited Zack to pick up the book and examine it. A quick glance confirmed this was a first edition of Dickens' *The Tale of Two Cities*. It was in immaculate condition.

The monsignor completed his call.

"Good afternoon, Detective. That's the copy I've wanted for years. It's in such pristine condition it could have just come off the press."

"Hello, sir. Even a gumshoe like me knows you must have incredible connections to find such a prize."

"I can thank the book dealers, Quarles & Brady. They're a New York concern with worldwide contacts. They have access to virtually anything…for a price."

Zack believed, but didn't say, that price had to be fairly exorbitant for such a prize. The Quarles & Brady firm was most likely overjoyed to have a client like the seminary president.

"I was sorry to hear about Ms. Watters' accident."

"Thanks for your concern, sir. But it wasn't an accident. She was the target of a hit-and-run. Our guess is that Evelyn Watters' mishap is somehow related to the death of Sister Katherine Small. We're certain the sister was a member of the *Lacrima Christi* group that's been conducting mercy killings. I thought I'd see if you knew anything about her or her affiliations that could help us in this investigation."

"I only knew her as an employee of the Brackett House. I would venture she was a private person who didn't associate with many others. The person you *should* talk to would be Sister Miriam. I know they had a close working relationship."

"I've already spoken to her, Monsignor. If you happen to think of anything that could be helpful, I'd appreciate a call."

"You can count on that, Mr. Gerrard."

On his way out the door, Zack said, "Give my regards to Father Riley. You know how much we hold him in high regard."

"I certainly do. We feel the same way."

TWENTY-SEVEN

Late afternoon showers had replaced the blazing heat and humidity with refreshingly clean air. Now, a pleasant breeze was whisking away the last remnants of the stormy clouds. The fragrance of flowering plants and the coolness found in early evening shadows combined in a soothing sensuality. It was the epitome of a summer day in Iowa as Riley leisurely returned home from work.

He was glad he had walked to work this morning so that he could luxuriate in these surroundings during his fifteen-minute stroll. It gave him an opportunity to unwind from the stress of the past few days. His office had been restored to a presentable condition with the exception of family photos and diplomas. Fortunately, his mom had kept the negative of her husband and son fishing that had been one of Riley's most prized possessions.

Upon reflection, he realized that his initial discovery of *Lacrima Christi* was when the stress began. Prior to that, his life had been predictable and rewarding and he hoped those days would return as soon as the *Lacrima* group was caught. Zack had promised to keep him apprised of progress in the investigation.

As he rounded a bend on Alpine Street, Riley could see the peaceful two-story home that housed his new apartment.

The brightly painted yellow building contained four rental units with his on the first floor just inside the front door. Retirees rented two of the neighboring units and the other was occupied by a traveling salesman who was seldom home. The extent of activity around the place was normally limited to someone retrieving their morning paper.

He noticed a young woman about fifty yards away heading toward him and it was a surprise to see her turn into the walkway of his complex. *The salesman must have a new girlfriend. Good taste*!

The woman had a great figure and, in her tight tennis top and shorts, not much was left to the imagination. Eight years ago, Riley might have been aroused. These days, considering his past indiscretion, a life of celibacy didn't seem to present a problem.

As the striking woman approached the entrance to the yellow house, Riley was close enough to read the "Gap" label on her rear pocket. Aware of him now, she turned and flashed a disarmingly friendly smile. However, with that gesture, she now appeared to have lost sight of the stairs, tripped and fell, her head colliding with the porch railing. Riley rushed towards her to slow her stumble. She was groggy and disoriented and grabbed her left leg in pain.

The young cleric stooped to help, but was afraid to touch her until she motioned for assistance. It was obvious that she was confused and had difficulty speaking. Her next gesture indicated she wanted assistance getting up. Riley could see swelling on her forehead but at least it wasn't bleeding.

With an arm around her slender body, Riley effortlessly raised her to a standing position. For a moment she seemed to be able to stand unassisted. Then a partial collapse caused her to lean against him. She brought her hand to her throat as if pleading for water.

Since Riley's apartment was only a few feet inside the entrance he supported her as she hobbled forward. Her petite figure required little effort on his part to guide her to the couch in his living room where he helped her to lie down.

"I'll be back in a minute with some water and a cold compress for your head," the concerned priest said, as he hustled to the kitchen.

As he was about to return to the injured woman, an outburst shook the walls.

"What the hell is going on in here? Jesus Christ look at her!" some man shouted. By that time Riley had reentered the room. He was aghast as he viewed his bruised guest. She was prone on the couch with all of her clothes removed except for skimpy bikini underwear. It took him more than a moment to survey the situation—and then, nearly dumbfounded, the light began to dawn.

A strange man leaning over the supposedly abused woman spoke: "What have you done to her? Tina, baby, what's happened?"

Tina, crying uncontrollably, couldn't respond.

A second stranger immediately returned with Riley's retired neighbor, Fred. The eighty-year old had difficulty speaking, as he was busy viewing sights he hadn't observed for more than half a century.

Riley was stunned as he comprehended what was happening. He was being set up.

Within twenty minutes the police were on the scene. Tina was clothed and being comforted by her bulky boy friend. Riley sat in the kitchen with Sergeant Murphy while Sergeant Skinner interviewed the woman and the two men. Neighbor Fred had returned to his apartment, thanking God that his eyesight was still good.

Sergeant Murphy couldn't help but believe Riley's account. He knew the Whitcombs well and Riley's reputation, impeccable before, had the added weight of newly ordained priesthood behind it.

The girl and her two friends gave Sergeant Skinner information to confirm their identities. All three had Illinois driver's licenses showing their residences as being in various Chicago suburbs. Tina explained that she was in town enrolling for the fall session at Clark College. She explained her reason for visiting Riley's apartment complex by saying, "I was just knocking on apartment doors to get a suggestion on available housing." The sergeant recorded all of the information including where they were staying and advised them, "A court hearing will probably take place in less than a week and in the interim I need to be informed of any changes in your addresses. It's mandatory that all three of you show up for the hearing, especially since it's your word versus Father Whitcomb."

After the police finished taking everyone's statements, Murphy and Skinner excused themselves from the others to compare notes. About twenty minutes later, the two police and the four involved parties met as a group.

"There are two very different versions to this story," Skinner said as she pointed to Tina and Riley.

Murphy added, "Due to the seriousness of the situation we just talked to the county attorney. Being that the three of you are from out of town, I think we can wrap up this whole matter fairly fast." He didn't want to convey his actual reasoning that Father Riley had lived an exemplary life and the judge would move on this as fast as possible due to the Whitcomb name. "The county attorney is confident a preliminary hearing can be held the first thing in the morning, the day after tomorrow. All the four of you have to do is be at the court house promptly at eight a.m." Murphy looked at the three accusers as he continued, "At that time the three of you can make your charges against Father Whitcomb and he can give his response. Should there be a change of time with the court Sergeant Skinner will personally notify you at your motel. You've got where they're staying, don't you, Sergeant?"

"I sure do."

~~~

As soon as everyone left, Riley phoned the Whitcomb family attorney who promised to be over within the hour. In the meantime the young priest pondered in disbelief. This was his second horrifying episode within a few days. *Lacrima Christi* had to be behind these attacks. Something had to be done about them. And soon.

Attorney Howard Allen had represented Riley's family for more than thirty years. He was well acquainted with all of the family members and he had no doubt of Riley's innocence. The priest recounted his experiences with *Lacrima* from day one and continued through this shakedown escapade. Howard was amazed.

After more than an hour, the discussion returned to the most immediate predicament. The police department said that sexual assault charges were being filed against Riley and he would be notified of a preliminary hearing. Howard believed the judge would move fast on this case as a courtesy to the Whitcomb name. Realizing there wasn't much that could be accomplished until after the hearing, Howard gave Riley as much encouragement as he could under the circumstances and said good night.

It was still early in the evening and Riley couldn't stand to be alone. He needed emotional support. The past few days had been severely upsetting and this was especially true of the past few hours. *My God, how can things like this happen to a man of the cloth?*

He was concerned that word could leak into the community about both the drugs and sexual abuse situations. If so, he wanted his mother to be aware of them before she heard the news from another source. Riley used the pretense of picking up more furniture for his apartment when he phoned his mom to see if he could drop by. When he hung up, he didn't know if he was up to telling her about the recent incidents by himself. As a result he called Will to see if he would accompany him.

Both his mother and Will were appalled to learn of the latest misfortunes. But there was no question of his innocence. They were supportive and consoled him.

"Mom, I know who's behind this. I know it sounds incredible: It's a secret group that's practicing euthanasia."

Riley related his encounters with *Lacrima Christi* from the start. His mom stared in disbelief. Will already knew most of it from Riley's plea to be there when he told his mom.

"Riley, honey, I'm so relieved you went to the police. Will, what else could we be doing?"

"I know the head of the investigation, Nell. I'm certain Detective Gerrard will be working 'round-the-clock on this since it directly involves his big case. They'll also probably be keeping an eye on Riley. Let's just hope they get to the bottom of this soon!"

Riley felt much better when he left his mom. He was glad Will had been there for support, too.

~~~

The next morning, the three investigators had been discussing the status of the *Lacrima* investigation with the chief in his office.

"Zack, what's the latest on the hit-and-run?"

"Forensics has been working on the partial fingerprints found on the vehicle. Now get this...in attempting to reconstruct a complete print, they discovered something quite remarkable: they believe the hit-and-run prints are identical to those partials found on the drug bag planted in Riley's office! Dr. Douglas, the forensic scientist, is willing to go on record to say the same person committed both crimes. We're hoping we can find a match for them through the national print files."

Lou said, "I think I have a handle on who the hit-and-run perp is. It could be Mack Wright, the head of maintenance at St. Peter's. I interviewed the woman who witnessed Evelyn being hit. Turns out our perp looked right at the witness as he drove away. She said the driver resembled a neighbor who lives a few houses down from her. Occasionally sees him at the grocery store. When I showed her Wright's photo from the St. Peter's directory, she said he could have been the driver."

"Could have been? Damn it, Lou, why can't she be certain!" The chief was tense.

"Here's the problem, chief. Her eyesight isn't that great. Plus, we had a little experience with her a year ago when she called in to report someone breaking into her neighbor's house. Come to find out the neighbor had broken his *own* window because he had locked himself out."

"God damn it!" the chief exploded. "The defense will murder her on the stand."

Zack chimed in to calm the chief down, "Lou is going to check into Mack Wright's background. I'm continuing to follow up with the founding members of *Casa del Christi*. With Sister Miriam's connections, she could well be part of the mercy-killing operation. We'll keep her under surveillance with the hope she may lead us to others. Also, I have an appointment with Dr. Brown at his home later this morning. Since he's the other founder of *Casa del Christi* and is on the House board, maybe he can shed some light on things."

~~~

Mrs. Brown welcomed Zack and suggested he wait in the study for the doctor, then excused herself to prepare coffee for them.

As the detective sat in the study he marveled at the sophisticated elegance. Rich walnut paneling surrounded a floor-to-ceiling bookcase, brimming with leather-bound books, reminding him of the monsignor's office. Zack took the liberty of thumbing through several volumes on the shelves. While the Browns' taste in literature was sophisticated, they didn't appear to have the monsignor's addiction for collectors' first editions.

By the time the coffee arrived, so had Dr. Brown.

Zack had one of the books in his hand. "I'd love to spend a cold winter's day with this on that snug leather couch by the fireplace."

"One of my favorite winter pastimes, Detective. Please have a seat." The doctor angled the two guest chairs in front of his desk so they could face one another. "Thanks for accommodating me by meeting here."

"I've heard so much about you; I'm glad to finally make your acquaintance. Dr. Brown, let me get down to business. I need to ask you a few questions about an organization known as *Lacrima Christi*."

As he mentioned that name, Zack noticed increased rigidity in the doctor's posture.

"Yes, go on, Detective."

"*Lacrima Christi* has been positively linked to several mercy killings in Dubuque over the past two years." Zack saw no advantage in also mentioning outright murder. "Sister Katherine of the House was a part of this group. That's confirmed. Since her death, our focus has been on two organizations in which she was involved, the Fallen Angels and the Brackett House. I'm here today because of your connection to the House and I'd like to understand more about their operation. Weren't you involved with an organization with a similar name?"

"To *Lacrima Christi*?"

"Yes."

"I was a founder of *Casa del Christi*. However, there's no connection to your *Lacrima Christi*. Our group was in existence solely to raise the initial funding for the Brackett House. When that was accomplished we dissolved. If you check the records you'll find this to be the case."

"Yes, we've discovered that, Doctor. So you know nothing of *Lacrima Christi*?"

"That's correct."

"The records indicate that Sister Miriam Barton and Arnold Greene were also founders. What ever happened to Mr. Greene?"

"Unfortunately, he passed away about the time we dissolved."

Zack asked, "Was that from a terminal illness?"

"Yes, it was, Detective." The doctor slowly rose from his chair, indicating he wanted to conclude the questioning. Zack remained seated for a few moments, mostly just to show the doctor that this was not a social call, partly to impress the fact that a policeman on a criminal investigation decides when the interview is over. Still, he could see that no other questioning would bring further details, so he allowed himself a graceful, if deliberate, amount of time to rise from his own chair.

"Well, thanks for your time, Dr. Brown. We'll just keep searching for this *Lacrima* group and we'd appreciate it if you remember hearing anything about it."

As Zack was shown to the front door he inquired, "Oh, by the way, one more question?"

"Certainly."

"Do you believe in euthanasia?"

"Yes, as a matter of fact I do. I believe it should be legalized...under strict controls, of course. Eventually, it will happen, but until then, we must make patients as comfortable as possible during their last days. Good morning, Detective." The doctor was officiously polite as he impatiently escorted Zack through the doorway and on to the street.

~~~

"Dan, I'm hoping you can help me out tomorrow," pleaded Riley. He had always been able to count on his dormitory friend, Dan Perkins. Over the past few years they had covered for each other when the need arose.

"What's up, Riles?"

"I have to go to court for a hearing on some trumped up sexual abuse scam that I fell into yesterday." Riley explained what had happened.

"Ain't that the shits? I hope they get those low-lifes with slander, perjury, or whatever. No matter what, Riley, I'm at your disposal."

"Thanks, friend. A couple of prospective students will be at Clark Hall around nine a.m. for a campus tour. I'm sure I could relieve you by eleven. I'll bet Sheila could get you off the paint detail for the morning."

Dan had a summer job with the seminary painting dormitory rooms. Sheila was in charge of all summer help.

~~~

It was a little before eight the next morning when Riley joined Howard Allen, his attorney, in the conference room adjacent to the courtroom. They were reviewing the procedure for the hearing that would take place shortly. When Sergeant Murphy did not come to get them, as he had promised, Mr. Allen decided to track him down. As he opened the conference room door Murphy made his entrance. He was excited. "Father Riley, you're off the hook. There'll be no hearing…at least at this time."

Bewildered, Riley said, "What're you talking about?"

"Tina and her goofy partners skipped town. Sgt. Skinner is in pursuit. When they didn't show up for the hearing she discovered they had all vanished. As soon as we nab them they'll be hauled in to answer for giving false statements in a police report. We'll need your assistance then. We knew they didn't have a case anyway. Whattya think of that?"

Riley was ecstatic. "Justice does prevail!"

All Howard could do was shake his head and smile.

~~~

It was ten o'clock at night and another *Lacrima* meeting was underway. Sister Miriam let her gravelly voice show her fury to the only other member.

"Damn it. You can't trust anyone. Tina and her idiot brothers couldn't scam an egg out of a chicken! Riley still has his due coming," the other said. "I can't understand why the police never charged him with drug possession."

"Well, I'm going to get back to Mack Wright for an encore. It may be time to cause a problem for one of his relatives."

The listener had nothing further to add. Her shrinking posture showed she didn't want to get in the way of Miriam's wrath.

TWENTY-EIGHT

Nell Whitcomb, Riley's mother, was a boon to the city of Dubuque. Financially, she was in a position to make large charitable donations with regularity. Her love was to help others.

This morning she wore her United Way hat. Since the depressed economy had cut deeply into their normal funding, Nell had fearlessly accepted the task of chairing the annual fundraising campaign hoping to finally put the campaign over its goal.

Nell was picking up the breakfast tab for a fundraiser for the area's business leaders at the Stonegate Country Club—one of the few places in town sufficiently impressive to induce attendees to ante up with sizeable donations.

Nothing seemed to be beneath her dignity for this kind of work, even the menial chores related to setting up the breakfast. Now she was scurrying about on one final task, bringing water from the club's kitchen for the flowers at the head table. Bustling from the kitchen, water pitcher in hand, she collided with an unsuspected, abrupt swing of the door...and the consequence could not have been more damaging as she was propelled head-over-heels down a flight of stairs.

The paramedics had arrived promptly. Fortunately, the extent of her injuries were limited to contusions and a compound fracture of her right femur. The shock to her system masked most of the pain.

At the hospital her doctor had her heavily medicated and scheduled surgery for the following morning. A pin would be inserted in her femur, strictly as a precautionary measure due to the angle of bone damage.

Riley was there to console her. "Mom, I feel so sorry for you. Dr. Crane told me you're lucky to escape with only a fractured leg. You've always been a tough cookie…must be the Keller genes."

Nell smiled weakly since the combination of the trauma and medication had taken their toll. "Thanks for coming, honey. I'm going to be all right. Shouldn't you be at St. Peter's though?"

"I've got things covered, Mom. As soon as I heard about your accident I called Dan Perkins. He agreed to sub for me this morning. All he has to do is pick up three prospects at the airport and give them a campus tour."

The mother and son were interrupted by a familiar voice. "Hello, Nell, Riley. I was sorry to learn of your accident, Nell. How're you feeling?" Dr. Brown was on his morning rounds when he heard about Nell's accident.

Nell replied, "Considering the circumstances, pretty good."

"Dr. Crane said the surgery should go well. Says you'll be hobbling around in no time," the doctor responded. "By the way Nell, I never did thank you for including Agnes and me at Riley's ordination and reception. It was a wonderful day for both of you and the community. Agnes said we should go out for dinner sometime soon. I don't know where the time has gone, but we haven't been together since Ted passed away.

"And Riley...I hear great things about you at the seminary. Keep up the good work. Well, I have to finish my rounds. It was nice seeing you both."

After he had left, Nell said, "Clifford is such a nice, considerate man, Riley. Ted thought a great deal of him."

"Mom, if you don't mind I'll stay with you for a while. My work is in good hands."

~~~

Those good hands were about to put themselves on the steering wheel of St. Peter's van. Dan saw the vehicle all shined and polished sitting next to the seminary maintenance building. Sheila had provided him with the names of the three seminary prospects and had assured him the van would be full of gas with the keys in the ignition.

Dan was in a hurry to get going because he was running behind schedule and he didn't think it would make a good impression to let the prospects feel they were stranded at the airport without the transportation that had been promised. As he hopped in the front seat, he saw Mack Wright wave and holler "Hi, Riley." There was no use correcting him, people got Riley and him confused especially from a distance.

The engine purred when Dan switched on the ignition. He fearlessly screeched out of the area leaving some of the tire rubber on the maintenance drive.

He had always enjoyed the winding and steep streets in this part of town, which he knew like the back of his hand. Driving the curves seemed like a roller coaster in slow motion. Being late for the pick-up only added to the challenge he relished. The young seminary student headed east on Loras Boulevard, zipping through intersections along a steep decline through light traffic. At the intersection of Dell the van began to shake and drifted into the oncoming lane of traffic. Dan's correction caused the front left wheel to separate, rolling downhill and causing the van to tip over onto the driver's side. The van slid uncontrollably into the intersection at Bluff Street where it smashed into a city Streets Dept. four-ton truck. Dan's panic was short-lived; death was instantaneous.

As it happened, Sergeants Skinner and Murphy had been patrolling not far away, heard the crash and were on the scene at once.

"Holy shit!" Skinner exclaimed. "That blue van's been totaled."

"Good thing nobody was in the city truck. Say, isn't that a St. Pete's van?"

"Yeah, I can tell by the license plate holder."

"Whoever was driving that didn't have a chance. Better give Gerrard a call. He'll for sure want to know about this."

~~~

"That can't be," exclaimed Mack into the phone. "I saw Riley get into the van!"

"God bless it all, Mack. You screwed up. I just got the story from one of our workers who was nearby when the van collided with a truck." Sister Miriam realized she had better calm down. Mack would be hanging out alone if the cause were discovered. Since she might need him for another job, she changed the subject. "I've got to give you credit though, you did good work with Riley's mom. Are you still available if we need you again?"

"Is the pay the same?" he asked.

"No, Mack. It's gonna be more. How's that?"

"Sounds good to me."

As she hung up Sister Miriam thought once again about the general incompetence of her hirelings to satisfactorily conduct crimes. She had to figure her next step carefully.

~~~

"We're getting our money's worth out of the state's forensics team. Didn't take them long to reconstruct the cause of the van's accident," said the chief. "Dale Douglas is already on his way with their report."

Almost before Zack and Lou could be seated, the forensic scientist arrived and started giving his report.

"This was no accident; the van was definitely tampered with. The driver died instantaneously. So what you've got is premeditated homicide. Here's what happened: The front wheel lug nuts on the driver's side had been loosened. In fact, we're amazed the vehicle got as far as it did! It was probably the stress of that final swerve that caused the wheel to come off. We discovered some fingerprints on the wheel well that could have been left when the lug nuts were loosened. However, those prints may only be considered circumstantial evidence. You'll have to run that by the DA. We'll document our findings before we head back to Des Moines."

Lou said, "Guess who has the responsibility for maintaining vehicles at St. Peter's? It's Mack Wright. Since he's also a suspect for the hit-and-run, I suggest we bring him in to be printed and questioned."

The chief responded, "You're probably right, Lou. I'd just hate to spook the guy if he has others involved in the mercy killings. Tell you what—let's keep a tail on him and bring him in tomorrow morning."

~~~

That evening Kristen drove to Galena to spend time with one of her college friends, sharing a pizza at Antonio's. Feeling a cold coming on, she called it an early night and was on her way home before nine. Even though she thought of herself as a good driver, as every college girl does, she wasn't fond of narrow, unfamiliar roads with turns and hills on a pitch-black night. Tonight, a sliver of moonlight was smothered by clouds giving her the illusion of a lighted candle that had just been snuffed out. Fortunately there was hardly any traffic. Suddenly two glaring lights raced up dangerously close behind her. *I'd pull off and let him go by if it wasn't for that embankment. I'll just slow down and he can pass when he has a chance.*

A bang into her rear bumper by the trailing car caused her head to lash backwards, the momentum pushing the car onto the shoulder. Gripping the steering wheel tightly, she steered the Volkswagen back to the highway. A second, much stronger blow to the car sent it careening across the road and down the steep embankment. As the car rolled, Kristen lost consciousness.

When she regained her senses and looked out of her side window in the inverted vehicle, she wondered how she had avoided a steep ravine and massive tree only a car length away.

Kristen managed to release her seat belt and extricate herself through the side window. She figured a hundred blows with a sledgehammer would have done less damage to the VW. But the Bug had served its purpose. And now, as though a sign from above, the moon broke through the clouds and she was able to see her reflection in the cracked backside window, looking a lot more like a Picasso painting than it ought to. She could see a mass of darkness on the side of her face. Touching the greasy area, she put a finger to the mouth, confirming the metallic taste of blood from a gash above her temple. Outside of incredible head and neck aches, her other injuries seemed minor. She could move her left arm even though hideous bruises were beginning to appear. Slowly, with pain, she made her way up the steep hill to the road. Cold and shivering on the hot and humid night, Kristen realized she was in shock. She had lost track of time. Twenty minutes later, the headlights of a pickup found her slumped form on the shoulder and slowed to rescue her.

~~~

"Dad, really I'm fine."

"I'll punch out and be over in thirty minutes," he replied anxiously. "Where did you say you were?" Zack couldn't remain at his night security job when he was worried about his daughter.

"I'm at the fire station on the south end of Main Street."

"Okay, babe. I'll be there right away."

Zack had no use for the speed limit tonight and he knew the Illinois Highway Patrol cops in the area would be sympathetic if they caught him speeding. In the race to Galena, he reviewed Kristen's description of the incident. No question this was another strike by his enemy, *Lacrima Christi*. They were upping the ante. Means we're getting awfully goddam close, he thought. *Now it's personal.*

TWENTY-NINE

Riley was devastated when he heard about Dan's death and Mack Wright's apparent involvement. At first, he was too crushed over the loss of his best friend to think of anything but Dan's family. He immediately went to the Perkins' home. Even though they were with their parish priest, Dan's parents took a moment to talk with Riley. He promised to return at a more convenient time.

It was only when he dragged himself to bed and was too wired up to sleep that he connected all the tragic events to his own involvement in the *Lacrima* investigation. He now realized *he* was the real target of the van crash.

He wasn't able to sleep continuously for more than a couple of hours and by the time he was fully awake he had formulated a plan to see whether Mack Wright was involved.

First he needed a set of legible fingerprints for a police comparison. Arriving at work, he got a key from the seminary's key rack in the Clark Hall kitchen. After wiping clean the tag on the key ring, he carefully placed it in his pocket and headed to the maintenance building to confront Mack Wright. On the way, he spotted Mack leaving Parks Hall and hailed him down.

"Mack! Got a minute?"

"Yeah, what do you want?" He did not hide his displeasure in seeing Father Riley.

"A while ago I tried this key to the marketing supply room." Riley carefully withdrew the key from his pocket, making sure he handled only the key itself. "I couldn't get it to work. Sometimes that lock seems a little tricky."

"Lemme see it," the maintenance chief barked. "Follow me." With the key in hand, he briskly led the way to the marketing supply room. Inserting the key, he opened the door with ease and pushed it wide. He shook his head with a demeaning look to confirm Riley's mechanical ineptitude.

"Boy, you sure know what you're doing," Riley exclaimed. While Mack stomped out of Parks Hall, Riley carefully disengaged the key and secured it in the handkerchief he had brought.

~~~

He awoke, startled. Zack couldn't believe it was after nine o'clock. He rushed in to check his daughter's status. She seemed to be resting peacefully.

Last night seemed long ago. The pickup driver had phoned 911 from his cell phone and within a few minutes, paramedics from the fire department arrived on the scene. Zack saw that Kristen had been well cared for. Her neck was placed in a cervical collar and her head lacerations were sutured and bandaged. Her father had been told by the fire marshal she was fortunate to have escaped with minimal injury. However, he suggested that she be taken to Dubuque's emergency ward at Finley Hospital for a more thorough exam.

By three in the morning, Kristen was released from the emergency ward to go home. Fortunately, the X-rays revealed no cervical fracture. The only apparent long-term injury was the neck strain, which would require therapy.

Now the detective was eager to be back on the trail of *Lacrima*. When he phoned the chief to say he'd be arriving late, he found the local police had already been apprised of Kristen's accident and her condition. After gently arousing Kristen to give her medication, he suggested she go back to sleep and call him later.

~~~

The young priest had been with Lou at the police station for about half an hour when Zack arrived. The lead detective asked the chief and Polly to join them to hear the results of Riley's detective work. "Damnation, Zack, this kid's collected some pristine prints!" Lou reported enthusiastically. He described how Riley obtained them and said, "They're a perfect match with several other items, namely, the hit-and-run Buick, the wheel well of the van, and the partial on the drug bag in Riley's office. This is one very busy perp."

"I'm definitely taking him off my Christmas card list." Riley said, drawing smiles all around.

The chief remarked, "The 'uniforms' are on their way to pick up Mack right now." He added, in a jovial tone, "If you guys aren't careful you could lose your jobs to this priest!"

Riley inquired, "Could I ask a favor?"

"Sure you can," the chief said.

"Is there any way I can listen in when you question Mack? I want to see his face when he hears how you caught him."

"That's the least we can do, Father Columbo," Zack interjected as he thought of the kid's resourcefulness.

~~~

By the time they brought Riley a sandwich Mack was being dragged into the interrogation room. Riley had a splendid view through the one-way mirror.

The detectives let Mack fidget alone for several minutes in the cubicle. When they did enter and gave him his Miranda, he responded, "I'm not talking to anyone until I see my attorney."

"That's certainly your prerogative, Mr. Wright. At this point we're not asking you to admit to anything. This is simply to inform you of the charges against you...and, not incidentally, how you were caught," Zack said.

"Well, I've got a right to know that. So go ahead tell me what you think I did."

"Mr. Wright, we have you for attempted murder in the Evelyn Watters hit-and-run, breaking and entering at Riley Whitcomb's office and with the planting of drugs, and, last but not least, tampering with the St. Peter's van, which resulted in the death of Dan Perkins. Seems you've been a busy fellow."

"How're you going to pin all those things on me?"

"With your fingerprints, Mack. There are partial prints on the Buick interior and the drug baggie, but forensics says there are enough common points of reference to assure certainty, which in my book spells 'conviction.' Your big problem is you weren't as careful with the van. The prints on the front driver's side wheel well are A-number-one.

"Perhaps you'd be interested in knowing how we obtained your prints so fast. The answer is sitting behind that mirror. Smile and say "hi" to Father Whitcomb. We'd all like to thank you for unlocking that door at Parks Hall this morning."

THIRTY

Hidden behind a growing stack of unopened mail and requests, Riley attempted to organize his busy schedule. Ever since his first experience with *Lacrima Christi,* it had been difficult to concentrate full-time on recruiting.

Sheila was out of the office, running errands for the monsignor. Janice, a part-time clerk, substituted for her. She meant well, but Riley offered a short prayer for Sheila's quick return.

Even as he was thinking that, Janice brought in a prospective student who recently graduated from Loyola. Riley was enjoying hearing how things were going at his undergraduate school when he heard voices in the lobby. Normally, he tuned this out; however, one of the voices sounded eerily familiar. At the first chance for a break, Riley politely excused himself. At that moment he recalled where he had heard that distinctive gravelly sound: above the main floor at the Omega Building where he had overheard the conversations during the *Lacrima Christi* meeting! By the time he reached the lobby, though, the people were gone. He asked Janice if she had noticed who was there a few minutes ago.

"I'm sorry, Father. I didn't recognize any of them. You know, I'm not really here enough to know who comes around," she said apologetically.

Riley felt irritated, not so much at her as at the situation "Can you even just *describe* who was here?"

"Well, there were two men, probably in their fifties, and a nun. She was about the same age."

"Thanks, Janice." Riley took a moment to calm himself. "I didn't mean to be so curt."

Riley returned to his prospect from Loyola. He knew his heart wasn't in the presentation and concluded the session as soon as decently possible. Doggone it, he thought, he had come so close to discovering the possible leader of *Lacrima*! When he had listened to the voice at the Omega Building meeting he couldn't tell if it was male or female. But at least it belonged to one of three people who came to the campus. This meant their paths might cross again.

~~~

Riley couldn't concentrate on work for the rest of the afternoon so he appreciated it when five o'clock finally came. Janice and the monsignor had just departed. As he hurried to lock the front door, he turned in haste and nearly bowled over a nun. She had been rushing from the other direction and also was not paying attention.

"Excuse me, Sister. I wasn't looking where I was going," he apologized as he picked up her briefcase and returned it to her.

"It's my fault, Father. I wasn't looking where I was going, either," the nun responded in a gravelly voice that came like a blow from a sledgehammer. Fortunately, her back was to him as his face registered shock and she quickly continued on her mission. Riley was stunned and took a moment to regroup. *Direct contact with the enemy! Why didn't I get her name?*

He decided to follow her. As he tracked her he realized her face was familiar, although they had never met. CEO of the Brackett House! He had recently seen her picture and

Cardinal Clancy's in the *Herald Tribune's* coverage of the Brackett House's dedication. *Strange they had never met.* Obviously, he couldn't nab her and take her to the police so he settled on seeing where she was going and planned to phone Zack with his discovery. Riley's familiarity with the seminary allowed him to pursue at a discreet distance.

His pursuit was aided by the presence of other pedestrians and within five minutes they were off campus grounds. She continued walking at a consistent, moderately fast pace and did not look over her shoulder. A block later Riley felt certain of her destination: Fallen Angels convent.

~~~

Riley found Zack had left for the day but Sergeant Murphy overheard Riley's urgent request and cut in on the call.

"Hey, Father, you just missed him but I'm sure he'll be home soon. Let me give you that number." Murphy couldn't resist adding, "By the way, you haven't been abusing any women lately, have you?"

Riley knew the sergeant's jibe was just a friendly tease and sat down to dial the detective.

"Hey, Riley. What's up?"

"I've got something big on the *Lacrima* case and I need to talk to you about it right away."

"What is it?"

"I think I've *made* the leader"

Gerrard rolled his eyes at the use of TV-cop jargon but figured that the priest-sleuth had probably earned the right.

"Fantastic! Who is it?"

"You'll hardly believe this…Sister Miriam!"

"Jesus! How'd you get that? Never mind, tell me when you get here…can you come over right now?"

"Absolutely!"

"Had dinner yet?"

"Nope."

"Good. I'm fixing spaghetti. I've got enough to feed an army. We'll plot the downfall of their ringleader over my famous pasta."

"That'd be great, Zack. Be right there." Address in hand, he hustled to his car and in less than ten minutes was knocking on Zack's door.

"Boy, you got here in a hurry."

"I couldn't wait to give you the news."

"Let's talk over dinner. How about a beer?"

As they ate Riley reported on his encounter. "I'm certain Sister Miriam is the leader of *Lacrima Christi*."

"Wow, that's heavy. The head of Brackett House! I hope you can back it up."

"Here's what happened. In my rush to leave work I bumped into this nun in the hallway. When I heard her voice there was no question she was the one in the Omega Building that night."

"Riley, her involvement explains a lot of things. She's the connection between the Fallen Angels and the Brackett House. She must've been using Mack Wright to do the latest dirty work."

"We don't know who else is involved, but I'm betting it's not too many," Riley replied.

Zack's eyebrows furled. "I'm especially concerned about Kate. Who knows what Sister Death is going to do next? Other *Lacrima* members could be around Kate's office," Zack noted. "In the meantime, there's a couple things we can do...but it'll mean getting cooperation from Brockton Starr and Mack Wright.

"We've just obtained a directory of the Fallen Angels with their photos. I'm going to see if Brockton can identify the person who injected his aunt.

"We might be able to break down Mack Wright...we've really got the goods on his ass. But I'm not so sure I'm ready to lighten his sentence if he cooperates. That guy has done too many awful things for us to show much compassion.

"I'll call the chief now and arrange a session first thing tomorrow to figure our next step with Sister Mary Tarantula. In the meantime, be extra careful, Father. These folks are deadly serious. And I do mean deadly."

~~~

Zack was more concerned than ever about Kate's safety. He'd wanted to be with her tonight but she was out of town for the evening, having taken Nicky and her mother with her father to the university hospital in Iowa City. With the possibility of a recurrence of cancer, his local physician thought it best if he returned to where he had treatments three years ago.

Finally, at ten p.m., he drove to her home and slipped a message under her front door asking her to call him immediately, regardless of the time. He also reminded her about not calling him from her office. She'd recognize this was a warning of danger from *Lacrima Christi* in the Brackett House.

~~~

Sister Miriam knew she had the flu bug that was making its rounds. She must have contracted the full-blown variety. God, her body ached and her forehead felt hot. Periods of sweat and chills alternated and the last thing she wanted to do was work, especially so late at night. Her concentration was terrible but she hoped her thinking was clear enough to do what was needed. Everything relating to *Lacrima Christi* had to be destroyed.

The head of Brackett House could almost feel the noose tightening around her and *Lacrima Christi*. The two members who had been squeamish about murder were long gone. Sister Katherine was dead. Now only she and Sister Renee were left to carry on the dream. And Mack was no longer…available.

Sister Miriam was in the large office located next to hers, a combination of Kate's office, library, and file storage. The *Lacrima* leader rummaged savagely for items relating to their secret actions. She had hidden many of the group's records in the cramped upstairs quarters of the Brackett House. Mostly the documents did not bear *Lacrima*'s name, at least in so many words, but the few that did were in two file drawers or on the wall-to-wall bookshelves marked "private M. Barton."

It felt spooky searching for documents with only the low light from Kate's desk lamp. But it was sufficient for her purposes and the lowered light would be less noticeable to any passerby. The single source of illumination created lengthy shadows that jerkily spackled the walls as she feverishly ransacked the place.

The sister was drawn to the back of the office where transparent sheeting temporarily formed the back wall during construction. Little headway had been made on enclosing the framing and exposed pipes directly below. With the aid of the meager light, she could barely see through the torn up flooring to the level below. But the image was engraved in her mind since she monitored construction progress several times each day.

She was eager for the project to be completed. This was the testament to her contribution to Catholicism. Granted, there was the unavoidable bending of the civil law regarding euthanasia. She was even oblivious to the murder of Molly Starr, because the money raised by *Lacrima* funded shining examples of charity for the elderly. To her, the end justified the means. It was what the money was *used for* that counted.

Her program would be copied near and far. What better praise? This was her tie to immortality.

Now her thoughts returned to reality and the project at hand. While she may be a suspect, no charges had been made. Any evidence was purely circumstantial. They only had the word of that aggravating new priest.

THIRTY-ONE

The phone rang and Zack picked it up, confused. Through bleary eyes he could see it was after midnight.

"I'm sorry to wake you, honey. We're back and the folks are home." Kate sounded relieved.

"It's so good to hear your voice, babe." Zack was still groggy. "How's your dad?"

"As good as can be expected. There weren't any signs of the cancer so they're just going to continue monitoring him. I read your note. What's happened?"

"Here's the deal: we're pretty sure your boss is part of *Lacrima Christi*, maybe the ringleader. Father Riley identified her as the voice he heard at their meetings."

"Oh my God! I guess I shouldn't be surprised, based on what you've been telling me though. I'm sort of scared, but I promise to be real careful. If anything happens I'll call you from another phone. Sorry I woke you. I'll see you soon. I love you."

Still in half-sleep mode, Zack was awake enough to realize something was different. Once again he was relieved to find that for the past several nights he had not been troubled by the nightmares of Joan's illness. If he had been more awake, he might have rushed to Kate's house and embraced her. Not for ending his bad dreams, but for making him realize he dearly cared for her. Instead he smiled contentedly, rolled over and returned to sleep.

~~~

There was little activity at the Brackett House the next morning. Sister Miriam had called in sick. She hoped to be well enough to come in later in the day.

The news put Kate more at ease as she headed to her office. She was frightened knowing her boss was a criminal…worse, a murderer!

Immediately, she could see that her office looked different. She never left things in such disarray. Piles of papers were stacked near the filing cabinets. A collection of folders leaned against one of the cabinets and some had slipped to the floor. Only a few people had access to this area. *Could this have been the work of Sister Miriam?* Kate could see the cleanup would take most of the morning. Fortunately, Miriam wasn't around. She noticed items on the top of her desk had also been moved around. Kate sat in her desk chair and examined the rearrangement. Everything was there, just in a different order. Evidently, someone had been using her desk as well.

Swinging her view to the left, she saw that her bookcase had some new gaps in it. Some reshuffling had taken place there, too. There was a large open space that had been occupied by orange-backed letter files. Since her first day on the job she had been warned they belonged to Sister Miriam and remembered they were marked "private M. Barton." The office manager was intrigued to see what else might be missing from the bookcase. As she approached she saw a narrow black book peeking over the top of books on the uppermost shelf. She hadn't seen that before. If her view hadn't been from that specific angle she wouldn't have noticed it.

Using the chair next to her desk, Kate thought she might be able to reach the thin black volume. She did so cautiously because the book was at the extreme left end of the shelves, precariously close to the plastic sheeting that temporarily replaced the office's back wall. Kate resisted looking directly down to the left where the construction in the kitchen was revealed a floor below. Kate didn't particularly like heights and so completed the task as fast as possible.

With the prize in hand, she sat at her desk to examine it. There was no identification on the black leather cover. The inside reminded her of a ledger. The first page contained hand lettering that jumped out at her: *Lacrima Christi*.

Astounded, she closed her eyes for moment thinking when she reopened them the delusion would be gone. No such luck; the menacing words were still there. Thank heavens Sister Miriam was gone for the day,...or the morning at least. Kate hurried to her door, closed it, and called the front desk to inform them not to disturb her under any circumstances.

In short order, her review of the contents suggested this book was *Lacrima*'s log of activities. Knowing this could be critical to the investigation, her mind was spinning with what to do. Zack had warned her not to phone him from her office. In spite of that, the police *had* to know about this as soon as possible. Never mind Zack's caution, it was time for an executive decision. Kate dialed the direct line number of the police detective division.

Millie answered.

"This is Kate. Is Zack there? I need to speak to him right away."

"I'm sorry, Kate. He's out for a while."

"How about Lou or Polly, is one of them there?"

"Polly's standing right here."

The investigators' newest member took over the phone.

"Hello, Kate. What can I do for you?"

The combination of anxiety and excitement caused Kate to rapidly spew forth her words. "Right now I'm in a terrific hurry. I need you to pick something up, immediately! It has to do with your investigation."

"Kate, please calm down. Can you take one minute to explain what's going on?"

"All right, I know I'm panicked. I'm holding a book that's entitled *Lacrima Christi*. Inside are about a dozen pages of initials, dates, and so forth. I'm sure it's very important to your investigation."

"That's incredible! That'll be key evidence when we question Sister Miriam. We're planning to arrest her today. Lou is actually waiting for Zack right now so they can pick her up together."

"She's not here, Polly. She called in sick, but could be here later."

"Well, until we get her, we don't want to do anything that might tip her off. How big is the book, anyway?"

"I'd say it's about nine by twelve inches, maybe twenty pages filled"

"Kate, since there aren't that many pages, why don't you run a copy of each page and return the book to where you found it. That way, if Sister Miriam is looking for it she won't know you're on to something."

"That's a good idea. I've got a copier right here in my office. I'll do it."

"Good, as soon as I hang up I'll track down Zack and tell him about what you found. Good luck. We'll be in touch."

Kate rushed to the copier on the other side of the room. Although the book was slightly larger than the eight-and-a half by eleven copy paper, she could reproduce each page in its entirety with careful positioning. She counted the pages. There were only fourteen. But after eight pages the copier froze up. *What the hell!* She remembered that the man from the office supply store was supposed to have come in yesterday to service the machine. *Where were those people when you needed them?*

Her only choice was to use the copier on the main floor. She gathered the eight completed copies and locked them in her desk drawer. With the *Lacrima* ledger concealed in a legal file, she raced down the stairs. At this hour, there was little activity in the House. Sister Renee was seated at the reception desk, talking on the phone while an elderly couple waited to talk to her. Kate waved as she flew by and headed for the copier that was within view and not far from the reception area. Kate was in a hurry, but wanted to be certain to get the entire page copied. Her first two attempts were inadequate. On the third try she had the system down pat. A short time later the remaining six copies had been made and were in satisfactory condition.

As she was about to return to her office, Sister Renee stopped her. "Kate, can I ask you a question?" Kate thought it was a hell of a time to be delayed.

"Please excuse me for one minute, folks." The sister grabbed a stack of papers from her desk and approached the nervous office manager. "Kate, this report is for the board meeting tomorrow. My numbers don't add up. Can I show you where I think the problem is?"

Kate's blood pressure was rising. "Sister, we have the rest of the day to resolve that. Why don't you give me a buzz when you're finished with this couple and we can sit down and figure it out?"

"Sure, Kate, but just look at this one page; you can probably spot any discrepancy in a minute."

A cursory glance at the numbers didn't reveal any problem. Kate responded, "I'll take this upstairs and give it a thorough going over. I'll talk to you later."

Kate was not used to this kind of stress. Upon her return to her desk she combined both sets of copies and confirmed every page had been reproduced. She placed all fourteen sheets in her desk and locked it once again. The chair that normally was by her desk was still positioned next to the bookshelf by the transparent temporary wall and so she climbed up to reposition her find. As she stretched to return the ledger to its original resting place, Sister Miriam burst in.

At first the CEO was not paying attention to the treasure in Kate's hands.

"I was feeling better and decided to come in to work. I didn't…" Then she recognized the black leather book Kate was holding. "Where did you find that? That's private property," shouted the sister as she hurtled forward to reclaim the secret volume.

Kate, in her state of shock, had remained standing on the chair. Both women were grasping the book as if it were the Holy Grail. A tug-of-war ensued. Then with a final jerk, Sister Miriam had the ledger. But she couldn't maintain her balance. She teetered on the edge of the flooring where the plastic sheeting formed the temporary back wall. Her hysterical grimace foretold what lay ahead. As her momentum thrust her through the sheeting, she grabbed Kate's arm in a desperate effort to keep from falling through. Somehow, Kate was able to cling precariously to the bookcase for an instant until the sister lost her grip.

The fall from sixteen feet would not necessarily have been life threatening. However, Sister Miriam hurtled towards the unfinished plumbing. The thud of her body impacting the floor caused Sister Renee, below, to bolt upright in her chair. This was accompanied by vibrations that rattled the cup and saucer on her desk less than thirty feet away.

In an instant, Renee dashed to the aid of Miriam, but it was soon obvious from her battered body that the CEO would not last long.

Incredibly, Miriam, impaled through her mid-section by an exposed kitchen pipe, was somehow able to turn her head in Renee's direction and seemingly focus on her friend. The leader's speech was distorted by the gurgling of blood-filled lungs. She gasped, "Our noble deeds…were…with…divine guidance." A Giaconda smile gradually formed as her eyes closed.

~~~

The ambulance, Zack and Polly arrived at virtually the same time. Kate was in shock and continued to shake as Zack held her firmly.

The paramedics discovered Sister Miriam had no vital signs and were certain she was dead. By that time, the police had cordoned off the area and strung blankets to hide the view of her body. Zack was the only one, other than the paramedics, to examine the deceased CEO. Sister Miriam's death scene had not been an easy one to witness. She was face down with part of a pipe exposed through her back. In her hand she continued to hold the *Lacrima Christi* ledger.

In spite of her condition, Kate related in detail the incident to Polly as Zack retrieved the ledger from the Sister's grasp. He hurriedly reviewed the contents apart from the group.

When he returned to the two women he said, "Kate, you need to go home and rest. This has been extremely traumatic. I'll have Polly drive you home and then Millie will come out to be with you. I'll call your folks and have them keep Nicky until tomorrow. Polly, as soon as you get her settled, come to the department conference room." He held up the ledger. "We may have all we need right here to make any other arrests."

~~~

Lou was at the county jail visiting Molly Starr's nephew.

"Brockton, We're going to take you up on the offer you made the other day. I've brought a directory of pictures of Fallen Angels convent members. See if you can find a picture of the woman who gave the injection to your aunt."

It only took a moment for Brockton to point to one of the photos. "She's the one...Sister Renee Norton."

"You sure about that?" Lou inquired.

"There's no doubt. I couldn't forget that face."

~~~

The detectives and Polly were in the conference room reviewing data from the *Lacrima* ledger. Each had a complete copy of the entries. About a week before, Polly had compiled a list of twenty-six deaths that in all likelihood could be attributed to *Lacrima Christi*. This was based on her analysis of the *Chris Crim* ads and the *Lacrima* website data that had been correlated with obituaries over the past twenty months. She compared this information with the entries in the *Lacrima* ledger.

"Gentlemen, I've gone through all of this information carefully," she said holding up her copy of the ledger. "This is a log of the murders in which *Lacrima* was involved. It shows every contact with their clients and the targeted victims in chronological order. It also reveals who was assigned to carry out each killing. Five people were active in committing the deaths based on the five different sets of initials."

Zack said, "Lou, why don't you write those initials on our blackboard and see how many we can identify? Go ahead and read those off, Polly."

"Okay, we've got: MB, KS, RN, CB, and TM." Lou wrote them on the board as he said, "MB was Miriam Barton, KS was Katherine Small. Those two are dead." Zack interrupted, "Brockton identified RN as Renee Norton. I think we can arrest her."

Lou responded, "That only leaves CB and TM. Zack, take a look at your Fallen Angels directory—are there any members with those initials?" After taking a couple of minutes to review the names in the directory, Lou said, "There's no CB but I did find a TM. That's probably Teresa McDonald."

"Boy, were we lucky to find this log," claimed Polly. "Zack, you're going to have to give Kate a medal."

Zack was quick to reply. "Don't worry, I'll give her more than that. Now let's go ahead and bring in the other deadly sisters."

THIRTY-TWO

Lou accompanied Sergeant Skinner to the Fallen Angels convent where they found one of the suspects, Sister Teresa McDonald. She did not resist arrest but was stunned and speechless, enough that she required assistance to get to the squad car.

The arrest of Sister Renee Norton occurred simultaneously at the Brackett House. She was picked up by Zack and Sergeant Murphy. Zack thought she looked as if she expected to be apprehended.

The two were taken to the police station where they were booked, processed and transferred to the women's section of the county jail. They were quartered at opposite ends of the cellblock to avoid any communication.

Their interrogations were being delayed until the conclusion of a meeting between investigators and forensic people of the state crime lab, which, it was hoped, could strengthen the cases against the two nuns.

For the previous eight hours the forensic scientist, Dr. Dale Douglas, and his associate, Matt Rodgers analyzed the *Lacrima* ledger and Polly's compilation of *Chris Crim* and *Lacrima* website activities. So much had rapidly taken place on the *Lacrima* investigation over the past few days that the chief had persuaded the two forensic specialists to stay over in Dubuque. At 8 p.m., Douglas and Rodgers met with the chief, the detectives and Polly to report on their findings.

"Some of what we've discovered regarding the *Lacrima* ledger only confirms what you've expected. However, if you'll bear with me, I'll start at the top." Douglas picked up his legal pad scribbled with notes. "Feel free to interrupt me at any time you have a comment or question.

"There are three sets of legible fingerprints on the journal. Sister Miriam Barton's and Kate O'Brien's are all over the book's cover. Theirs are also on the corners of pages along with those of the late Sister Katherine Small.

"As you pointed out, the journal amounts to a log of activities relating to each of the murders committed by this organization. Entries are grouped into twenty-seven sections, one for each of their victims. Actually only twenty-six deaths occurred. The twenty-seventh referred to your sting operation with Bob Watters.

"Each victim and the contact person who requested the killing are listed, along with addresses and phone numbers. There's detailed information concerning each case. It lists the date of the initial request for help and the associated medical problems, the preferred time and date for the euthanasia to occur, and the date and amount of cash payment as well as the date of the killing. It confirms your theory that fifty thousand dollars was charged for twenty-four of the murders, one for one hundred thousand and one for twenty-five thousand.

"A column adjacent to each case has initials which we believe are specific members of *Lacrima*. These appear to be the parties responsible for each killing. As a personal aside, I'd say you have to give *Lacrima*'s scribe an 'A' for good record keeping. The thoroughness should enable you to identify each of the killers."

Zack remarked, "I think we've identified almost all of them. All except one are either dead or in our custody. We're still missing the one designated 'CB.'"

The chief was pleased with the forensic work. "Dale, thanks for the speedy and thorough analysis of all aspects of this case. Your work on the van and the hit-and-run car should remove any uncertainty about those crimes when we go to court."

"Oh, Chief, that reminds me—by next week we should complete the DNA comparison between the hair found in the hit-and-run car and Mack Wright's"

"Great. Well, thank you, gentlemen. It's not that we don't like you, but I hope we won't have a reason to invite you back to Dubuque for a long time."

~~~

Even though it was nearly nine p.m., the detectives were anxious to question Sister Renee. They had plenty of ammunition to convict her and the icing on the cake would be Brockton's identification of her as the one who injected his aunt.

She was brought to the interrogation room. Prior to her arrival Zack and Lou reviewed the background information gathered by Sergeant Skinner through interviews with her fellow nuns.

Sister Renee had found life tough as a teenager. She was an orphan who was used to fending for herself. Numerous petty thefts led to serving two years in juvenile detention. She found God, thanks to the perseverance of a nun dedicated to saving souls of young women. After that, it was an easy transition to the Fallen Angels.

The Sister did not talk. Her early years had steeled her against threats of punishment making her as tight-lipped as she was unyielding. Her only comment was a request for an attorney.

The detectives decided to let her sleep on the charges against her. They planned to wait until the next day to spring Brockton Starr on her for a surprise reunion.

Lou suggested they talk to Teresa McDonald—TM—in the morning. It had been a long day and Zack was agreeable. Plus, he was eager to be with Kate; however, first he wanted to phone Riley.

Riley reacted to Zack's highlights of the day's incidents by saying, "Word travels fast. Sheila told me about Sister Miriam's death. What a terrible way to go."

"You were right, Riley. In addition to being the leader, she was plenty nasty. You may not be aware that Kate found a journal detailing all of the murders they committed. There were twenty-six victims, not counting the botched attempt on Bob Watters. Molly Starr appears to be the only murder which was not for the purpose of euthanasia.

"The other good news is, we have a handle on nearly all the other members of *Lacrima*. Two are dead, two have been arrested, and only one is still at large."

"What you're saying, Zack, sounds like they were compassionate killings, except for Molly Starr."

"Yeah, I think they just got carried away raising money for the Brackett House. I'm sure Sister Miriam's praise from the pope and cardinal didn't help the situation.

"We still have one loose end to tie up. We're missing a *Lacrima* member with the initials CB. Maybe you'll have an idea who that might be. Do you think you could stop by around eleven in the morning and we'll discuss that? It shouldn't take very long."

"Sure, Zack."

"We'll see you, then, in the detective conference room."

~~~

"Hi, Millie, how's the patient doing?"

"Hello, Zack. Kate seems fine. The sedatives knocked her out for a couple of hours. Since then she's been lying around for the most part."

"I'm sorry it took so long to relieve you. This has been one heck of a day."

"You *should* feel good. I'd think we're nearing the end of the *Lacrima* problem."

"I hope you're right, Millie. Why don't you go home and get some rest. I'm sure the chief won't mind if you don't come in until noon tomorrow. You deserve some time off."

As she was about to leave she turned and said as she pointed to Kate's bedroom, "Zack, she's a keeper. How she puts up with you is beyond me."

As soon as Millie left, the detective hurried into the bedroom and found Kate asleep. He stripped to his underwear, carefully got in bed, kissed Kate on the arm and cuddled with her. He was soon asleep himself.

~~~

Despite bags under her eyes, Sister Renee appeared to have rejuvenated energy. She had met with her attorney and the two of them were in the interrogation room when Zack and Lou arrived after ten that morning. Her confident scowl made it immediately apparent the police could expect no cooperation from this tough nun.

Anticipating this, Zack decided the timing was right to unveil their surprise witness after she had been read her rights. He said, "Sister, I'd like to bring in someone who can shed some light on your situation." He gestured with a welcoming motion to the two-way mirror. Within a moment the door opened and the nephew of Molly Starr made his entrance. Brockton said, "Well, hello, again. I didn't realize you were a nun when you visited my aunt. Have you given many injections lately?"

Sister Renee Norton visibly wilted. Sergeant Skinner assisted her back to her temporary domicile.

The two detectives remained in the interrogation room. Within moments, Sister Teresa McDonald took her place at the table.

It was only a short time into the interview when Zack realized this woman was what he would have called a dingbat if she weren't a nun—and a surprisingly pretty one at that. He could practically visualize a sensuous figure through the prison garb. He reckoned it wouldn't be long before she would be a much sought after commodity at the State Prison for Women in Mitchellville.

After a few minutes of conversation, he figured Sister Teresa's IQ somewhere below his daughter's 79 bowling average. She pled ignorance to all of the charges, which was no surprise because she definitely was ignorant. When asked about *Lacrima*, she thought they were talking about the white liquid you put in coffee. "Lou, let's get back to this woman later. We're not making any headway. I imagine Sister Renee's attorney will be representing her. In the meantime, we need to get to our eleven o'clock."

Zack and Lou headed for the detective conference room where Polly, the chief and Riley were already present. Millie, who had come in earlier than expected, had everyone equipped with coffee.

Prior to the arrival of the two detectives, the other three had been reviewing the notes on the blackboard and brainstorming about the identity of the last remaining *Lacrima* member.

As Zack and Lou entered the conference room, Riley piped up, "Zack, I think I know who CB is. I thought about this when I went to bed last night. It was nagging at my subconscious. You know how it is when the answer is there, buried in you innermost mind and…"

"Father Riley, can you get to the point?" Lou sounded exasperated.

"CB could be Dr. Clifford Brown. Both Brown and Sister Miriam were members of the original *Lacrima*. They're both members of the Brackett House Board of Directors. In addition, he's admitted to being a supporter of euthanasia."

"I'll bet you're right," the lead detective said. "He's tied to that group in several ways and his medical expertise would be a natural contribution to them."

Riley's concentration suggested he was working out a way to confirm Dr. Brown's involvement. A moment later he recommended, "I think I know how we can confront him…Let me talk to him about this. I have a perfect entrée. He and my father were best friends. He knows I've been involved in this investigation. I could play up the angle of continuing to assist the police. After I mention who's been arrested, I could report overhearing that he is considered a possible member and might be brought in for questioning."

Zack thought Riley had a creative approach to law enforcement. If he was half as good at the priesthood as he was as an investigator, he might be a bishop by the age of thirty.

Riley continued to promote his approach. "What have we got to lose? It's unofficial and I'm just trying to help him out."

The chief spoke. "Father Riley, you have good instincts but there's really nothing to be gained from the department's point of view in 'confronting' a suspect off the record. That's strictly for Tom Cruise movies. And by the way…" the chief pursed his lips as though to bite off an ill-considered remark, "the last I checked you're still a priest, not a cop. Despite what you see on TV, we don't like to send civilians in to do our dirty work."

THIRTY-THREE

Zack had used his lunch hour to visit Kate at her home. Her recovery from yesterday's life-and-death struggle with Sister Miriam was going as well as could be expected.

As he returned to his office, the phone rang.

"Zack, Lou. I've been called to the residence of Dr. Brown. When I arrived an ambulance was there. One of the medics reported the doc's body was sprawled on the study floor. Our conclusion is he died from a self-inflicted gunshot wound. No need for you to come over, just wanted you to know what's up. I'll keep you posted on whatever happens."

Zack dialed the young priest.

"Oh, my God, Zack," Riley replied upon hearing the news. "I can't believe he could've been a party to any murder. When you look at assignments listed in the *Lacrima* ledger he hadn't taken an active role for at least a month. That means he was only involved in euthanasia activities!"

"I understand where you're coming from Riley, if you justify euthanasia as not murder. Just remember, the law recognizes those as criminal activities and he didn't bother to come forward to expose *Lacrima* during their last few weeks of brutality."

Sister Renee wanted to talk. She and her attorney were waiting when the detectives arrived at the interrogation room that afternoon. Once she began, she had to tell the whole story. "Dr. Brown was a good man. He had great courage in helping those that suffered. I want to absolve him of any wrongdoing. I know from personal experience there was no one with more compassion than Dr. Brown. He was there for me when I needed him. I had a drug problem as a teen. During my darkest days he helped me overcome my addiction. Without him, I would have died. I'd do anything for him. That's why I want to clear his name." She wiped away a tear before continuing.

"Dr. Brown's caring for others did him in. Our first mercy killing was Arnold Greene. He pleaded with the doctor to end his suffering. He even offered to make a large gift to the Brackett House if we would do so. That's how our business started. We only wanted to stop people's suffering and then we realized we could use the money for the House.

"For the first year or so, we had the best of both worlds. Then, Sister Miriam was told by Archbishop O'Donnell that the country's Catholic leaders were impressed with what we did for the older people. At that point Sister Miriam became obsessed with getting national attention. She said we could get it by doing more for the elderly. That meant raising more money. So we more than doubled the number of mercy killings. Then, through carelessness, Brockton Starr sucked us into murdering his aunt. We…"

Zack interrupted, "He what? What do you mean 'you were sucked in'?"

"Detective, we did have a moral code. It's just that not everyone accepts it…and granted it's considered illegal. Our sole intent was to ease the suffering of the terminally ill. We did it through euthanasia only when requested. But we blew it with Brockton. He falsified Ms. Starr's medical records. We thought she was terminally ill like the others."

Good God, Zack thought, Brockton was sucking us in, too. He made it look like Lacrima had no problem committing murder. We know the difference between euthanasia and killing is splitting hairs according to the law. But, at least, Lacrima was taking a higher road of only performing it for those who suffered when no hope was left. Zack said, "I can see Mr. Brockton Starr has more explaining to do."

"We're all guilty for being part of this. But not Dr. Brown. When he found we had been tricked, he left our group. He cut off all communication with us from then on. There's no way he would do anything but euthanasia and then, only if the terminally ill patient was suffering in his last stages. I've prayed for forgiveness. Now I pray for Dr. Brown. He only did what he thought was right. "

Both Zack and Lou were silent. They'd had interrogated Sister Renee enough for the day. She was returned to her cell.

"Lou, I don't know about you, but personally I'm beginning to feel *Lacrima* was a mixed bag. If a person believed in euthanasia and it was near the end of a life of suffering, one could possibly make a case for many of *Lacrima*'s activities."

"I know what you're saying, Zack. But where do you draw the line?"

~~~

"Lou, let's get Brockton in here right now. That son-of-a-bitch is going to get what he deserves."

A couple of minutes later Brockton arrived at the interrogation room sporting a smug smile. "Well, you got that Sister Renee good, huh?"

"Sit down, Mr. Starr," the lead detective said in a somber tone. Lou and Zack pulled their chairs as close to Brockton as they could considering the table between them. "Sister Renee did confess all right…and when she did, she shed a little more light on your aunt's tragic death. You sold them a bill of goods on your aunt's health, didn't you?"

"Well, I…I…," the suspect stammered.

"You should be stuttering, Brockton. It just confirms the pathetic piece of shit I knew you were. You're going down big time, fella! Nobody's going to give you any compassion."

Zack opened the interrogation room door and yelled, "Hey, Murph, take this piece of crap back to his hole." And to his partner he said, "C'mon Lou, lets go celebrate an end to this mess."

~~~

That evening all who had been involved in the investigation met at the home of the lead detective. Riley and Millie joined Lou, Polly, the chief, Murphy, Skinner and Brenda. Kate and Zack prepared the meal.

Originally, all had agreed to hold a celebration when *Lacrima Christi* was closed down. But with the revelation of Dr. Brown's involvement and his subsequent death the tone of the occasion had changed. Nevertheless, all were relieved that the final chapter in the case was completed. And there was definite satisfaction to have the worst of them, Sister Miriam, the instigator who considered herself above justice, vanquished.

"We've wrapped up the worst killing spree in this city's history. Let's drink to that…" And then, while still raising his arm, the chief added solemnly, "…and to all the innocent suffering souls caught in the middle of it."

Riley made his own silent toast to Dan, his fallen friend, who forfeited his life in Riley's place.

THIRTY-FOUR

One more confession this morning and the last piece of the *Lacrima* puzzle would be in place, Zack thought. He and Lou were once again in the interrogation room. Sister Teresa was present with a court-appointed attorney.

Thirty minutes of alternating grilling by the two detectives resulted in absolutely nothing. Zack kept asking himself, *what's she doing here?* There was no way she could have been a participant in *Lacrima Christi*. She couldn't kill a cockroach. How could she assist in a suicide? He doubted she could pray and chew gum at the same time.

This young, well-proportioned holy woman was as ditsy as they come. Maybe that was part of her problem, he thought. Pursuing that further, he pressed Sister Teresa to talk about why she became a nun and it soon became clear that, for her, the convent was a refuge from the unwelcome advances of the male chauvinist pigs of the world—*not that she had any idea what that phrase meant.* Apparently she preferred being a gopher for her sister nuns to being hit upon by every Tom, Dick, and Horny.

Finally, Zack said aloud, "Detective Davis, would you join me outside for a minute?"

As soon as they were outside the room, Lou spoke. "Zack, I know what you're going to say. I feel the same way. I think we're gonna have to cut her from the *Lacrima* list."

"Yeah, let's let her go now. We'll have to go back to the drawing board for that last member."

They returned to Sister Teresa and her attorney to give them the news. The suspect said, "I don't have any hard feelings. You were just doing your job. Besides I appreciated a couple days' rest from all the errands I do for the other nuns."

The two law enforcers could only smile as they returned to the conference room where they invited the chief and Polly to join them and rethink their next step. Shit, thought Zack, I could sure use a few days off.

The first order of business was a review of the Fallen Angels members and Brackett House employees. No other TM surfaced except the monsignor, Timothy Mulcahey.

"It's a long shot but, considering how strange this has been, I suppose he *could* be the one," Zack noted dourly. "Although he's paid well, he's supporting a very expensive hobby. Maybe the others were letting him siphon off some of the funds to invest in his first-edition masterpieces. Some of those books have to cost a lot more than a couple of grand."

The chief said, "There's a couple other reasons: He controls the seminary physical plant—Mack Wright reports to him—and he's on the board of the Brackett House. Give me a couple of minutes and I'll probably come up with some other reasons."

Zack replied, "We can't easily pin a cash flow from one of the Brackett House accounts to him. But it would be interesting to see how he comes up with the twenty or thirty thousand a year that I would think is a minimum to support his habit. His supplier of the first editions is Quarles and Brady, a dealer in rare books located in Manhattan. Polly, why don't you call them and check out his purchases? In the meantime, I'll nose around Clark Hall to see what I can find."

~~~

"Good afternoon, Cindy Lou. We'll have the usual…a Coke and an iced tea."

Zack and Riley were back at Denny's where the seminarian revealed *Lacrima Christi* to the detective for the first time.

Zack explained their belief that Sister Teresa McDonald was not part of the group. They were now considering Monsignor Timothy Mulcahey as the elusive TM, the final member of the group to be ID'd.

Zack noted, "I really thought we had the case wrapped up, Riley."

"Yeah. I guess we can't expect something this difficult to come easy. However, my intuition is that the monsignor *isn't* the one you're looking for. He's tough, all right, as well as brilliant. I think he's just too smart in too many ways to get wrapped up in such a thing. You might be able to pry something out of Sheila, though. The two work close together. Chances are she'll have an idea how he funds his rare book purchases."

"Okay, I'll do that. When would be a good time to approach her?"

"This afternoon would probably be perfect. The monsignor is at a meeting in Des Moines for the day. I can smooth the way a bit, if you like."

"Okay. Let's go over there and talk to her."

Ten minutes later the detective and young priest were chatting with the seminary's assistant to the president over coffee.

"I've been hearing rumors about the *Lacrima* case. I understand it's all wrapped up," Sheila said.

"We thought so until we closely examined our evidence against Sister Teresa. We're still missing the elusive TM."

"Wait a minute! We're not just having coffee here, are we Detective? You're thinking the monsignor has the right initials and now you're trying to get me to help you prove he's part of a murder conspiracy? What on earth have you been smoking back at the PD! And Father Riley...I'm surprised at you. Of all people!"

"Well," Zack said, "he does have connections with the Brackett House; he's Mack Wright's boss, a guy who's guilty of several crimes related to this investigation; and he needs a great deal of money to support his rare book habit. *Lacrima* was collecting a large amount of money from their euthanasia activities. Even though those funds were channeled into the Brackett House, who's to say some *Lacrima* members didn't dip into the till. The monsignor needs plenty of money to buy those first-edition books."

Sheila responded with rolling eyes and a wry smile, "You're right about the books costing a lot. That's his addiction. Some months he spends three thousand dollars or more for them. Has an open account with the supplier. But, if you'd bother to get Father Columbo here checking around you'd have found that he inherited several hundred thousand bucks when his uncle passed away three years ago. You could probably buy a *Tale of Forty Cities* with that kind of dough."

It was Zack's turn for his jaw to drop, as did "Father Columbo's."

"Gentlemen, the monsignor once told me he thought rare books were a better investment than the stock market. He could enjoy them and build a nest egg for retirement at the same time. Not that he needs much, since the diocese pretty much takes care of all that, but I don't think he fancies a cot in an old priests' home. And another thing: I happen to know the monsignor believes strongly in the Church's position on the sanctity of life. I used to overhear arguments in his office with Dr. Brown. Detective, I believe I know the monsignor fairly well. You're just barking at a tree…and it's the wrong tree at that."

The detective was fairly taken aback at the strength of the administrator's argument, as well as the intensity of her presentation.

"You've built one heck of a strong case for your boss, Sheila. I'll have to re-think this for sure."

After thanking both Sheila and Riley for their time, Zack decided to return to his office. He was heading to the Toyota when his cell phone rang.

"Zack, where are you? I need you in a hurry."

"What's up, Lou?"

"One of your good friends just died."

"Who're you talking about?" *Christ…what now? Is there no end to all this!*

"Father Will. Will Meloy. He was in a car accident in Bellevue. The Bellevue PD just called. His Datsun is being fished out of the Mississippi even as we speak. He drowned."

Lou continued to talk, but Zack was not listening. He couldn't believe what he heard. His mind was in another world. "…still looking for his body. Zack…Zack, are you still there?"

Zack was stunned. Finally he forced himself back to reality. "Yeah, Lou, I'm still here."

"Do you want me to go to Bellevue with you?"

"I think that's a good idea. I'll pick you up at the station. I'm on my way."

The return drive to the police station was strictly by instinct, the built-in cruise control someone has when the mind is lost in thought. Will's death didn't seem possible. What did Lou mean? Were they still looking for his body? Maybe there was an outside chance he wasn't dead.

The Toyota barely had to stop; his partner was waiting on the police station curb. They headed south to the sleepy town on the Mississippi. Bellevue, a haven for campers and fishermen, was less than a forty-minute drive.

There was little conversation during the trip. Zack was lost in thoughts of Will. Occasionally, he would make a remark about his professor friend. It was as if he were thinking out loud. Lou realized no conversation was required.

The Bellevue PD was easily recognizable on Main Street. A cop on his break was leaning against the building on the shaded side, having a smoke.

Lou rolled down his car window and inquired, "Excuse me, officer. I'm Detective Davis from the Dubuque police. Could you direct us to the scene of the Meloy accident?"

"Accident? Buddy, he drove straight through the retaining fence and the car flew off the bluffs down there, right into the river. That was no accident; check the tire tracks yourself." He pointed down the road with his cigarette. "It's about a half mile south of town. You're headed in the right direction. You can't miss the activity."

As they neared their destination they could see the river on the left and gigantic bluffs to the right.

"The Bellevue State Park is up there," Lou said as he nodded in the direction of the monstrous cliff.

Zack replied, "Must be at least fifty yards high."

"Yeah, and it's straight down to the road…and the river."

Zack saw several vehicles including an ambulance and fire truck circled around the crash site near the river, resembling the protective formation of a wagon train the pioneers would have used here more than a hundred years ago. He remarked, "That winch is extracting what's left of Will's car from the Mississippi."

Lou was in awe. "Nobody could have survived that crash."

They were directed to stop some distance from the activity. When they had walked to the scene Lou recognized the chief of police.

"Hi, Vic, shake hands with my partner, Zack Gerrard. Zack, this is Vic Dobbs."

The two lawmen shook hands.

Zack spoke first, "I see Father Meloy's vehicle, but not him. Did an ambulance already remove his body?"

"Nope. Haven't found it yet. And…I suspect we may *not* locate it. You see how that current is flowing there?"

A large, partially submerged rock formation not far from the riverbank interrupted the normally calm flow of the Mississippi River and caused a perpetually swift current at the spot.

"What do you think happened, Vic?" Lou asked.

"Well…the vehicle crashed through a fence up there." As he spoke he pointed almost directly overhead. "The cliff's one hundred and eighty two feet high at that point. No way this could be considered an accident. The vehicle had to be traveling at a minimum of thirty miles an hour and was headed perpendicular to a mighty sturdy barrier fence. But see, that isn't the direction of the road, which means the driver had to go to a lot of trouble to hit the fence. When the vehicle landed down here it had enough momentum to clear the highway, nose-dived on the embankment and flipped into the river. The car, or what was left of it, was upside down, submerged in the water. You can see what the river current's like in this area. Hell, we've had people fall in this spot and never been seen again! Last October one of our local DUIs missed this turn and was never found. And he was driving on the *road*, not flying off some damn cliff."

The detectives returned to Dubuque with Lou driving. Zack, in no condition to be steering a car, sat quietly in the front passenger seat as he tried to understand how all of this had come about.

THIRTY-FIVE

As they neared Highway 61 and the city limits Zack felt like talking.

"Lou, something doesn't ring true about Will's suicide. With his faith in God, it's hard to believe he would end his life that way."

Zack followed his intuition by directing the driver. "Lou, take a left up ahead instead of going into town."

"Don't you want to go back to the office?"

"Something tells me we should go to Will's house. Have to eventually, anyway. Might as well be now."

"Okay." Lou shook his head in wonderment. "You'll have to give me directions. I don't know where he lived."

Fifteen minutes later after circumventing the city to the south by a circuitous route, they turned to its western outskirts. Zack directed the way to the winding entrance of the Meloy residence.

"Will was always misplacing his key to the house. He kept a spare one in a niche under the front porch. Let me see if it's still there."

Zack rummaged around under the front steps. The prize was where he expected it.

"Got it, Lou. Let's go in and look around."

Everything seemed in order. It was as if Will had not planned to leave. Dirty dishes were in the sink. Clothes were in the closet. All the signs of continuing a normal existence were there.

~~~

"Hey, Zack, found something on the mantle…envelope addressed to you."

Zack had returned from the workshop building. He took the parcel and sat on the edge of Will's lounge chair in anxious anticipation of its contents. Lou sat across from him on the lumpy davenport. Zack nervously opened the envelope and pulled out three handwritten pages, which he read to himself.

> My friend, Zack,
>
> What can I say except I'm sorry? I feel I owe it to you to explain…

"What's it say?" Lou said impatiently. "Can't you read it out loud?"

Zack wanted to read the letter by himself.

"He was my friend, Lou, and this is addressed to me. Let me read it first and then I'll decide."

Lou looked agitated as he got up, "I'm going to the kitchen for some water."

Zack returned to his reading:

> I feel I owe it to you to explain my involvement in Lacrima Christi. Sister Miriam, Cliff and I formed this group with the best of intentions. Arnold gave us the idea when he asked us to end his life of suffering. The doctor said he only had a few months to live. He agreed to pay for the euthanasia. And that payment helped

fund Brackett House activities. The mercy killing had gone so well Sister Miriam thought we should do more to raise money. She recruited two other Sisters, Katherine and Renee. Soon we were doing it once or twice a month. They weren't careful in checking out Molly Starr's health. The nephew had deceived them. When Cliff and I heard they had murdered her we were through with the group. The three Sisters did all of the injections. They wanted the money to help the Brackett House grow.

Sister Miriam was the brains and leader of Lacrima. When we started, she got me involved by secretly agreeing I could have a small retainer if I participated. Since she, alone, controlled the funds I was given three thousand dollars a month. The money wasn't for me and she knew it. I sent it all to my mom to pay for the care of my brother who had Guillain-Barre syndrome. He had long outlived his life expectancy and the cost of maintaining him had made my mother destitute.

I cannot face up to what I have done. This is the end for me.

Good-bye, my friend....

Zack found it hard to believe Will was part of *Lacrima*, but he could almost understand Will's rationalization. Heck, he thought, he might have done the same thing so long as it was only for euthanasia.

"Here, Lou, see what you think of this," Zack said as he handed him Will's letter.

Upon finishing the letter, Lou said, "I'd say that wraps up the case. We've now accounted for all the guilty parties. But I've got one question. The final member of *Lacrima* had the initials TM. How does that work for Father Will Meloy?"

The lead detective had to chuckle. "The T stands for Teddy, Will's nickname since birth. You see, his mother gave him that name because he was born so large she thought he was like a teddy bear. He eventually got her to not use it, but I imagine someone like Sister Miriam knew him well enough to know about that name and used it to show who was calling the shots."

Lou said, "Let's give the news to the chief and Polly."

Zack locked the house and replaced the key in its hidden location. The drive downtown was especially quiet. Zack was lost in his thoughts. He didn't mention to Lou that two important items had been missing in their search of Will's home. Those two things were especially dear to Will. Why would they be missing? One was the clay sculpture Will had kept on the mantle above his fireplace. He had been so proud of it. Possibly a mold was being made from which bronze statues would be produced. The other item was the photo of Will, his mother, and brother that was taken forty or more years ago. It had been hung in a grouping with other important memorabilia in the living room. With two of Will's most cherished items gone, it occurred to Zack that he might still be alive. He would never go away without taking the photo and sculpture with him. Perhaps

Will had constructed an elaborate suicide hoax. Zack knew he would probably always keep this secret to himself. Was euthanasia a crime? More and more he was thinking…it was the only humane thing to do.

~~~

Within the hour the investigative quartet convened in the detective conference room. The chief and Polly had already learned of Will's death.

Zack reread his letter aloud for the benefit of the two others who were not aware of it. It came as a surprise that Will was part of *Lacrima*, just as it had been when Dr. Brown was found to be involved.

The chief spoke, "Now that *Lacrima Christi* has been eliminated, it's time for some damage control. Because euthanasia is illegal, every one of the members committed a crime. But Dr. Brown and Father Meloy were connected only with the terminally ill who were about to die. I'm not suggesting we hide the facts, but I do suggest we put as good a face on this as possible for those two men. They've contributed so much of value to the community. I hope the public will remember them for all their goodness. If we're done here, I'm going to visit the *Herald Tribune*."

As the chief was about to leave, Lou piped up, "They helped the suffering die to help the old people live. I'd call that 'mercy.'"

Polly responded, "Lou, I'd call it 'mercy, mercy!'"

The lead detective thought, there's a lot of truth to that. The Lacrima members thought they were being noble, at least until the last month.

Once the chief departed, the other three members remained in their chairs. After a few moments, Zack said, "Polly and Lou, it's hard for me to communicate how proud I am of both of you. This has been the most dedicated law enforcement team I've ever been associated with." None of them were in the mood to celebrate, but all appeared relieved that the biggest criminal case in the annals of Dubuque had been solved.

As the lead detective left the meeting and returned to his office, he noticed that he was being followed. Entering Zack's office, Lou closed the door and extended his hand. "You did one hell of a job on this case, man. You deserve to be the detective-in-charge. I really appreciate you covering my ass when I planted that evidence. You can rest assured I'll never do such a stupid thing like that again. Thanks, friend."

After shaking hands, Zack's associate humbly backed out of the room and closed the door.

Dubuque's lead detective leaned back in his swivel chair. He knocked a precariously placed stack of files on the floor as he plopped his feet on his desk, crossed them, closed his eyes and let a smile of satisfaction form on his haggard face. God, it felt good in spite of the fact he was mentally and emotionally drained.

~~~

Zack and Kate took the day off. Kate prepared a hearty breakfast in Zack's kitchen. He felt it meant something important was happening in a relationship when one party knew the location of the other's pots, pans and utensils. Nicky entertained Kristen in the living room. The couple in the kitchen had been making small talk as Zack inspected the *Tribune*. He commented, "The chief must have been persuasive with the paper's editor. Ryan managed as good a spin as possible on the various aspects of our investigation. Boy, did we get the coverage. Page one has the story of our successful elimination of *Lacrima Christi* with an explanation of Dr. Brown and Father Will leaving the group when it turned from the positive aspects of euthanasia. Next to it is an article praising Dr. Brown for his generous civic contributions over the years. On page two, Will is fondly remembered as the professor emeritus of St. Peter's. Even though his body had not been found, the Bellevue police were convinced it was lost in the Mississippi as so many others had. And, look at this. There's almost a full page editorial entitled, 'Should euthanasia be legalized?'"

As Kate was ready to serve the meals, she said, "Say, Detective, after we give the kids a boat ride, what would you say to starting your next big investigation?"

"Huh?" Zack lowered the paper and looked into those emerald green eyes as he wondered what she was talking about.

"On me, you idiot, I'm your next investigation. Just the two of us at my pad and you'd better be thorough."

"Now, that's quite a chore. That could take at least a decade or two."

Epilogue

The *Lacrima Christi* investigation was no longer the talk of the town. It was a little over six months since a memorial service had been held for Father Will Meloy.

Zack still missed his friend, giving him an idea for the perfect wedding gift for Kate. With that in mind, he drove to Davenport and located the Darnell Gallery in the upscale retail area on North Third where Will had mentioned he hoped to market his work. In the store he noticed sculptures at the back of the building. A swift glance brought his attention to an exquisite bronze statue with smooth flowing lines. It was familiar to him. He strained his neck to see the rear base of the statue where he found the artist's signature. In this case there was only one letter, a T. The piece, priced at forty-two hundred dollars, was entitled *Madonna and Child*.

Eagerly, Zack sought out the salesperson, who presumably was also the owner. "What can you tell me about the artist of this piece?" the detective inquired as he pointed to the sculpture marked with a T.

"Oh, that's by Ted DeBeer. It's very fine work, don't you think? We've only had this work a couple of months and already five have been sold. One of his new sculptures will be released to us soon. Would you like to see a photo of what it will look like?"

Zack nodded.

"Please follow me."

The owner took Zack to his desk where he extracted a file entitled DeBeer from which he pulled a photo. "This is the clay sculpture that was recently completed. Would you please excuse me for a moment? I think someone needs my help."

As the owner walked away, Zack studied the photo. It showed a sitting mother, holding a baby with a child leaning against the mother, looking at the baby. The detective wondered, *could that be a family portrait of Will?* Was Ted DeBeer, Teddy the Bear? It seemed like Will's sense of humor.

The DeBeer file was within easy reach. Zack peeked inside and found an address, "1780 N. Elm Street, Decatur, Illinois." He wrote it on the back of one of his calling cards, told the owner he would consider purchasing the *Madonna and Child*, and went to his car phone.

"Hi, babe," he had reached Kate. *Now I have two babes!* "Something critical has come up on one of my investigations. It means driving to Decatur, Illinois. I'll check in with you tonight. I love you."

Zack had not prepared for an overnight. He stopped at a Target and outfitted himself with another set of clothing and purchased a razor and deodorant. This was too important to not follow up on. He had to learn if Ted DeBeer was Will.

The drive to Decatur was all by interstate. During his drive he had decided on his plan of action. First, he'd check out the premises, unobtrusively, and hope to find who resided at 1780 N. Elm Street. If that didn't work, he'd worry about an alternate plan later.

Zack positioned his Toyota about a quarter of a block away from the residence, a two-story white house, sadly in need of paint and repair in this crowded working-class neighborhood. It was two-fifteen in the afternoon. Fortunately, he had purchased a *USA Today* to occupy himself during his wait. It was going on three o'clock when a vehicle pulled into the drive of the house. Two people got out of a blue 80s-vintage Chevy. An older, stoop shouldered woman and a heavyset, large man took several bags of food from the trunk. The trunk was left open, suggesting that at least one of them would make another trip. While the old Chevy was unattended, Zack moved his car directly across the street from its driveway. He was only thirty to forty feet from the open trunk when both residents returned for another load. As the man closed the trunk, Zack tapped lightly on his horn. They both looked at him as he stuck his head out of the open window and his eyes made contact with the man.

Zack winked and extended his fist in a thumbs-up position. The man responded in like manner but immediately turned his back to return to the house.

Zack did not move as he watched them enter their home.

~~~

"Hello, babe. My trip was for naught, someone gave us a bad lead. I'm spending the night in Davenport, be home tomorrow by noon. See you then."

At ten in the morning Zack was at the Darnell Gallery when it opened and left the store carrying the *Madonna and Child*.

~~~

A month later, Kate and Zack were married at Allee Chapel, with Father Riley officiating. As the couple drove off afterwards, Zack was amused to see Kristin, Lou, the chief and Polly all pointing toward the back of the car as they waved them off. It wasn't until the next day that it occurred to Zack and Kate to open the trunk...where they found twelve bottles of the Italian red wine, Lacrima Christi, and a note from Lou:

"Let us know if you need help with this case!"

Photo by Larry Coplin

Jerry Maples grew up in Cedar Rapids, Iowa. He received a B.A. degree from Cornell College and an M.A. from the University of Iowa. After nearly twenty years in banking, he owned and operated an art gallery in Milwaukee. For the past seven years he has divided his time between landscape painting and writing. Jerry lives in Fountain Hills, Arizona with his wife, Linda. In addition to three children, Jerry has several grandchildren.

Ordering additional copies of

divine misguidance
by Jerry Maples

Autographed copies are available for $13.95 each, plus postage and handling ($2.50 first copy, $1.00 for each additional copy, not to exceed $4.50).

Checks are the only acceptable method of payment.

Mail request and check to:
    Ms. Tree Publishing
    7119 E. Shea Blvd., Suite 109 #293
    Scottsdale, AZ 85254

Ship to:
Name _____

Address _____

City _____ State/ZIP _____

    Book total   _____
    Sales tax   _____
    ($ 1.24/book, if shipped within Arizona)
    Postage and handling   _____

    Total amount due   _____

Please allow 2 – 3 weeks for delivery.
This offer is subject to change without notice.

The e-mail address for the author or publisher is:
    mstpub@earthlink.net